"To The Rocks You Loved, Old-Timer. May God Save Your Soul."

It was going to take Al considerable time to fill that deep grave.... Only a few more heavy stones! But where to find them? He had sacked the desert of its loose fragments....

While allaying his thirst at the stream Al espied the dull yellow gleam of a rock out in a little pool, rather deep.

He waded out to secure it. It lifted easily enough, until he heaved it out of the water. Then it felt like lead....

He gave it a kick with his wet boot. Dull yellow and white stripes appeared on this queer looking stone.... Frantically he crawled into the stream and grasped up handfuls of wet sand. Specks of gold! They were as many as the grains of sand.

"Jim! Jim!" he shouted, panting with rapture.

Silence and loneliness emanated from the camp. They struck at Al's heart....An empty space marked where Jim's bed had lain in the shade.

Books by Zane Grey

ZANE GREY

AMBER'S MIRAGE
AND OTHER STORIES

PUBLISHED BY POCKET BOOKS NEW YORK

Another *Original* publication of POCKET BOOKS

POCKET BOOKS, a division of Simon & Schuster, Inc.
1230 Avenue of the Americas, New York, N.Y. 10020

ISBN: 0-671-55461-1

First Pocket Books printing March, 1983

10   9   8   7   6   5   4   3

POCKET and colophon are registered trademarks of Simon & Schuster, Inc.

Printed in the U.S.A.

Contents

Introduction	7
Amber's Mirage	9
The Horse Thief	57
The Saga of the Ice Cream Kid	163
Don: The Story of a Lion Dog	183
Fantoms of Peace	209

Introduction

Readers of Zane Grey know of him primarily as a novelist. Probably not many are aware that in addition to the sixty-one novels, ten full-length fishing books, and several full-length baseball stories and boys' books, he wrote over two hundred shorter works. Although most of these were outdoor fishing and hunting stories, there were a number of novelettes and short stories in this prodigious output. Some of them were expanded into novels, and many of the others were published in magazines, but never appeared in book form. However, one story in this volume, "The Saga of the Ice Cream Kid," to our knowledge, has never before been published in *any* form. I discovered it, along with several other unpublished manuscripts, among my brother Romer's personal effects after he passed away in 1976.

The lead story in this volume, "Amber's Mirage," has never been published in paperback form. It first appeared in *The Ladies' Home Journal* in 1929, and like most of Zane Grey's writings, it has a timelessness which transcends the years. It is the strange and poignant tale of an old prospector who, in his dying moments, recounted having had a vision of a towering, shining cliff at the base of which was a spring whose sands were heavy with gold. This "mirage," as most prospectors in the region called it, could not be found on any map. The story's young hero, who stays with the old prospector until his end rather than riding back to claim the girl he loves, ultimately finds his reality in Amber's Mirage.

As are the other stories in this volume, it is done in the grand Zane Grey manner which has always captured the reader's interest from beginning to end.

Loren Grey
Woodland Hills, California

Amber's Mirage

1

Now that it was spring again, old Jim Crawford slowly responded to the call of the desert. He marked this fact with something of melancholy. When he was once more out on the lonely wasteland, hunting for the gold he had never found or to which he had given the best years of his life, he seemed a little more loath to bring in his burros back over the long trail. He sat on the sunny side of the mountains and pondered. The peaks were glistening with snow and the lower slopes showed patches and streaks of snow above the black pines; but the foothills were clean and beginning to green and purple over. High time to be up and doing, if he were ever to find the treasure at the foot of the rainbow.

"I've grown fond of this lad, Al Shade," soliloquized the old prospector as he refilled his pipe. "An' I just had to leave for the desert with things the way they are."

Crawford's shack stood at the edge of the pine woods opposite the lumber mill, and was the last habitat on the outskirts of Pine, a small town devoted to sheep and cattle

raising. The next house toward town was a picturesque log
cabin, just up in the pines and within town, as Jim had
found to his sorrow. Jim's neighbor was a mill hand, a
genial and likable fellow with one fault, an overfondness
for drink. He had a complaining wife and five children, the
oldest of whom, Ruby Low, seventeen years old, red-haired,
with eyes of dark wicked fire, had been no little contention
in the community.

Crawford had seen Ruby carrying on with cowboys and
lumberjacks in a way that amused him, even thrilled him a
little. His impulses were not yet dead to the charm of beauty.
But when Ruby attached Al Shade to her list of conquests,
the circumstances grew serious for old Jim. He pondered
of that now, while he listened to the melodious whine of
the great saw, and watched the yellow smoke rise from the
mill stack, and felt the old call of the desert in the spring;
it was something he had not resisted for thirty years.

Long ago in a past slowly growing clear again in memory,
he had been father to a little boy who might have grown
into such a fine lad as Alvin Shade. That was one reason
Jim had taken such a liking to Al. But there were other
reasons, which were always vivid in mind when Al appeared.

A cowboy galloped by, bright face shining, with scarf
flying in the wind. Jim did not need to be told he would
stop at the Low cabin. His whistle, just audible to Jim,
brought the little slim Ruby out, her hair matching the cowboy's scarf. He was a bold fellow, unfamiliar to Jim, and
without a glance at the open cabin door or the children
playing under the trees, he snatched Ruby off the ground,
her heels kicking up, and bending, he gave her a great hug.
Jim watched with the grim thought that this spectacle would
not have been a happy one for Al Shade to see.

The cowboy let the girl down, and sliding out of his
saddle, he led her away into the edge of the woods, where
they found a seat on a fallen pine, and then presently slipped
down to sit against the tree on the side hidden from the
cabin. They did not seem to care that Jim's shack was in

sight, not so very far away. Most cowboys were loverlike and masterful, not to say bold, but this fellow either embodied more of these qualities than any others Jim had seen with Ruby, or else he had received more encouragement. After a few moments of keen observation, Jim established that both possibilities were facts. He saw enough not to want to see more, and he went into his shack sorrowing for the dream of his young friend Alvin.

Straightaway, Jim grew thoughtful. He had more on his hands than the task of getting ready for his annual prospecting trip. If a decision had not been forced on him, it certainly was in the cards. Dragging his pack saddles and camp equipment out on the porch, he set morosely to going over them, but stealing more glances in the direction of the Low cabin.

Eventually the mill whistle blew. The day was over and the mill hands got off at an early hour. Not minutes afterward the old prospector heard a familiar step and he looked up gladly.

"Howdy, old-timer," came a gay voice. "What ya doin' with this camp truck?"

"Al, I'm gettin' ready to hit the trail," replied the prospector.

"Aw, no, Jim. Not so early! Why, it's only May. Snow isn't off yet," protested the young man.

"Set down a little. Then I'll walk to town with you. I'm goin' to buy supplies."

Al threw down his dinner pail and then his hat. He stood a moment looking at Crawford. Al was a tall, rangy young man, about twenty-one, his overalls redolent of fresh sawdust. He had a rough, handsome face, keen blue eyes which were now shaded with respect, square chin covered by a faint silky down. He plumped down on the porch.

"I'm sorry to see you goin'," said Al.

"It's good of you, Al, if you mean you'll miss me," replied the prospector.

"I sure do mean that. But there's somethin' else. I'm not growin' any younger, an' you—well, these trips on the desert must be tough, even for an old-timer like you. Forgive me, but I've seen you back four, five times now, an' each time, you seem done up. Jim, you might die out there."

"'Course I might. It's what I want when my time comes."

"Aw, but that should be a long while yet. Jim, you've taken the place of my Dad."

"I appreciate that, son," replied Crawford warmly.

"Then you come live with Mother and me," suggested Al.

"You'd take care of me?"

"I didn't mean that, Jim. You can work. We've got a ranch, even if it is mortgaged. But if we cultivate it, buy a couple of horses—the two of us . . ."

"It's not a bad idea, I've thought of that before. There's plenty of work left in me yet. But I'd only want to after I'd made a strike. Then we could pay off the mortgage, stock the place an' farm right."

"So you've thought of that?" asked Al.

"Yup, a lot," replied Crawford.

"I didn't know you thought so much of me. Gosh, that'd be grand!" Then his face fell and he added ruefully, "But you old prospectors never make a strike!"

"Sometimes we do," replied Jim, vehemently nodding. "Our hopes are like the mirages you tell about. Haven't I told you of Amber's Mirage?"

"That's a new one. Come on, old-timer—if it don't take too long."

"Not today, son. Tomorrow, if you come over."

"I'll come. Ruby has flagged me again for another cow-puncher," rejoined Al with evident pathos.

"Who is he?" queried Jim, looking up.

"He's a new one. A flash cowboy, good-lookin', son of a rich cattleman who has a lot of the ranches around here."

"Reckon I remember hearin' 'bout Raston. But he hasn't paid for those big range interests yet, has he? Is young Raston sweet on Ruby?"

"Shore, same as all these other galoots. Only he's a hot shot. An' Ruby is powerful set up about him."

"Does she encourage him?" asked Jim, going over to pick up a saddle cinch.

"She sure does," burst out Al in disgust. "We've been over that enough."

"You're deep in love with Ruby?" asked Crawford.

"Head over heels. I'm drownin'," replied Al with a frank laugh.

"Are you engaged yet?"

"I am to her, but I guess she ain't to me—at least not all the time. Jim, it's this way, I think she likes me better than any of the others, but she sure plays around with other fellows more than with me. Ruby loves to ride an' dance. She's full of the devil. There's more than one fellow like Raston who'd like to take her away, but she always comes back."

"What does your mother think about all this?"

Al hesitated, then replied, "When Ruby comes over to our house, Mom doesn't exactly approve of her. She says Ruby is half good an' half bad, but my mother believes if I could give Ruby what she craves—why, she'd turn out all right. Jim, that's what I hope."

"But you can't afford that on your pay," protested Jim.

"I know I can't. But I save all the money I can. Jim, I don't even own a horse. But if I can get ahead somehow—unless something awful happens—Jim, I can't compete with a dude like Raston."

"I can't help but wonder. Al, do you really think Ruby is worth this . . . this love an' devotion of yours?"

"Yes, she is," replied Al indignantly. "You don't love someone because he or she is so 'n so. You can't help yourself."

"You're right at that," replied the prospector. "But suppose a . . . suppose a woman is no good."

"You're not insinuatin' . . ." ejaculated Al, aghast.

"I'm just askin' on general principles, since you made a general statement."

Then Al seemed to take on an older and yet gentler expression than Jim had ever observed before. Slowly he said, "It oughtn't to make no difference."

"Mebbe it oughtn't, but it sure does with most people. There's only one way for you to fulfill your dreams if it's at all possible."

"How's that?" queried Al sharply.

"You've got to get money quick."

"Lord, don't I know that. Haven't I lain awake at nights thinkin' about it. But, Jim, I can't rustle cattle or hold up the mill on payday."

"Reckon you can't. But, Al Shade, I'll tell you what you can do. You can go with me."

"Jim Crawford! On your next prospectin' trip?"

"You bet. The idee just come to me, Al. I swear I never thought of it before."

"Gosh almighty!" stammered Al.

"Isn't it a stunnin' idee?" queried Jim, elated.

"I should smile—if only I dared."

"Wal, you can dare. Between us we can leave enough money with your mother to take care of her while we're gone. An' what else is there?"

"Jim—you ask that!" burst out Al violently. "There's Ruby Low, you dreamin' old rainbow chaser! Leave her for eight months with that Raston around? It can't be did!"

"Better than forever," retorted Crawford ruthlessly. He was being impelled by a motive he had not yet defined.

"Jim!" cried the young man.

"Al, it's you who's the rainbow chaser. You've only one chance in a million to get Ruby. Be a good gambler an' take it. Ruby's a kid yet. She'll think more of fun than marriage yet for a while. You've just about got time. What do you say, son?"

"Say, man, you take my breath."

"You don't need any breath to think," responded the old prospector, strangely thrilled by a subtle conviction that he would be successful. "Come, I'll walk to town with you."

On the way the sober young man scarcely talked and Jim was content to let the magnitude of his suggestion sink deeply.

"Gosh, I wonder what Ruby would say!" murmured Jim to himself.

"Wal, here's where I stop," said Jim heartily as they reached the store. "Al, shall I buy grub an' outfit for two?"

"Aw . . . give me time," implored Al.

"Better break it to your mother tonight an' come tomorrow," returned Jim, and left Al standing there mouth open, his eyes dark and startled.

Seldom did the old prospector answer to unconscious impulse. But he seemed driven here by something beyond his immediate understanding. Through it flashed the glimpse he had taken of Ruby Low and the love he took to be young Raston. Jim felt that he was an inspiration. One way or another—a success or failure—he would make Al Shade's dream and spare him of heartache. Some content of Amber's Mirage ran like a stream through Jim's thought.

He bought supplies and outfits for two, and most generously, as he'd been ever careful of his funds. Leaving orders for the purchases to be delivered out to his place, Jim started back with quickened steps.

It was a great project. It had an allurement which never before had happened on the prospecting trips, though they all had been exciting enough. He tried to evade queries and doubt with the present, well knowing that when he had been claimed by the lonely desert, doubt would vanish. Then came impatient sensations—a nostalgia for sight of leagues of lonely land, the bleak rocks, canyons, the dim, hazy purple distances, the smell of cedar smoke, the sifting of sage, the wailing coyote, the cry of the night, passed over him like a magic pervading his soul. How could he wait so long?

A gay voice calling disrupted Jim's thoughts. Already he had reached the outskirts of town and was opposite the Low cabin, with Ruby meeting him at the gate. Her red hair flamed and her lips were like cherries. She transfixed him with a dazzling smile.

"Uncle Jim, I was layin' for you," she said archly. "I hate to ask you, but I need some money."

Ruby sometimes borrowed—on two occasions Jim could remember.

"Wal, lass, I'm about broke, but I can rake up five. Will that help?"

"Thanks, Uncle Jim. I want to buy somethin' for to-night's party," she said as she took the bill, then ran her arm through his. "I'll walk with you to your house."

Jim could not reproach Ruby, and it was often that she told him of her troubles with the boys.

"Another party, huh? I guess you're goin' with Al," rejoined Jim.

"No. He didn't ask me. Besides, Al an' I have fought some lately. He's jealous."

"Wal, hasn't he cause?"

"I suppose he has, Uncle," she answered. "I'm not . . . quite altogether his girl. I do like the other boys."

"I see. But it's pretty hard on Al. Ruby, do you really care for Al? Set me straight."

"Uncle Jim!" she exclaimed.

"Wal, I just wondered. I saw you over back of that pine log."

"You saw me, with Joe Raston?" she exclaimed confusedly.

"I don't know Joe. But the cowboy—you was kissing this cowboy."

"That was Joe. An' you watched—that's not fair!"

"Ruby, I didn't mean to spy on you. An' when you slipped off together, I didn't look long." They sat down on the porch steps.

"Uncle, did you give me away to Al?" she asked, and a tinge of scarlet showed under her clear skin. She was ashamed, yet no coward.

Jim gazed down upon her, somehow seeing her as never before. He realized that he had reason to despise her, but he did not. At least he could not when she was actually present in the flesh. Ruby had seen only seventeen summers, but she did not seem a child. Her slim form had the contours of a woman. And like a flaming wildfire, she was beautiful to look at.

"No, Ruby. I didn't give you away to Al," replied Jim.

"You're not goin' to, Uncle?"

"Wal, as to that . . ."

"Please don't. It'll only hurt Al, an' not do a bit of good.

He has been told things before. But he didn't believe them. An' he thrashed Harry Goddard. Of course he'd believe you, Uncle Jim. But it wouldn't make no difference. An' . . . an' . . . what's the sense?"

"Ruby, I reckon there wouldn't be much sense in it. Not now, anyway, me on a long prospectin' trip."

"What?"

Jim motioned to the pack saddles and harness strewn upon the floor, the tools and utensils.

"Oh, no. Don't take him, uncle," she cried, and now her checks were pale as pearl. She caught her breath. The sloe-black eyes lost their wicked darts. They softened and shadowed with pain. "Oh, Uncle, I . . . I couldn't let Al go."

"Wal, lass, I'm afraid you'll not have anythin' to do with it."

"But Al would never go—if I begged him to stay."

Jim believed that was true, though he did not betray it. He felt gladness at a proof that Ruby cared genuinely for Al, though no doubt her motives were selfish.

"Mebbe not, lass. But you won't beg him."

"I sure will. I'll crawl at his feet."

"Ruby, you wouldn't stand in the way of Al's coming back home with a big lot of gold."

"Gold!" she echoed, and a light leaped up in her eyes. "But Uncle, isn't prospectin' dangerous? Mightn't Al get killed or starve on the desert?"

"He might, sure, but he's a husky lad, an' here I've been wanderin' the desert for thirty years."

"How long would you be gone?"

"Till winter comes again."

"Seven . . . eight months! I . . . I don't believe I could bear it," she faltered weakly.

"Ruby, you'll make a deal with me not to coax him off— or I'll tell him what I saw today."

"Oh, Uncle Jim!" she retorted, though she winced. "That would be mean. I really love Al."

"Ahuh. You acted like it today," replied Jim dryly. "Reckon you're tryin' to tell me you love two fellows at once."

"I'm not tryin' to tell you that," she flashed hotly. "If you want to know the truth, I love only Al. But I like Joe—an' the other boys. I'd quit them in a minute if Al had anythin'. But he's poor. He's poorer than I am. An' I hate to be poor. An' I don't see why I should give up havin' fun while I wait for Al."

"Did Al ever try to make you give them up?" queried Jim.

"No. He's pretty decent, even if he is jealous. But he doesn't like me to go with Joe."

"Wal, do we make a bargain, Ruby?"

Her red lips quivered. "You mean you won't give me away if I don't try to keep Al home?"

"That's it."

"Wh-when are you leavin'?"

"Wal, I reckon tomorrow sometime, late afternoon."

"All right, Uncle, it's a deal," she replied soberly, and with slow reluctance she laid the five silver dollars on the porch. "I won't go to the party tonight. I'll send for Al."

"Wal, Ruby, that's good of you," said Jim warmly. "I'm goin' over to Al's after supper to see his mother, an' I'll fetch him back."

"She'll be glad to have Al go," rejoined Ruby bitterly. "She doesn't approve of me."

Jim watched the girl walk slowly down the path, her bright head bent, her hands locked behind her. What a forlorn little creature. Suddenly Jim pitied her. After all, vain and shallow as she was, he found some excuse for her. Under happier circumstances the good in her might have dominated. The old prospector's mind was active, revolving phases of the situation he had developed, while he prepared a hasty supper. It was dark when he started out for town. The lights were flickering and the wind from the peaks carried a touch of snow. Al lived on the other side of town, just outside the limits, on a 160-acre farm his father had homesteaded, and which, freed from debt, would be valuable someday. Jim vowed the prospecting trip would clear that land, if it did no more. A light in the kitchen of the cottage guided Jim, and when he knocked the door appeared to fly open, disclosing Al, flushed and excited, with the bright light of adventure in his blue eyes. Jim needed no more than that to set his slow heart beating high.

"Come in, old-timer," shouted Al boisterously. "No need to tell you I've knuckled. An' Mother thinks it's a good idea."

Al's mother corroborated this, with reservations. She seemed keenly alive to the perils of desert treasure seeking, but she had great confidence in Jim, and ambition for her son.

"What's this Amber's Mirage my boy raves about?" asked Mrs. Shade presently.

"Wal, it's something I want to tell Al," replied Jim, serious because he could never think of Amber in any other way. "I knew a wonderful prospector once. An' for twenty years I've looked for his mirage on the desert."

"Gracious, is that all? How funny you gold hunters are! Please don't graft any of those queer ideas on Al."

"Say, Jim, haven't you seen this Amber's Mirage?" asked Al.

"Not yet, son. But I will this trip. Wal, good night an' good-by, Mrs. Shade. Don't worry about Al. He'll come back, an' mebbe rich."

"Alas! I wonder if that is not the mirage you mean," returned the mother, and sighed.

Al accompanied Jim back to town and talked so fast that Jim could not get a word in, until finally they reached the store.

"No, don't come in with me," said Jim. "You run out to see Ruby."

"Ruby! Aw, what'd you want to make me think of her for? She's goin' out with Joe Raston tonight."

"Al, she's stayin' home to be with you this last night."

"Gosh!" ejaculated Al rapturously, yet incredulously. "Did you tell her?"

"Yes. An' she sure got riled. Swore she'd never let you go. I reckon she cares a heap for you, Al. An' I'm bound to confess I didn't believe it. But I talked her into seein' the chance for you, an' she's goin' to let you go."

"Let me go!" stammered Al, and he rushed away down the street.

The old prospector lingered to watch the lithe, vanishing form, and while he stroked his beard he thought sorrowfully of these two young people, caught in the toils of love and fate. Jim saw no happy outcome of their love, but he clung to a glimmering hope for them both.

And an hour later, when he trudged homeward, thoughts of Al and Ruby magnified. It was youth that suffered most acutely. Age had philosophy and resignation. Al was in the throes of sweet wild passion, fiercer for its immaturity. He would be constant, too. Ruby, considered apart from her bewildering presence, was not much good. She would fail Al, and failing, save him from ruin, if not heartbreak. Yet she, too, had infinite capacity for pain. Poor pretty little moth. Yet she seemed more than a weak, fluttering moth— just what, Jim could not define. But they were both facing an illusion as tragic, if not so beautiful, as Amber's Mirage.

Jim felt tired when he reached his shack and was glad to sink upon the porch. The excitement and rushing around during the day had worn upon him. He bared his head to the cold, pine-scented wind. The pines were roaring. The pale peaks stood up into the dark blue, star-studded sky. And to the south opened the impenetrable gloom of the desert. A voiceless call seemed to come up out of the vast windy space, and that night it made him wakeful.

But he was up at dawn, and when it was light enough to see, he went out to hunt up his burros. They never strayed far. With the familiar task at hand again, there returned the nameless pleasurable sensations of the trail. High up on the slope he found the four burros, sleek and fat and lazy, and when he drove them again, the first time for months, he had strange, dark, boding appreciation of the brevity of life. That succumbed to the exhilaration of the near approach of the solemn days and silent nights on the desert. In a few hours he would be headed down the road.

The supplies he had ordered came promptly after breakfast, and Jim was packing when Al bounded in from the porch, so marvelous in his ecstasy of flamboyant youth that Jim's heart almost failed him.

"Howdy, son," he managed to get out. And then: "I see you come light in heart as well as in pack."

"Old-timer, I could fly this mornin'," exclaimed Al fervently.

"Ahuh! Ruby must have sprouted wings on you last night," ventured Jim.

"Gosh, she was sweet. I'm ashamed to death of the things I felt an' thought. We said good-by nine hundred times— an' I sure hope it was enough."

"Wal, she'll be over before we leave, you can bet on that."

"Aw, no. I stayed late last night—gosh it was late. Mom waited up for me. Jim, old-timer, that red-headed girl was hangin' on to me at one o'clock this morning."

Al delivered that amazing statement with a vast elation.

"You ought to have spanked her."

"Spank Ruby? Gosh! It would be like startin' an avalanche or somethin'. Now, Jim, you start me packin' an' you'll think an avalanche hit this shack."

Jim did not require many moments to grasp that Al would be a helpful comrade. He was indeed no stranger to packing. But they had just gotten fairly well started when Ruby entered like an apparition in distress. She wore her white Sunday dress and looked lovely, despite her woeful face and tearful eyes.

"Aw . . . now, Ruby!" ejaculated Al, overwhelmed.

"Oh, Al!" she wailed, and throwing her arms around his neck, she buried her face on his breast. "I didn't know I loved you so—or I'd been different."

Jim turned his back on them and packed as hurriedly and noisily as possible. But they had forgotten his very existence. And presently he proceeded with his work almost as if these young firebrands were not present. But they were there, dynamic, breath-arresting with the significance of their words and actions. Jim was glad Al would have this poignant parting to remember. He sensed, and presently

saw, a remorse in Ruby. What had she done? Or did her
woman's intuition read a future alien to her hopes and long-
ings? Perhaps, like Al, she lived only in the pangs of the
hour.

Nevertheless, in time he wooed her out of her inconsistent
mood and kissed away her tears and by some magic not in
the old prospector's ken restored her smiles. She was ador-
able then. The Ruby that Jim had seen did not obtrude here.
She entered into Al's thrilling expectancy, helped with the
packing, though she took occasion now and then to peck at
Al's cheek with her cherry lips, and asked a hundred questions.

"You'll fetch me a bucketful of gold?"

"I sure will, sweetheart," promised Al with fire and pride.

"A whole bucketful, like that bucket I have to lug full
of water from the spring. Al, how much would a bucketful
of gold buy?"

"I haven't any idea," returned Al, bewildered at the enchanting prospect. The light in his eyes, as it shone upon
her, hurt the old prospector so sharply that he turned away.
"Hey, old-timer, what could I buy Ruby with a bucketful
of gold?"

"Wal, a heap of things an' that's no lie," replied Jim
profoundly. "A house an' lot in town, or a ranch. Hosses,
cattle, a wagonload of pretty clothes, an' then have some
left for trinkets, not to forget a diamond ring."

Ruby screamed her rapture and swung round Al's neck.

It went on this way until at last the burros were packed
and ready. Jim took up his canteen and the long walking
stick, and shut the door of the shack with a strange finality.

"Son, I'll go on ahead," he said thickly. "You can catch
up. But don't let me get out of sight down the road. Ruby,
you have my blessin' an' my prayers. Good-by."

She kissed him, though still clinging to Al, but she could
not speak.

"Get up, you burros," called Jim, and he drove them
down the road.

After a while he looked back. The young couple had
disappeared and were very likely in the shack saying good-

by all over again. Jim strode on for half a mile before he
turned once more. Ruby's white form gleamed on the little
porch. Al had started. He was running and looking back.
Jim found himself the victim of unaccountable emotions,
one of which seemed a mingling of remorse and reproach.
Would it have been possible to have done better by Al? He
did not see how. After a while he gained confidence again,
though the complexity of the situation did not clear. All
might yet be well for Al, and Ruby too, if the goddess who
guarded the treasure of gold in the desert smiled quickly.

At the turn of the road Al caught up, panting from his
run.

"Gosh, but that was . . . tough!" he panted.

He did not glance back, and neither did Jim. Soon they
turned a bend between the foothills. The sun was still high
enough to shed warmth, though the air was cooling. They
were leaving the mountains and descending into the desert,
glimpses of which could be seen through the passes. Piñons
and cedars took the place of pines, and the sage and bleached
grama grass thickened.

Al regained his breath and kept pace with Jim, but he
did not have anything to say.

Jim wanted to reach Cedar Tanks before dark, a campsite
that was well situated for the initiative, for it regulated
succeeding stops just about right. This first water was down
on the flat, still some four or five miles distant. Jim found
a spring in his stride that had been missing for months. He
was on the heels of the burros, occasionally giving one a
slap.

The last foothill, rather more of a mound than a hill, was
bare of cedars and had a lone piñon on top, and the skies
were flush with a weed that took on a tinge of pink. When
this obstruction had been rounded, the desert lay below.

No doubt Al had seen it before from that vantage point,
but never with the significance of this moment, which halted
him stock-still.

The sun was setting red and gold over the western confines, where the lights were brilliant. Just below the travelers
there were flats of grass and belts of cedars and, farther on,

bare plains of rock, all in the ruddy shadow. Leagues away, buttes and mesas stood up, sunset flushed, and, between them and farther on, wild, broken outlines of desert showed darkly purple. A bold and open space it was, not yet forbidding, but with a hint of obscure and unknown limits.

One long gaze filled Jim Crawford with sustaining strength. His eye swept like that of an eagle. This was a possession of his soul, and whatever it was that had clamped him in perplexity and doubt faded away.

It was dark when they reached Cedar Tanks, which consisted of a water hole at the head of a rocky ravine. Here Al found his tongue. The strain of parting gave precedence to the actuality of adventure. While they unpacked the burros he volleyed questions, which Jim answered when it was possible. He remembered the stops all the way across the border. Turkey Creek was the next, then Blackstone, then Green Water, Dry Camp, Greasewood, and on to Coyote Wells, Papago Springs, Mesquite, and then a nameless trail that had as its objective the volcanic peak of Pinacate.

Al picked up water and wood, and built a fire while Jim prepared their first meal, a somewhat elaborate one, he said, to celebrate the start of their expedition. Not in many years had Jim Crawford had a companion in camp. He had been a lone prospector, but he found this change a pleasure. He would not have to talk to the burros or himself. After all, the start had been auspicious.

"Jim, have you ever been to Pinacate?" asked Al.

"Yes. It's an infernal region in midsummer. But I've never been to the place we're headin' for."

"An' where's that?"

"Wal, I know an' I don't know. I call it Three Round Hills. They lay somewhere in from the Gulf of California, a couple of hundred miles below the mouth of the Colorado. It's in Sonora. We get through Yaqui country an' then right into the land of the Seris."

"An' who're the Seris?"

"Wal, they're about the lowest order of humans I know anythin' about. A disappearin' Indian tribe. Cannibals, accordin' to some prospectors I've met. They live in the Gulf durin' the dry season. But when it rains an' the water holes are full, they range far up an' down the coast an' inland. So we've got to dodge them."

"Gosh, you didn't tell Mother or Ruby that," remarked Al.

"No, I didn't. An' I reckon I haven't told you a great deal yet."

"Then there's gold in this Seri country," asserted Al, thrilled.

"There sure is. All over Sonora, for that matter. But somewhere close under Three Round Hills a wash starts an' runs six miles or so down to the Gulf. I met a prospector who dry-panned gold all along the wash. So rich, he never tried to find the lead from which the gold came. An' he never dug down. Gold settles, you see, He was afraid the Seris would locate him an' poison his water hole. So he didn't bother to stay in long, an' after that he couldn't find the Three Round Hills again."

"An' you're goin' to find them?"

"Reckon we are, son. I feel it in my bones. I believe I can locate them from Pinacate. I brought a powerful field glass, somethin' I never had with me before. If I can locate them, we'll travel at night along country across the Pinacate, instead of workin' down to the Gulf. That would take weeks. We'll travel at low tide so the water would wash out our tracks. An' then we couldn't find those hills from the shore. I've been savin' this trip for ten years, Al."

"Gosh. An' where does Amber's Mirage come in?" went on Al, who had forgotten his supper for the moment.

"Wal, it won't come in at all unless we see it."

"Who was Amber, anyhow?"

"I don't know, 'cept he was a prospector like myself. Queer character. I always wondered if he was right in his mind. But he knew all about the desert."

"Well! Jim, what was the difference between his mirage an' any other?"

"Son, did you ever see a mirage?" asked Jim.

"Sure. Lots of them. All alike, though. Just sheets of blue water on flat ground. Pretty, an' sort of wonderful."

"Wal, you never really saw a mirage, such as I have in mind. The great an' rare mirages are in the sky. Not on the ground. An' mostly they're upside down."

"Jim, I never heard of such a thing."

"Wal, it's true. I've seen some. Beautiful lakes an' white cities. An' once I saw a full-rigged ship."

"No!" exclaimed Al.

"Sure did. An' they were sights to behold."

"Gosh! Come, old-timer, tell me now about Amber's Mirage," cried the young man impetuously, as if lured on against his will.

The old prospector laid aside his cup, as if likewise impelled, and wiping his beard, he bent solemn gaze on the young man, and told his story.

Al stared. His square jaw dropped a little and his eyes reflected the opal lights of the cedar fire.

"An' Amber died after seein' that mirage!" gasped Al.

"Yes, son. There's two men livin' besides me who heard him tell about it an' who saw him die."

"But, old-timer," expostulated Al, sweeping his hand through his yellow locks, "all that might have been his imagination. What's a mirage but an illusion?"

"Sure. Perhaps it's more of a lyin' trick of the mind than the sight. But the strange fact, an' the hard one to get around, is that soon after Amber's death a great gold strike was made there. Right on the spot!"

"Jim, you old prospectors must get superstitious," returned Al.

"No. The desert is like the earth in the beginnin'," replied the old prospector sagely. "After a while it takes a man back to what he was when he first evolved from some lower organism. He gets closer to the origin of life an' the end of life."

"Gosh, old-timer, you're too deep for me," said Al with a laugh. "But if it's all the same to you, I'd just as soon you didn't see Amber's Mirage this trip."

2

It was June, and Jim Crawford had been lost in the desert for more than a week. At first Jim endeavored to conceal the fact from his young friend, but Al had evidently known for quite some time. One morning from the black slope of desolate Pinacate, the prospector had located the dim blue Gulf, and the mountains in Pedro del Martir, and then, away to the southward, the round hills. He had grown tremendously excited and nothing could have held him back. These colorful hills seemed far away to the younger man, who ventured a suggestion that it might be wise to make for the cool altitudes instead of taking a risk of being caught in that stark and terrific empire of the sun. Even now at midday, the naked hand could not bear contact with the hot rock.

They went on down into the labyrinth of black craters and red canyons, and across fields of cactus, ablaze with their varied and vivid blossoms. The paloverde shone gold in the sun, the ocotillo scarlet, and the dead palo christi like soft clouds of blue smoke in the glaring sand washes. The magnificent luxuriance of the desert growths deceived the eye, but at every end of a maze of verdure there loomed the appalling desolation and decay of the rock fastness of the earth.

From time to time the gold seekers caught a glimpse of the Three Round Hills that began to partake of the deceitfulness of desert distance. They grew no closer, apparently, but higher, larger, changing as if by magic into mountains. These glimpses spurred Crawford on, and the young prospector, knowing that they were lost, grew indifferent to the peril and gave himself fully to the adventure.

They had been marvelously fortunate about locating water holes. Crawford had all the desert rat's keenness of sight, and the judgment of experience to this was the fact that only Jim's burro, Jenester, could scent water at these distances. But one night they had to camp. The next day was hot. They had to find water. And that day the Three Round Hills disappeared as if the desert had swallowed them. Cool, sweet desert dawn, with them in the east, found the adventurers doubly lost, with no landmark to strive for. Everything appeared about the same—barren dark cones, stark and naked shining ridges, rising mountains in the distances.

But Crawford pushed himself and became more bowed every day, and lame. The burro became troublesome to drive. Jenester wanted to quit and the others were dominated by her instinct. Jim, however, was ruthless and unquenchable. Al walked, no longer with blind faith, but with the perturbation of a man guided by some blind sixth sense.

Nevertheless, soon Jim changed their order of existence. They slept in the daytime and went on at night. Pre-dawns, soft and gray and exquisite, the glowing sunrises, seemed to hold the younger man, as well as the gorgeous sunsets. As for the other hours, he slept in the shade of a tree, bathed in sweat; and tortured by night, he stalked silently after the implacable prospector.

They talked but little. Once Crawford asked how many days were left in June, and Al replied that he guessed about half.

"August is the hot month. We can still get out," said the

prospector, rolling the pebble in his mouth. And by that he probably meant they could find gold and still escape from the fiery furnace of the desert. But he had ceased to pan sand in the washes or pick at the rocks.

The days multiplied. But try as Crawford might, he could not drive the burros in a straight line. Jenester edged away to the east, which fact was not manifest until daylight.

Another dry camp, with the last of the water in their canteens used up, brought the wanderers to extremity. Crawford had pitted his judgment against the instinct of Jenester, and catastrophe faced them.

Darkness brought relief from the sun, if not from overwhelming dread. The moon came up from behind black hills and the desert became a silvered chaos, silent as death, unreal and enchanting in its beauty.

This night Crawford gave Jenester her head, and with ears up she led to the east. The others followed eagerly. They went so fast that the men had to exert themselves to keep up. At midnight Al was lending a hand to the older man, and when dawn broke, the young man was half supporting the old prospector.

But sight of a jackrabbit and the sound of a mockingbird in melodious song saved him from collapse. Where these living creatures were, it could not be far to water.

Crawford sank less weightily upon Al's strong arm. They climbed, trailing the tracks through the aisles between the cactus thickets, round the corners of cliffs, up a slow rising ridge above the top of which three round peaks peeped, and rose and loomed. Crawford pointed with a shaking hand and cried out unintelligibly. His spirit was greater than his strength; it was Al's sturdy arm that gained the summit for him.

"Look, old-timer!" panted Al hoarsely.

Three symmetrical mountains, singular in their sameness of size and contour and magnifying all the mystery and glory of reflected sunrise, dominated a wild and majestic reach of desert.

But the exceeding surprise of this sudden and totally unexpected discovery of the three peaks that had lured and betrayed the prospectors instantly gave way to an infinitely more beautiful sensation—the murmur of running water. A little below them ran a swift, shallow stream.

Crawford staggered to the shade of a shelving rock and fell with a groan that was not all thanksgiving. Al, with a thick whoop, raced down the gentle declivity.

The water was cold and sweet. It flowed out of granite or lava somewhere not far away. Al filled his canteen and hurried back to his comrade, who lay with closed eyes and pallid, moist face.

"Sit up, Jim. Here's water, an' it's good," said Al, kneeling. But he had to lift Jim's head and hold the canteen to his lips. After a long drink, the old prospector smiled wanly.

"Reckon . . . we didn't . . . find it any . . . too soon," he said in weak but clear voice. "Another day would have cooked us."

"Old-timer, we're all right now, thanks to Jenester," replied Al heartily. "Even if we are lost."

"We're not lost, son. We've found our Three Round Hills."

"Is that so? Well, it's sure great to know. But if my eyes aren't deceivin' me, they're sure darned big for hills," rejoined Al, gazing up at the three peaks.

"Make camp here. We'll rest," said Crawford.

"You take it easy, Jim. I'll unpack."

The old prospector nodded with the reluctant air of a man who had no alternative.

By stretching a tarpaulin from the shelving rock where Crawford reclined, Al made an admirable shelter. He unrolled his comrade's bed and helped him on it. Then he unpacked utensils and some food supplies, whistling at his work. The whole world bore a changed aspect. What a miracle water could perform!

He built up a stone fireplace, and then, ax on his shoulder, he sallied down in search of wood.

Late in the afternoon Al discovered his companion wide-awake, lying with head propped high.

"Gee! I feel like I've been beaten," exclaimed Al. He

was wet and hot. "Howdy, Old Rainbow Chaser. Are you hungry?"

"Reckon I am," replied Crawford.

"Gosh, I am, too. I'll rustle a meal pronto. Whew! Strikes me it's warm here."

"Al, looks like the hot weather is comin' early," rejoined Crawford seriously.

"Comin'? Say, I think it's been with us for days."

"Wal, what I meant was hot."

"Jim, you're a queer one. What's the difference between hot an' hot?"

"Son, when it's hot you can't travel."

Al stared at his old friend. What was he driving at? At the moment, the idea of travel apparently refused to stay before Al's consciousness. But a sober cast fell upon his countenance. Without more ado he got up and busied himself around the fireplace.

When the meal was ready, he spread it on a canvas beside Crawford's bed. The old man could not sit up far, and he had to be waited upon, but there was nothing wrong with his appetite. This pleased Al and reacted cheerfully upon him. While they were eating, the burro Jenester approached, her bell tinkling.

"I'll be darned. There's Jen. She's sure well trained," said Al.

"I reckon. But if you'd lived with burros on the desert long as I have, you'd see more in it."

"Aw, she's only lookin' for some tin cans to lick," replied Al.

Nevertheless, the covert significance Crawford attached to the act of the burro seemed not to be lost upon Al. While doing the camp chores, he no longer whistled. The sun grew dusky red and when it sank behind the mountains it was as if a furnace door had been closed. Presently with the shadows a cool air came across the desert. Then twilight fell. Silence and loneliness seemed accentuated.

The old prospector lay propped up, his bright eyes upon the peaks. Al sat with his back to the rock, gazing out to see the moon come up over the weird formations of desert.

"Jim," said Al suddenly, as if a limit had been passed. "We spent weeks gettin' to your three old hills. Now what're we goin' to do now that we are here?"

"Son, we used up our precious time," replied Crawford sadly. "We got lost. We're lucky to be alive."

"Sure, I'm thankful. But I'm hopin' you'll be up to-morrow, so we can look around."

If Crawford nursed a like hope, he did not voice it, which omission drew a long, steady look from the younger man. In the gloaming, however, he could not have gleaned much from his observation.

"Old-timer, I hope, too, that you had more in mind than Amber's Mirage when you headed for these triplet hills."

If Al expected his sole reproach to stir Crawford, he reckoned without his best, for the old prospector vouchsafed no word on that score. Al's attempt to foster conversation, to break the oppressive silence, resulted in failure. Crawford was brooding, aloof.

Another day dawned, and with it unrest.

After breakfast Crawford called his young companion to his bedside.

"Set down an' let's talk," he said.

"Sure, an' I'll be darn glad to," returned Al cheerfully, though his scrutiny of his friend's face noted a subtle change.

"Son, you've a lot on your mind," began Jim with a fleeting smile that was like a light on the dark worn face.

"Ahuh, I just found it out," replied Al soberly.

"Worried about bein' lost?"

"Sure. An' a hundred other things."

"Ruby, for one?"

"Well, no, I can't say that. Ruby seems sort of far off—an' these close things are botherin' me."

"Wal, we'll dispose of them one at a time. First, then, about bein' lost. We are, an' we aren't."

"I don't savvy, old-timer."

"Listen. I know where we are now, though I've never been anyways near here. You recall the prospector who told me about these Three Round Hills? Wal, he seen them from a ridge top down near the Gulf. He sure described them to a T. An' I reckon now he wasn't ten miles from them. The wash he dry-panned so much gold from is almost certainly this one we're on. Water is scarce down here. An' he said water ran down that wash in the flood season. So I reckon we're now less than ten miles from the Gulf. This stream peters out, of course, in the sand below here someplace. Probably halfway down, I reckon."

"Ahuh. An' what of all this?" queried Al suspiciously.

"Wal, a fellow could mosey on down, stoppin' in likely places to shake a pan of gold, an' in a few days reach the Gulf with at least a couple thousand dollars' worth. Then he'd have, I reckon, about six days' travel along the Gulf, bein' careful to go only by night an' at low tide, to the mouth of the Colorado. Then Yuma, where he could cash his gold dust. An' then if he happened to live in Arizona, he could get home pronto by stage."

"Sure would be wonderful for that particular fellow," returned Al, almost with sarcasm. "Funny, old-timer, now we're sittin' right under these amazin' Three Round Hills, that we don't give a damn much about the gold diggin's they're supposed to mark?"

"Not funny, son," reproved the grave old prospector, "but sure passin' strange. Gold makes men mad, usually. Though I could never see that I was, myself . . . If we'd only had good luck!"

"To my notion, we're most darned lucky," declared Al vehemently.

"No. If that were so, we'd got here weeks ago an' I wouldn't be on my back. We'd have had time to fill some sacks an' then get out before the hot weather came."

"Oh, I see, the hot weather."

"It takes a while to heat up this old desert. Then after a while the rock an' sand hold the heat over an' ever' day grows hotter, until it's a torrid blastin' hell, an' white men don't dare exert themselves."

"Ahuh. Then I'd say we haven't many days to waste," said Al significantly.

"You haven't, son," replied the other gently.

"Me!"

"Yes, you, Al."

"I don't get your hunch, old-timer. You strike me queer lately."

"Wal, even if I do, I've a clear mind now, an' you may be grateful for it someday. It may have been my dream of gold that made me drag you into this hellhole, but I've got intelligence now to get you out."

"Me! What about yourself?" demanded Al sharply.

"Too late, Al. I will never get out."

The younger man rose with passionate gesture and bent eyes of blue fire down upon his reclining comrade.

"So that's it, old-timer!" he asserted fiercely, clenching his fist.

"What's it, son?" queried Crawford.

"You're knocked out an' need days to rest up. But you don't want me to risk waitin', so you would send me on ahead."

"Ah, I meant to lie to you an' tell you that. But I can't do it, now I face you."

"What you mean?" flashed Al suddenly, dropping back on his knees.

"Wal, son, I mean I couldn't follow you out."

"Why couldn't you?"

"Because the rest-up I'm to do here will be forever," replied Crawford.

"Jim, you're . . . talkin' queer again," faltered Al, plucking at his friend.

"No, son. I overreached my strength. My body was not up to my spirit. I cracked my heart . . . an' now, Al, pretty soon I'm goin' to die."

"Aw, my God!. . . . Jim, you're only out of your mind," cried Al.

The old prospector shook his shaggy head. He scarcely needed to deny Al's poignant assertion. "Listen," he went on: "You put water beside me here. Then pack Jenester an' one other burro. Pack light. But take both canteens. Start tonight an' keep in the stream bed. In the mornin' early, pan some gold. But don't let the madness seize on you. It might. That yellow stuff has awful power over men. An' remember when you reach the Gulf to travel at low tide after dark."

"Jim, I couldn't leave you," rejoined Al, mournfully shaking his head.

"But you must. It's your only chance. I'm a tough old bird an' I may live for days."

"I won't do it, old-timer," returned Al, his voice gaining.

"Son, you'll make my last days ones of grief an' regret."

"Jim, you wouldn't leave me," said Al stubbornly.

"That would be different. You have everythin' to live for an' I have nothing."

"I don't care. I won't . . . I can't do it."

"There's your mother to think of."

"She'd be the last to want me to desert my friend."

"An' Ruby. You mustn't forget that little red-headed girl."

Al dropped his face into his hands and groaned.

"Perhaps I misjudged Ruby. She really loves you. An' you can't risk losin' her."

"Shut up, Jim!"

"Al, if you don't go now, soon it'll be too late. I won't last long. Then you'll be stuck here. You couldn't stand the torrid months to come. You'll go mad from heat an' loneliness. But if you did survive them an' started out in the rainy season, you'd be killed by the Seris."

"I'll stick," rasped out Al, the big drops of sweat standing on his pallid brow.

"Ruby loves you, but she'll never wait that long," declared Crawford, ruthless in his intent.

Al's gesture was one of supplication.

"Ruby won't wait even as long as she promised," went on Crawford inexorably. "That Joe Raston will get round her. He'll persuade her you're lost. An' then he'll marry her."

"Aw, Ruby will wait," rejoined Al, swallowing hard.

"Not very long. She's weak an' vain. She needs you to bring out the good in her. Joe Raston or some other flash cowboy will work on that, if you don't hurry home."

"You're lyin', old-timer," replied Al huskily.

"I saw Raston gettin' her kisses," said Crawford. "That very day before we left."

"Honest, Jim?" whispered Al.

"I give the word of a dyin' man."

Al leaned against the rock and wrestled with his demon. Presently he turned again, haggard and wet of face.

"All right. I always was afraid. But we weren't really engaged till that Saturday night."

"She can't be true to you unless you're there to hold her. Go home now, Al."

"No. I'll stand by you an' I'll trust Ruby."

"Go, Al. I'm beggin' you."

"No."

"For your mother's sake."

"No!"

"Then for Ruby's. An' for those kisses you'll never . . .never get unless you go . . . now," shouted Crawford as, spent with passion, he sank back on his pillow.

"No!" yelled Al ringingly, and strode away down into the desert.

At length he came to a wide spreading paloverde where the shade was dense and had a golden tinge. Half the yellow blossoms of this luxuriant tree lay on the ground, and it was that color rather than the shade which had halted Al. He cast himself down here, sure indeed of a mocking loneliness. And in the agony of that hour, when he fought to be true to his passionate denial of Crawford's entreaty, he acted like a man overwhelmed by solitude and catastrophe, yet laboring to victory under the eye of God. It was well indeed that the old prospector, who had brought him to this sad pass, could not likewise see him in his extremity. And what would it have meant to the wayward girl, whom he was losing in that bitter hour, to see him ascend the heights?

When it was over, he rose, a man where he had been a boy, and retraced his steps to camp. The sun appeared to burn a hole through his hat. He found Crawford asleep, or at least he lay with closed eyes, a tranquillity new to his face transforming it. Al had the first instance of his reward, outside of his conscience.

That very day the hot weather Crawford had predicted set in with a vengeance. Al, awaking out of a torrid slumber, sweltered in his clothes. And Al began his watchful vigil. That day dispelled any hope, if one had really existed, of his old friend recovering. Crawford drank water often, but he wanted no more food. Al himself found hunger mitigating.

"Al," said Crawford, breaking his silence at sunset, "you're stuck here—till the rains come again."

"Looks like it, old-timer," replied Al cheerfully. "Perhaps that's just as well. Don't you worry."

"Quién sabe?" replied the prospector, as if he pierced the veil of the future.

At night they conversed more freely, as the effort cost less, but neither again mentioned gold or Ruby Low. The oppression of heat was on their minds. Crawford had before given stock of his desert wisdom, but he repeated it. Where he had been violently solicitous for Al to go, now he advised against it.

The days passed, wonderful in spite of their terror. And the nights were a relief from them. Al did not leave the old prospector's side except when absolutely necessary. And as Jim imperceptibly faded away, Al made these times more and more infrequent.

One afternoon upon awakening late, Al became at once aware of a change in the sky. Clouds were rare in this section during the hot dry season, yet the sky appeared obscured by pale green-yellow mushrooming clouds through which the sun burned a fierce magenta hue.

Al rubbed his eyes and watched, as had become his habit. A hard hot wind that had blown like a blast from a furnace earlier in the day had gone down with the sinking sun. The yellow rolling canopy was dust and the green tinge a reflection cast by desert foliage.

"What you make of that sky, old-timer?" asked Al, turning to his companion. But Crawford, who was usually awake

at this hour and gazing through the wide opening to the
desert, did not make any response. Al bent quickly, as had
become his wont lately, to scrutinize the masklike face.

Getting up, Al set about his few tasks. But the lure of
the sky made him desist from camp work and set him out
to drive up the burros.

Meanwhile, the singular atmospheric conditions had augmented. The sun, now duskily gold, set behind Three Round
Hills, and the canopy of dust, or whatever it was, had begun
to lift, so that it left a band of clear dark air along the desert
floor, a transparent medium like that visible after a flash of
lightning.

The phenomenon was so marvelous and new that Al
suffered a break in his idle attention. This stirred his consciousness to awe and conjecture as had no other desert
aspect he had watched. Presently he thought to ask the old
prospector what caused it and what it signified. To this end
he hurried back to camp.

Crawford leaned far forward from his bed, his spare
frame strung like a whipcord, his long lean bare arm out-
stretched. He pointed to the west with quivering hand.

Al wheeled in consternation and he called in alarm, "Hold
on, old-timer."

"Look!" cried Crawford exultantly.

"What you see?"

"Amber's Mirage!"

Al flashed his gaze from the prospector's transfigured
countenance out across the desert to see weird rocks and
grotesque cacti exquisitely magnified in the trailing veil of
luminous gold.

"Jim, it's only the afterglow of sunset," cried Al, as if
to try to convince himself.

The old prospector had fallen back on the bed. Al rushed
to kneel beside him.

"Oh, God! He's dead! . . . . An' I'm left alone!"

Al crouched there a moment, stricken by anguish. To be
prepared for calamity was not enduring it. The sudden sense
of his terrific loneliness beat him down like a mace. Pres-

ently when the salt blindness passed from his sight he observed that Jim had died with eyes wide open.

He closed the eyelids, to have them fly open again. Al
essayed a gentle force, with like result. Horrified, he shut
the pale lids down hard. But they popped up.

"Aw!" he exclaimed, breathing hard.

Al had never seen a dead man, much less a beloved
friend, who even in death persisted in a ghastly counterfeit
of life. Suddenly Al saw strange shadows in the staring
eyes. He bent lower. Did he imagine a perfect reflection of
the luminous golden effulgence in the sky, with its drifting
magnifying veil? Or were there really images there? He
wiped the dimness from his own sight. He was like a man
whom shock had gravely affected. There was something
stamped in Jim's eyes. Perhaps the mirage engraved upon
his soul! Or the sensitive iris mirroring in its last functioning
moment the golden glow of a rare sunset. Al trembled in
his uncertainty.

Then he recalled the story of Amber's Mirage. And he
sustained another shock. According to Jim, the miner Amber
had died raving about a mirage of gold, with wide-open
eyes in which flamed a proof of his illusion and which would
not stay shut.

"It's only the mind," muttered Al. A monstrous trick of
the imagination, natural to these prospectors, a lie as false
as any mirage itself!

But there shone that beautiful light in Crawford's sight-
less eyes. And the sky had shaded over. The gold had
vanished. The mysterious veil might never have transformed
the desert. Al covered the old prospector's face with a blanket.

That night Al Shade kept reverent vigil beside the body
of his departed friend; the desert seemed a sepulcher.

With the retreat of the somber shadows came a necessity
for practical tasks. He ate a meager breakfast. Then he
wrapped Jim in a blanket and tarpaulin and bound them
securely. Whereupon he stalked forth to find a grave.

It would never do to bury Jim in the sand. Of all the

desert mediums, sand was the most treacherous. It would blow away, and so he hunted for a niche in the rocks. He found many, some too large and others too small. At last under a cliff he had overlooked he discovered a deep depression, clean and dry, as fine a last resting place as any man could desire. And it would be sweet to the old prospector. It was sheltered from rain and flying sand, yet it looked out upon the desert. If properly filled and sealed, it would last there as long as the rocks.

He carried Jim—now how light a burden—and tenderly deposited him in the hole. Then Al tried to remember a prayer, but as he could not, he made one up.

"To the rocks you loved, old-timer. May God save your soul."

It was going to take considerable to fill that deep grave.

Small stones, such as he could lift, were remarkably scarce, considering it was a region of stone. It would be necessary to fill the grave full or the scavengers of the desert would dig poor Jim out and strew his old bones over the sands.

Al went further afield in search of rocks. Now he would gather a sack of small ones and then he would stagger back under burden of a heavy one. He performed Herculean labors.

The time came when his task was almost done. Only a few more heavy stones! But where to find them? He had sacked the desert of its loose fragments.

While allaying his thirst at the stream, he espied the dull yellow gleam of a rock out in a little pool, rather deep.

Al waded out to secure it. His feet sank in the sand, and as the water was knee-deep, he had to bend to get the stone. It lifted easily enough, until he heaved it out of the water. Then it felt like lead.

All this toil in the hot sun had weakend him, or else the stone, which was not large, had exceeding weight; in fact, it was so burdensome that Al floundered with it and at the shore would have fallen if he had not let it drop.

Bare flat rock edged on the stream there, and Al's stone, as it struck, gave forth a curious ring. He gave it a kick with his wet boot, shaking off some of the sand that adhered to it. Dull yellow and white stripes appeared on this queer-looking stone Al had carried out of the stream.

Then he scraped his hobnailed boot hard on the surface. Bright threads caught the sunlight.

Frantically he crawled into the stream and grasped up handfuls of wet sand. He spread them to the sun, gazed with piercing eyes.

Specks of gold! They were as many as the grains of sand.

Al tore up the bank, his fists shut tight on his precious discovery.

"Jim! Jim!" he shouted, panting with rapture. "Look ahere! A strike! An' old Three Round Hills is her name!"

He got no response to his wild outcry.

"Jim!"

Silence and loneliness emanated from the camp. They struck at Al's heart with reality. An empty space marked where Jim's bed had lain in the shade.

3

The second Christmas had come and was far gone when Al Shade set foot in Pine again. It was the last of winter and fine weather for that high country. It was an unlikely circumstance for Pine not to have a cold winter. The mountaintops were shining, snowy domes, and that pure smooth white snow slipped far down into the timber, but it had not yet encroached upon the lower slopes. A bracing wind blew out of the west, whipping dust down the main street of Pine.

The stage had but few passengers that day and Al Shade was one of them. He wore a new suit and overcoat, and he carried a small satchel. His lean, clean-shaven face was nearly as dark as an Indian's. He got out to button his coat and turn up the collar. An icy breath of winter struck within him, coincident with a recurrent and thrilling emotion that had beset him at times on the long ride up from Yuma.

The hour was still a little short of noonday. Al's first act was to hurry into the bank. He approached the teller's window.

"Hardwick, do you remember me?" he asked.

"Don't say I do," replied the teller after a close scrutiny. "But your face seems familiar."

"Al Shade. You used to cash my check Saturdays when I worked for the lumber mill."

"Al Shade! Now I know you. But you've changed—into a real fine man. Say, didn't you leave Pine with an old prospector a couple of years ago?"

"Yes, but it actually wasn't that long ago," replied Al.

"You were reported lost in the desert."

"That was true enough. But I got out. Hardwick, I want to deposit considerable money."

"Glad to hear it," returned the teller heartily. "Come into Mr. Babbitt's office."

Babbitt did not recall Al, nor the circumstance of his departure from Pine.

"Mr. Babbitt, I have a large amount of money to deposit." Al emptied the contents of the satchel on the desk before the bank officials, and then he stripped from his waist a thick roll of green-backs. "I'm sure glad to be rid of this," he continued. "Please count it all and give me a bankbook."

"This here's a lot of money for a young man," exclaimed the banker. "I congratulate you—you must be rich."

"It's a little worth for what I've been through," returned Al. "My partner, Jim Crawford, died on that trip. He is buried on the desert."

"That's too bad. I remember the old man. Shade, you look as though you really earned this—the hard way. I hope you use it wisely," said the bank official.

"Reckon I will," replied Al with a richer note in his voice. "I promised someone that I'd fetch back a pot of gold." After his business was concluded, he left the bank.

For many months the possession of gold, and then for days its equivalent in cash, had been a nuisance and a dread. Soon he would need to consider the possession of much gold—Ruby's. The moment was at hand. No word had he heard of her, of mother, of friends.

The door opened to disclose an older woman. But she had the face, the flaming hair of the girl pictured in Al's mind.

"Al!" she screamed in amazement. "Alive? We heard you was dead."

"Ruby!" he cried, his voice hushed, his arms spread wide to envelop her.

"You desert wanderer!" she exclaimed. "How you've grown . . . changed."

Al laughed with a happy wildness and was about to kiss her when out of the tail of his eye he saw a figure standing in the open doorway. Releasing Ruby, he faced round squarely, confusion added to his rapture.

A sneering man, fastidiously attired in fancy rider's apparel, stood there, with something familiar about him that stung Al.

"Howdy, Shade. I see your hunt for gold hasn't improved your manners," he said mockingly. "But maybe you didn't know you were hugging a married woman."

"Joe Raston!" burst out Al in an agony of recognition.

"Sure . . . the same," replied Raston, his white teeth gleaming. He had the same red face, the same hard blue eyes, with dark puffs under them. His attire now smacked of the city dandy instead of the cowboy.

Al wheeled to Ruby. "Is it true—you . . . you're . . . ?" he queried hoarsely, breaking off.

"Yes, but—"

Raston stepped down off the threshold, almost between them.

"Married, with a girl baby," interrupted Raston. "Another redhead girl to make trouble."

"Hush up, Joe. Let me tell him," cried Ruby, recovering from glad surprise to anger.

"My God!" choked Al with horrified stare. Then he turned and ran.

"Wait, Al . . ." screamed Ruby after him.

But Al ran on, blindly at first, down the clattering boardwalk, and almost into town before he could check his mad flight. Out of breath, he slowed down near Ben Wiley's blacksmith shop. Terror at the thought of being a subject for town gossip and ridicule drove him to swallow his conflicting emotions. What an awful blunder he had made! But had he not expected that very thing? He should have asked questions, have learned something before calling upon Ruby. That sneering devil, Raston. Ruby had married . . . a baby girl! Al fought off a deathly sickness, and in sheer desperation he turned into the blacksmith's shop.

"Howdy, Ben," he said, confronting the burly, grizzled giant, who let his hammer fall.

"Jumpin' jackrabbits! It ain't you, Al?" boomed Wiley.

"Sure is, Ben. How are you?"

"Sun of a gun, if it ain't Al Shade. Wal, by gum! I am shore glad to see you," replied the blacksmith, and it was well Al possessed a bony, tough hand. "So thet story of you bein' daid on the desert ain't so. You're a healthy-lookin' ghost. An' shore you're a prosperous-lookin' gent."

"Ben, I struck it rich. Jim Crawford took me down into Sonora. We got lost. Jim died, an' afterward I struck gold."

"You don't say! Thet's staggerin' news. Sorry old Jim cashed. He was the salt of the earth."

"Indeed he was. Ben, I've been down the road," said Al haltingly. "But not home . . . yet. How's my mother?"

"Say, Al, haven't you heard nothin' all this time?" queried Wiley with concern.

"Not a word."

"Wal, that's tough. To come home with a stake an' find . . . all changed!"

"Ben, I didn't expect anything else. Tell me."

"Wal, Al, it's not a long story, anyway. After you left, Raston took the farm away from your mother. Mortgage come into his hands through a deal, an'—"

"Raston? You mean the cattleman who took over the Bar X an' some of the valley ranches? Not Joe Raston?"

"Joe's father. Thet's the man. Left everythin' to Joe. He's been playin' high jinks heah. Al, he owns the lumber mill now an' Halford's store. But nobody has any use for him."

"Go on—about my mother," returned Al, fortifying himself.

"Wal, she went to Colorado an' . . . an' died there. Let's see. Must have been last summer. My wife will know.

She read about it in the paper. An' this is the first you've heahed aboot it, Al?"

"Yes. But I've been afraid," replied Al huskily as he turned away his face.

"It's hard, Al. I'm shore sorry I had to be the one to break it. I reckon you better come to see my wife. She was friendly with your mother."

"Thanks. I will, Ben. An', Ben, can you tell me anything 'bout my girl, Ruby Low?"

"Thet redhead! Wal, I'll be doggoned! You're in for more bad news, Al."

"Ahuh. Come out with it, then."

"Ruby's married."

"Married? Joe Raston?"

"Haw! Haw! Why, Joe Raston wouldn'ta married Ruby, as everybody knows. Joe is the high flier round town now. Father left him all his interests."

"But, Ben!" ejaculated Al, aghast. "I thought Ruby . . . it must be Joe Raston."

"Wal, like some other folks, an' Ruby herself—so they say—you figgered wrong. Joe jilted Ruby cold. It went so hard with her that she up an' married Luke Boyce."

"Luke! Why, he an' I went to school together. Luke Boyce! He was a pretty nice boy, if I remember. Younger than me. So it's Luke? An' not Raston!"

"Luke's not a bad sort. Used to work for me heah. Things have gone agin' him, an' thet's no joke. He was ridin' for the Bar X an' broke a laig. Raston fired him. After he was able to be aboot agin, he worked heah an' there, at odd jobs. But when winter set in, he was thrown out of work. An' he's hangin' too much around the saloons."

"How long has he been married?"

"Most a year. Ruby has a baby."

"Things happen—even in a short year!" rejoined Al ponderingly. "Well, Ben, good day. Remember me to Mrs. Wiley. I'll come over some night."

"Do, Al. We'll be plumb glad to see you. An' Ma can tell you all the news."

Returning to town, Al went to the hotel and engaged a

room with a fireplace, before which he huddled the rest of the day. When darkness came, he had parted with his mother and the sweet part of the past in which she had figured.

Al had never been given to drink. But now an urge to seek oblivion almost overcame him. It was memory of old Jim Crawford that gave him the final strength to abstain. The sooner he faced the whole fact of his calamity, the sooner he might consider how to meet it. He sensed a vague monstrous obstacle between him and the future. He went out to meet it.

It was in one of the side-street saloons that Al finally encountered Luke Boyce. The recognition was instantaneous on Al's part, but Boyce at first glance failed to see in Al an old schoolmate.

"Howdy, Luke, don't you know me?"

"I don't, but I'll bet you're Al Shade. Everybody's talkin' about you."

They shook hands. Boyce's surprise and pleasure were shortlived, owing, no doubt, to shame at his condition and embarrassment before Ruby Low's old fiancé. Boyce looked like a cowboy long out of a job and verging on the condition of a tramp. He tried to pass off the meeting with a lame remark and to return to his game of pool on the dingy table. But Al would have none of that. "Come, Luke, let's get out of here. I'm sure glad to meet you, an' I want to talk."

Boyce was not proof against such warmth. He left the saloon with Al, and by the time they arrived at the hotel his constraint had disappeared.

"I reckon you want to talk about Ruby?" queried Luke bluntly.

"Why, sure, Luke, but not particular, an' there's no hurry," replied Al frankly. "Naturally I want to hear how things are—with my old girl. I want to know a lot else, too."

Boyce laid aside his hat and turned back the collar of his thin coat, and held lean blue hands to the fire.

"Let's get it over, then," he said with the same bluntness, but devoid of resentment. "I didn't double-cross you with Ruby."

"That never entered my mind, Luke," rejoined Al hastily.

"I was always sweet on Ruby, as you know," went on Boyce. "But I never had a look-in while you an' the other fellows were around. When you went away, Ruby quit the boys for a while."

"What?"

"I didn't know it then, Al, but she told me later. After I married her. Ruby didn't go around with anyone for half a year, I guess. You promised you'd be back that Christmas, she said—an' she was true to you. But when rumors drifted up from Yuma that you'd been lost on the desert, she took up with Joe Raston again. It didn't last long. Only a few months. Joe wasn't the marryin' kind. He gave Ruby a dirty deal—jilted her. That took the starch out of Ruby. I married her in spite of the fact she swore she didn't an' couldn't love me. But I loved her. We got along fine while I was earnin' money. Ruby likes pretty clothes. She was gettin' fond of me. Once she said she liked me better than any beau she ever had, except you. Well, I broke my leg, an' that started us downhill. Joe Raston had me fired. I got well again, but nobody would believe I could ride. An' I had to take odd jobs anywhere. Lately I've been out of work. Then Ruby had a baby, and now I reckon she hates the sight of me. We're poor as dormice. I've borrowed until my old friends dodge a corner when they see me. An' if somethin' doesn't turn up this spring, I'll sure lose Ruby an' the baby."

"Somethin' will turn up, Luke," rejoined Al confidently. "Things are never so bad as they seem. Maybe I can help you. Spring will be here before long, an' that's the time to get a job or start somethin'. You might even see Amber's Mirage."

"Al, you don 'pear to have been drinkin'," said Boyce bluntly. "But your talk is plumb good. Sounds like music to me. An' what's Amber's Mirage?"

"I never quite satisfied myself about that," replied Al seriously. "Old Jim Crawford used to talk as if Amber's Mirage was more than fortune to a man. I took it to be a real mirage an' somethin' he imagined. Somethin' close to love an' death—somethin' that proved the passion for gold was terrible an' selfish—a waste of life, unless the strivin' was for some noble purpose. Anyway, just before Jim died, he saw the mirage. Or he was out of his head an' thought so. But he didn't seem crazy. He looked like the great poet I read about—who just before dyin' sat up with wonderful eyes an' said: 'More light!' Jim's end was like that."

"Wal!" exclaimed Boyce, deeply stirred. "It shore must have been somethin'. Al, I'll try once more, an' if I can't make a go of it, an' get Ruby back, I'll leave Pine. I've stood a heap, but I couldn't stand to see Raston get Ruby."

"Ahuh. So he's after her now—since you're married!"

"Sure is. Ruby went back to her mother, an' Raston goes there. Ruby admitted it. But she doesn't trust him."

"Luke, it strikes me you ought to stop Raston."

"How? He's powerful here in Pine. Runs everythin'. If I thrash him, I'll get thrown into jail, where I haven't been yet. What can I do?"

"I'll say a word to him."

"Shade, am I to understand you . . . you want to be my friend?" asked Boyce incredulously.

"I reckon. What else? But keep your mouth shut about it."

"I think it fine of you," burst out Boyce.

"I've seen Ruby—out at her old home. Raston was there. I—like a jackass—thought he was her husband. But, Luke, I'll stand by you, as you stood by Ruby, an' it's not too late to save her."

Boyce leaped up, radiant, but he could not speak.

"Shake on that. There!" added Al.

"Let me get this straight," gasped Boyce.

"Are you in debt?" went on Al imperturbably.

"Yes, an' pretty deep. It was a quarrel over debt that made Ruby leave me. She would run bills an' I couldn't pay. I tell you, Al, if it wasn't for my hard luck, Ruby would turn out all right."

"How deep are you in debt, Luke?"

"Somethin' over two hundred," replied Boyce abjectly.

Al laughed. He had long been apart from the struggles and miseries of men. He had no idea of values. He had seen a million dollars in gold in the bed of a stream!

"Come in to see me tomorrow morning," said Al. "I want to . . . to lend you the money to pay those debts."

Long after the bewildered Boyce had left, Al sat there watching the fire through dimmed eyes. Then he went out to look for Raston.

The street, the saloons, failed to disclose him, but the lobby of the hotel ended his search.

"Raston, I've been lookin' for you," said Al deliberately.

"Yes? About the little joke I have on you?" queried the other maliciously.

"You have no joke on me. My old friend Luke Boyce told me you were tryin' to ruin his wife."

"That's his business, not yours," snapped Raston.

"Well, I'm sort of footloose, an' I can make most anythin' my business," went on Al, stepping closer.

"Sure. And now you'll cut me out. You're welcome to the redhead flirt. She'll be easy for you, now you're lousy with gold. I told her so and reminded her—"

Al struck out with all the might of unspent misery and wrath. The blow laid Raston his length upon the lobby floor.

"Hold on," he called out.

"Get up, you dog!"

Raston rose shakily, not very much the spectacle of a man. His hand went to a bleeding and puffing lip.

"Shade, I had some right to say what I did," he began hurriedly, backing away. Yet he appeared resentful, as if he had been wronged. "I couldn't get Ruby, by hook or crook. She always flirted and let me spend my money on her. But no more. And lately, when I lost patience, she swore there'd never been but one man who could make her disloyal to Boyce. And that man was dead. She meant you, Al."

That staggered Al to an abrupt abandonment of the encounter.

"Raston, you leave Ruby alone, now," returned Al passionately, and went his way.

It was afternoon of the next day, somber and still, with storm out in the foothills.

Al, running down the road to catch up with his burros, did not look back, as once he had looked to wave good-by to Ruby. He had just knocked loudly on the cabin door, thrilling in his cold, sick heart to Ruby's voice: "Come in." But he had needed only the assurance of her presence. Then he had set down a heavy bucket before the door. Ruby's bucketful of gold that he had promised to fetch her from the desert! It was heavier by far than any bucketful of water she had ever lugged so complainingly from the spring. Like a horse freed from a burden, he had sped down the road.

A cry pierced his ears, and as he ran on, again, but fainter.

Still he ran, soon crowding his pair of lightly packed burros. As a criminal in flight or a coward at the end of his tether he ran until he turned the bend in the road. Then he strode on, the panting from his breast like hard sobs. Free! The gray hills, the yellow road, the blue haze of desert far on proclaimed it.

Free from that vise-clamp round his heart! The gates of locked, unnatural calm burst at last. It was not so much that he had held in his passion, but that it had been only forming, mounting, damming. He had brooded, planned, talked, while this unknown and terrible chaos had taken possession of him.

A storm mourned down from the shrouded peaks and enveloped Al, so black, so furious, that he had to walk beside his burros to keep from losing them.

Al lifted his face to the elements. There was an anguished ecstasy in this kindred spirit, this enveloping and protective storm. It was his gratitude for the return to loneliness. He had escaped from four walls, from streets and houses, from people, from eyes, eyes, eyes, curious, pitying, wondering, ridiculing, hateful eyes that knew his story, yet would never understand. But he was pursued still, down the naked shingle of this winding road, by the tortures he had invited, by the pangs of relinquished love, by the glory of something too great for him to bear.

As he descended toward the desert, he gradually drew out of the storm. Gray space, with a light shining low down to the west, confronted him. Then Cedar Tanks and night halted him. Habit was stronger than nature. Mechanically he performed the first camp tasks, then sat on a stone, peering into the mocking golden heart of the fire, then crawled like a dog under the cedars, beaten and crushed. Half the night a desert wind wailed the requiem of boyish dreams, half the night he slept. And the dawn broke cold, still, gray.

Al packed and took to the road.

Blackstone, Green Water, Dry Camp, Greasewood— day by day they were reached and passed. Coyote Wells, Papago Springs, Mesquite, and then at last Bitter Seeps, where the seldom trodden trail headed off the road toward Pinacate.

Bitter Seeps marked another change—the rebellion of physical nature against the havoc of grief. Al Shade lifted his head. There was a ring in his call to his burros. He faced the desert and saw it with clearing eyes. He was entering the empire of the sun. And the desert was abloom with the blossoms and sweet with dry wild fragrance.

Slowly the scales of mortal strife fell from Al Shade's eyes. And there came a regurgitation of the dominance of the senses. Far, far behind lay Pine and the past.

Four days' travel brought him to the slope of Pinacate.

Next morning he climbed the black slope to the point where Jim Crawford had made his observations that fatal day long ago.

The morning was clear. The heat haze had not come to obscure the wondrous and appalling panorama. Below, to the west, seemingly close, lay the blue Gulf, calm and grand, and across it loomed San Pedro del Martir, dim and purple against the sky. But it was the south that held Al Shade's gaze.

The wild desert, like a vivid mosaic, stretched its many leagues of jagged lava and colored cacti and red stone, down to where Three Round Hills, pale in outline, infinitely strange, appeared to mark its limits.

Only the hard bitter life of that wasteland, only the torment of its heat and thirst, the perils of its labyrinthine confines, only such loneliness and solitude and desolation and death as were manifested there could have brought an exultant, welcoming cry from Al Shade's lips. He would keep lonely vigil by Jim Crawford's grave.

He descended to camp, found and packed his burros, and with a trenchant call he drove them south.

There was peace in the desert. The pervading stillness engendered rest in him. He would have liked to dispense with spiritual consciousness, as he had with memory. But it took time for the desert to perform miracles.

At noon he halted to rest the burros in the shade of an ironwood tree on the edge of an elevation. The desert dropped away here. When he gazed out on a level, he encountered sky and mushrooming thunderclouds that were rising above a distant range.

It was drowsily warm and he fell asleep, leaning against the tree. He dreamed of his old friend Jim, and the spell lingered on into his awakening.

Al rubbed his eyes.

He could not have slept until approach of sunset, for the sun stood at its zenith. But there appeared to be a clear, dark amber glamour over sand and bush, rock and cactus. Then he gazed straight out from the elevation.

The southern sky had become transfigured by mountains of golden mushrooming clouds. They moved almost imperceptibly, rising, spreading, unfolding. Then they changed until they were no longer clouds. A sharp level line cut across the floor of this golden mass, and under it shone the clear, dark, amber desert, weird only in that it had color at noonday.

Above it glimmered a long blue ripple of gentle waves, lapping the line, overcast by golden tinge. Foliage faintly of the same hue bordered shoreline far into the dim verge. And the broad water spread to the marble steps and balustrades and terraces and doors and golden walls of a magnificent city. Empty streets led upward into halls of pearl and chambers of opal and courts of porphyry, all burned

through with lucent gold. A lonely city of shining amber!
Tiers of walls rose one above the other, towering with a
thousand pillared arches and trellises and sculptured images
of lifeless gods and wingless eagles, with niche on niche,
and window on window of shimmering treasure, all rising
to flaming turrets that perished against the pitiless truthful
sky.

A mellow drowsy hum of insects seemed to float mur-
muringly to Al on the dry air. The tinkle of a burro bell
further emphasized the silence. Dark veils of heat, like
crinkled transparent lace, rose from sand and stone.

Had he really seen the mirage, or was that shining city
in the clouds the mansion to which the souls of men must
climb?

The Horse Thief

1

The lone horseman rode slowly up the slope, bending far down from his saddle in the posture customary for a range rider when studying hoof tracks. The intensity of his scrutiny indicated far more than the depth or direction of these imprints in the dust.

Presently the rider sat up and turned in his saddle to look back. While pondering the situation, his eagle eyes swept the far country below. It was a scene like hundreds of others limned upon his memory—a vast and rugged section of the West, differing only in the elements of color, beauty, distance and grandeur that characterized the green Salmon River Valley, the gray rolling range beyond, the dead-white plain of alkali and the purple sawtoothed peaks piercing the sky in the far distance.

That the tracks of the stolen Watrous thoroughbreds would lead over the range into Montana had been the trailer's foregone conclusion. But that the mysterious horse thieves had so far taken little care to conceal their tracks seemed a proof of how brazen this gang had become. On the other hand, Dale Brittenham reflected that he was a wild-horse hunter—that a trail invisible to most men would be like print to him.

He gazed back down the long slope into Idaho, pondering his task, slowly realizing that he had let himself in for a serious and perhaps deadly job.

It had taken Dale five hours to ride up to the point where he now straddled his horse, and the last from which he could see the valley. From here the stage road led north over the divide into the wild timbered range.

The time was about noon of an early summer day. The air at that height had a cool sweet tang, redolent of the green pines and the flowered mountain meadows. Dale strongly felt the beauty and allurement of the scene, and likewise a presentiment of trouble. The little mining town of Salmon, in the heyday of its biggest gold-producing year—1886— nestled in a bend of the shining white-and-green river. Brittenham had many enemies down there and but few friends. The lonely life of a wild-horse hunter had not kept him from conflict with men. Whose toes might he not step upon if he tracked down these horse thieves? The country was infested with road agents, bandits, horse thieves; and the wildest era Idaho had ever known was in full swing.

"I've long had a hunch," Dale soliloquized broodingly. "There're men down there, maybe as rich and respectable as Watrous himself, who're in cahoots with these thieves. . . . 'Cause if there wasn't, thick slick stealin' couldn't be done."

The valley shone green and gold and purple under the bright sun, a vast winding range of farms, ranches, pastures, leading up to the stark Sawtooth Mountains, out of which the river glistened like a silver thread. It wound down between grassy hills to meander into the valley. Dale's gaze fastened upon an irregular green spot and a white house surrounded by wide sweeping pastures. This was the Watrous ranch. Dale watched it, conscious of a pang in his heart. The only friendship for a man and love of a woman he had ever known had come to him there. Leale Hildrith, the partner of Jim Watrous in an extensive horse-breeding and trading business, had once been a friend in need to Brittenham. But for Hildrith, the wild-horse hunter would long before have taken the trail of the thieves who regularly several times a year plundered the ranches of the valley. Watrous had lost hundreds of horses.

"Dale, lay off," Hildrith had advised impatiently. "It's no mix of yours. It'll lead into more gunplay, and you've already got a bad name for that. Besides, there's no telling where such a trail might wind up."

Brittenham had been influenced by the friend to whom he owed his life. Yet despite his loyalty, he wondered at Hildrith's attitude. It must surely be that Hildrith again wanted to save him from harm, and Dale warmed to the thought. But when, on this morning, he had discovered that five of Edith Waltrous's thoroughbreds, the favorite horses she loved so dearly, had been stolen, he said no word to anyone at the ranch and set out upon the trail.

At length Brittenham turned his back upon the valley and rode on up the slope toward the timberline, now close at hand. He reached the straggling firs at a point where two trails branched off the road. The right one led along the edge of the timberline, and on it the sharp tracks of the shod horses showed plainly in dust.

At this junction Dale dismounted to study the tracks. After a careful scrutiny he made the deduction that he was probably two hours behind the horse thieves, who were plainly lagging along. Dale found an empty whiskey bottle, which was still damp and strong with the fumes of liquor. This might in some measure account for the carelessness of the thieves.

Dale rode on, staying close to the fir trees, between them and the trail, while he kept a keen eye ahead. On the way up he had made a number of conjectures, which he now discarded. This branching off the road puzzled him. It meant probably that the horse thieves had a secret rendezvous somewhere off in this direction. After perhaps an hour of travel along the timber belt, Dale entered a rocky region where progress was slow, and he came abruptly upon a

wide, well-defined trail running at right angles to the one
he was on. Hundreds of horses had passed along there, but
none recently. Dale got off to reconnoiter. He had stumbled
upon something that he had never heard the riders mention—a trail which wound up the mountain slope over an
exceedingly rough route. Dale followed it until he had an
appreciation of what a hard climb, partly on foot, riders
must put themselves to, coming up from the valley. He
realized that here was the outlet for horse thieves operating
on the Salmon and Snake river ranges of Idaho. It did not
take Dale long to discover that it was a one-way trail. No
hoof tracks pointing down!

"Well, here's a rummy deal!" he ejaculated. And he
remembered the horse traders who often drove bands of
Montana horses down into Idaho and sold them all the way
to Twin Falls and Boise. Those droves of horses came down
the stage road. Suddenly Dale arrived at an exciting conclusion. "By thunder! Those Montana horses are stolen, too.
By the same gang—a big gang of slick horse thieves. They
steal way down on the Montana ranges . . . drive up over
a hidden trail like this to some secret place where they meet
part of their outfit who've been stealin' in Idaho . . . then
they switch herds . . . and they drive down, sellin' the
Montana horses in Idaho and the Idaho horses in Montana . . . Well! The head of that outfit has got brains. Too
many to steal Jim Watrous's fine blooded stock! That must
have been a slip. . . . But any rider would want to steal
Edith Watrous's horses!"

Returning to his mount, Dale led him in among the firs
and rocks, keeping to the line of the new trail but not directly
upon it. A couple of slow miles brought him to the divide.
Beyond that the land sloped gently, the rocks and ridges
merged into a fine open forest. His view was unobstructed
for several hundred yards. Bands of deer bounded away
from in front of Dale, to halt and watch with long ears erect.
Dale had not hunted far over that range. He knew the Sawtooth Mountains in as far as Thunder Mountain. His wild-
horse activities had been confined to the desert and low
country toward the Snake River. Therefore he had no idea

where this trail would lead him. Somewhere over this divide, on the eastern slope, lived a band of Palouse Indians. Dale knew some of them and had hunted wild horses with them. He had befriended one of the number, Nalook, to the extent of saving him from a jail sentence. From that time Nalook had been utterly devoted to Dale, and had rendered him every possible service.

By midafternoon Brittenham was far down on the forested tableland. He meant to stick to the trail as long as there was light enough to see. His saddlebag contained meat, biscuits, dried fruit and salt. His wild-horse hunts often kept him weeks on the trail, so his present pursuit presented no obstacles. Nevertheless, as he progressed he grew more and more wary. He expected to see a log cabin in some secluded spot. At length he came to a brook that ran down from a jumble of low bluffs and followed the trail. The water coursed in alternate eddies and swift runs. Beaver dams locked it up into little lakes. Dale found beaver cutting aspens in broad daylight, which attested to the wildness of the region. Far ahead he saw rocky crags and rough gray ridgetops. This level open forest would not last much farther.

Suddenly Brittenham's horse shot up his ears and halted in his tracks. A shrill neigh came faintly to the rider's ears. He peered ahead through the pines, his nerves tingling.

But Dale could not make out any color or movement, and the sound was not repeated. This fact somewhat allayed his fears. After a sharp survey of his surroundings, Dale had led his horse into a clump of small firs and haltered him there. Then, rifle in hand, he crept forward from tree to tree. This procedure was slow work, as he exercised great caution.

The sun sank behind the fringe of timber on the high ground and soon shadows appeared in thick parts of the forest. Suddenly the ring of an ax sent the blood back to Dale's heart. He crouched down behind a pine and rested a moment, his thoughts whirling. There were campers ahead, or a cabin; and Dale strongly inclined to the conviction that the horse thieves had halted for the night. If so, it meant they were either far from their rendezvous or taking their time waiting for comrades to join them. Dale pondered the situation. He must be decisive, quick, ruthless. But he could not determine what to do until he saw the outfit and the lay of the land.

Therefore he got up, and after a long scrutiny ahead, he slipped from behind the tree and stole on to another. He repeated this move. Brush and clumps of fir and big pines obstructed any considerable survey ahead. Finally he came to less thick covering on the ground. He smelled smoke. He heard faint indistinguishable sounds. Then a pinpoint of fire gleamed through the thicket in front of him. Without more ado Dale dropped on all fours and crawled straight for that light. When he got to the brush and peered through, his heart gave a great leap at the sight of Edith Watrous's horses staked out on a grassy spot.

Then he crouched on his knees, holding the Winchester tight, trying to determine a course of action. Various plans flashed through his mind. The one he decided to be the least risky was to wait until the thieves were asleep and quietly make away with the horses. These thoroughbreds knew him well. He could release them without undue excitement. With half a night's start he would be far on the way back to the ranch before the thieves discovered their loss. The weakness of this plan lay in the possibility of a new outfit joining this band. That, however, would not deter Dale from making the attempt to get the horses.

It occurred to him presently to steal up on the camp under cover of the darkness and if possible get close enough to see and hear the robbers. Dale lay debating this course and at last yielded to the temptation. Dusk settled down. The night hawks wheeled and uttered their guttural cries overhead. He waited patiently. When it grew dark he crawled around the thicket and stood up. A bright campfire blazed in the distance. Dark forms moved to and fro across the light. Off to the left of Dale's position there appeared to be more cover. He sheered off that way, lost sight of the campfire, threaded a careful approach among trees and brush, and after a long detour came up behind the camp, scarcely a hundred yards distant. A big pine tree dominated an open space lighted by the campfire. Dale selected objects to use for cover and again sank to his hands and knees. Well he knew that the keenest of men were easier to crawl upon than wild horses at rest. He was like an Indian. He made no more noise than a snake. At intervals he peered above the grass and low brush. He heard voices and now and then the sputtering of the fire. He rested again. His next stop would be behind a windfall that now obscured the camp. Drawing a deep breath, he crawled on silently without looking up. The grass was wet with dew.

A log barred Dale's advance. He relaxed and lay quiet, straining his ears.

"I tell you, Ben, this hyar was a damn fool job," spoke up a husky-voiced individual. "Alec agrees with me."

"Wal, I shore do," corroborated another man. "We was drunk."

"Not me. I never was more clearheaded in my life," replied the third thief, called Ben. His reply ended with a hard chuckle.

"Wal, if you was, no one noticed it," returned Alec sourly. "I reckon you roped us into a mess."

"Aw, hell! Big Bill will yelp with joy."

"Mebbe. Shore he's been growin' overbold these days. Makin' too much money. Stands too well in Halsey an' Bannock, an' Salmon. Cocksure no one will ever find our hole-up."

"Bah! That wouldn't faze Big Bill Mason. He'd bluff it through."

"Aha! Like Henry Plummer, eh? The coldest proposition of a robber that ever turned a trick. He had a hundred men in his outfit. Stole damn near a million in gold. High respected citizen of Montana. Mayor of Alder Gulch. . . . All the same, he put his neck in the noose!"

"Alec is right, Ben," spoke up the third member in his husky voice. "Big Bill is growin' wild. Too careless. Spends too much time in town. Gambles. Drinks. . . . Someday some foxy cowboy or hoss hunter will trail him. An' that'll be about due when Watrous finds his blooded horses gone."

"Wal, what worries me more is how Hildrith will take

this deal of yours," said Alec. "Like as not he'll murder us."

Brittenham sustained a terrible shock. It was like a physical rip of his flesh. Hildrith! Those horse thieves spoke familiarly of his beloved friend. Dale grew suddenly sick. Did not this explain Leale's impatient opposition to the trailing of horse thieves?

"Ben, you can gamble Hildrith will be wild," went on Alec. "He's got sense if Big Bill hasn't. He's Watrous's pardner, mind you. Why, Jim Watrous would hang him."

"We heard talk this time that Hildrith was goin' to marry old Jim's lass. What a hell of a pickle Leale will be in!"

"Fellers, he'll be all the stronger if he does grab thet hoss-lovin' girl. But I don't believe he'll be so lucky. I seen Edith Watrous in town with that cowboy Les Crocker. She shore makes a feller draw his breath hard. She's young an' she likes the cowboys."

"Wal, what of thet? If Jim wants her to marry his pardner, she'll have to."

"Mebbe she's a chip off the old block. Anyway, I've knowed a heap of women an' thet's my hunch . . . Hildrith will be as sore as a bunged-up thumb. But what can he do? We got the hosses."

"So we have. Five white elephants! Ben, you've let *your* cravin' for fine hossflesh carry you away."

An interval of silence ensued, during which Dale raised himself to peer guardedly over the log. Two of the thieves sat with hard red faces in the glare of the blaze. The third had his back to Dale.

"What ails *me*, now I got 'em, is can I keep 'em," this man replied. "Thet black is the finest hoss I ever seen."

"They're all grand hosses. An' thet's all the good it'll do you," retorted the leaner of the other two.

"Ben, them thoroughbreds air known from Deadwood to Walla Walla. They can't be sold or rid. An' shore as Gawd make little apples, the stealin' of them will bust Big Bill's gang."

"Aw, you're a couple of yellow pups," rejoined Ben

contemptuously. "If I'd known you was goin' to show like this, I'd split with you an' done the job myself."

"Uhuh! I recollect now thet *you* did the watchin' while Steve an' me stole the horses. An' I sort of recollect dim-like thet you talked big about money while you was feedin' us red likker."

"Yep, I did—an' I had to get you drunk. Haw! Haw!"

"On purpose? Made us trick the outfit an' switch to your job, huh?"

"Yes, on purpose."

"So. . . . How you like this on purpose, Ben?" hissed Alec, and swift as a flash he whipped out a gun. Ben's hoarse yell of protest died in his throat with the bang of the big Colt.

The bullet went clear through the man to strike the log uncomfortably near Dale. He ducked instinctively, then sank down again, tense and cold.

"My Gawd! Alec, you bored him," burst out the man Steve.

"I shore did. The damn bullhead!. . . . An' thet's our out with Hildrith. We're gonna need one. I reckon Big Bill won't hold it hard agin us."

Dale found himself divided between conflicting courses— one, to shoot these horse thieves in their tracks, and a stronger one, to stick to his first plan and avoid unnecessary hazard. Wherewith he noiselessly turned and began to crawl away from the log. He had to worm under spreading branches. Despite his care, a dead limb, invisible until too late, caught on his long spur, which gave forth a ringing metallic peal. At the sudden sound, Dale sank prone, his blood congealing in his veins.

"Alec! You hear thet?" called Steve, his husky voice vibrantly sharp.

"By Gawd I did!. . . . Ring of a spur! I know thet sound."

"Behind the log!"

The thud of quick footsteps urged Dale out of his frozen inaction. He began to crawl for the brush.

"There, Steve! I hear someone crawlin'. Smoke up thet black patch!"

Gunshots boomed. Bullets thudded all around Dale. Then one tore through his sombrero, leaving a hot sensation on his scalp. A gust of passion intercepted Dale's desire to escape. He whirled to his knees. Both men were outlined distinctly in the firelight. The foremost stood just behind the log, his gun spouting red. The other crouched peering into the darkness. Dale shot them both. The leader fell hard over the log, and lodged there, his boots beating a rustling tattoo on the ground. The other flung his gun high and dropped as if his legs had been chopped from under him.

Brittenham leaped erect, working the lever of his rifle, his nerves strung like wires. But the engagement had ended as quickly as it had begun. He strode into the campfire circle of light. The thief Ben lay on his back, arms wide, his dark visage distorted, ghastly. Dale's impulse was to search these men, but resisting it, he hurriedly made for the horses. The cold sick grip on his vitals eased with hurried action, and likewise the fury.

Presently he reached the grassy plot where the horses were staked out. They snorted and thumped the ground.

"Prince," he called, and whistled.

The great stallion whinnied recognition. Dale made his way to the horse. Prince was blacker than the night. Dale laid gentle hands on him and talked to him. The other horses quieted down.

"Jim . . . Jade . . . Ringspot . . . Bluegrass," called Dale, and repeated the names as he passed among the horses. They all were pets except Jade, and she was temperamental. She had to be now. Presently Dale untied her long stake rope, and after that the ropes of the other horses. He felt sure Prince and Jim would follow him anywhere, but he did not want to risk it then.

He led the five horses back, as nearly as he could, on the course by which he had approached the camp. In the darkness the task was not easy. He chose to avoid the trail, which ran somewhere to the left. A tree and a thicket here and there he recognized. But he was off his direction when his own horse nickered to put him right again.

"No more of that, Hoofs," he said, when he found his animal. Cinching his saddle, he gathered up the five halters and mounted. "Back-trail yourself, old boy!"

The Waltrous horses were eager to follow, but the five of them abreast on uneven and obstructed ground held Dale to a slow and watchful progress. Meanwhile, as he picked his way, he began figuring the situation. It was imperative that he travel all night. There seemed hardly a doubt that the three thieves would be joined by others of their gang. Anyone save a novice could track six horses through a forest. Dale meant to be a long way on his back trail before dawn. The night was dark. He must keep close to the path of the horse thieves so that he would not get lost in this forest. Once out on the stage road, he could make up for slow travel.

Trusting to Hoofs, the rider advanced, peering keenly into the gloom. He experienced no difficulty in leading the thoroughbreds; indeed they often slacked their halters and trampled almost at his heels. They knew they were homeward bound, in the charge of a friend. Dale hoped all was well, yet could not rid himself of a contrary presentiment. The reference of one of the horse thieves to Ben's double-crossing their comrades seemed to Dale to signify that the remaining outfit might be down in the Salmon River Valley.

At intervals Dale swerved to the left far enough to see the trail in the gloom. When he could hear the babble of the brook, he knew he was going right. In due time he worked out of the open forest and struck the grade, and eventually got into the rocks. Here he had to follow the path, but he endeavored to keep his tracks out of it. And in this way he found himself at length in a shallow, narrow gulch, the sides of which appeared unscalable. If it were short, all would be well; on the other hand, he distrusted a long defile, where it would be perilous if he happened to encounter any riders. They would scarcely be honest riders.

The gulch was long. Moreover, it narrowed and was dark

as pitch except under the low walls. Dale did not like Hoofs's
halting. His trusty mount had the nose and ears of the wild
horses he had hunted for years.

"What ails you, hoss?" queried Dale.

Finally Hoofs stopped. Dale, feeling for his ears, found
them erect and stiff. Hoofs smelled or heard something. It
might be a bear or a cougar, both of which the horse disliked
exceedingly. It might be more horse thieves, too. Dale listened and thought hard. Of all things, he did not want to
retrace his steps. While he had time then, and before he
knew what menaced further progress, he dismounted and
led the horses as far under the dark wall as he could get
them. Then he drew their heads up close to him and called
low, "Steady, Prince . . . Jade, keep still . . . Blue, hold
now . . ."

Hoofs stood at his elbow. It was Dale's voice and hand
that governed the intelligent animals. Then as a low tram-
pling roar swept down the gully, they stood stiff. Dale
tingled. Horses coming at a forced trot! They were being
driven when they were tired. The sound swelled, and soon
it was pierced by the sharp calls of riders.

"By thunder!" muttered Dale, aghast at the volume of
sounds. "My hunch was right!. . . . Big Bill Mason has
raided the valley. . . . Must be over a hundred head in that
drove."

The thudding, padded roar, occasionally emphasized by
an iron-shod hoof ringing on stone, or a rider's call, swept
down the gully. It was upon Dale before he realized the
drove was so close. He could see a moving, obscure mass
coming. He smelled dust. "Git in thar!" shouted a weary
voice. Then followed a soft thudding of hoofs on sand.
Dale's situation was precarious, for if one of his horses
betrayed his whereabouts, there would be riders sheering
out for strays. He held the halters with his left hand, and
pulled his rifle from its saddle sheath. If any of these raiders
bore down on him, he would be forced to shoot and take
to flight. But his thoroughbreds, all except Jade, stood like
statues. She champed her bit restlessly. Then she snorted.
Dale hissed at her. The moment was one to make him taut.

He peered through the gloom, expecting riders to loom up, and he had the grim thought that it would be death for them. Then followed a long moment of sustained suspense, charged with incalculable chance.

"Go along there, you lazy hawses," called a voice.

The soft thumping of many hoofs passed. Voices trailed back. Dale relaxed in immeasurable relief. The driving thieves had gone by. He thought then for the first time what a thrilling thing it was going to be to return these thoroughbreds to Edith Watrous.

Hard upon that came the thought of Leale Hildrith—his friend. It was agony to think that Leale was involved with these horse thieves. On the instant, Dale was shot through with the memory of his debt to Hildrith—of that terrible day when Hildrith had found him out on the range, crippled, half-starved and frozen, and had, at the risk of his own life, carried Dale through the blizzard to the safety of a distant shelter. A friendship had sprung up between the two men, generous and careless on Hildrith's part, even at times protective. In Dale had been engendered a passionate loyalty and gratitude, almost a hero worship for the golden-bearded Hildrith.

What would come of it? No solution presented itself to Dale at the moment. He must meet situations as they arose, and seek in every way to protect his friend.

Toward sunset the following day Dale Brittenham rode across the clattering old bridge, leading the Watrous thoroughbreds into the one and only street of Salmon. The dusty horses, five abreast, trotting at the end of long halters, would have excited interest in any Western town. But for some reason that puzzled Dale, he might have been leading a circus or a band of painted Indians.

Before he had proceeded far, however, he grasped that something unusual accounted for the atmosphere of the thronged street. Seldom did Salmon, except on a Saturday night, show so much activity. Knots of men, evidently in earnest colloquy, turned dark faces in Dale's direction; gaudily dressed dance-hall girls, black-frocked gamblers, and dusty-booted, bearded miners crowded out in the street to

see Dale approach; cowboys threw up their sombreros and
let out their cracking whoops; and a throng of excited young-
sters fell in behind Dale to follow him.

Dale began to regret having chosen to ride through town,
instead of fording the river below and circling to the Watrous
ranch. He did not like the intense curiosity manifested by
a good many spectators. Their gestures and words, as he
rode by, he interpreted as more speculative and wondering
than glad at his return with the five finest horses in Idaho.

When Dale was about halfway down the wide street, a
good friend of his detached himself from a group and stepped
out.

"Say, Wesley, what'n hell's all this hubbub about?" queried Brittenham as he stopped.

"Howdy, Dale," returned the other, offering his hand.
His keen eyes flashed like sunlight on blue metal and a huge
smile wrinkled his bronzed visage. "Well, if I ain't glad to
see you I'll eat my shirt. . . . Just like you, Dale, to burst
into town with thet bunch of hosses!"

"Sure, I reckoned I'd like it. But I'm gettin' leary. What's
up?"

"Hoss thieves raided the river ranches yesterday,"
replied the other swiftly. "Two hundred head
gone!. . . . Chamberlain, Trash, Miller—all lost heavy.
An' Jim Watrous got cleaned out. You know, lately Jim's
gone in for cattle buyin', an' his riders were away somewhere. Jim lost over a hundred head. He's ory-eyed. An'
they say Miss Edith was heartbroke to lose hers. Dale, you
sure got the best of her other beaux with this job."

"Stuff!" ejaculated Dale, feeling the hot blood in his
cheeks, and he sat up stiffly. "Wes, damn you—"

"Dale, I've had you figgered as a shy hombre with girls.
Every fellow in this valley, except you, has cocked his eyes
at Edith Watrous. She's a flirt, we all know. . . . Listen.
I been achin' to tell you, my sister Sue is a friend of Edith,
an' she says Edith likes you pretty well. Hildrith only has
the inside track 'cause of her father. I'm tellin' you, Dale."

"Shut up, Wes. You always hated Hildrith, an' you're
wrong about Edith."

"Aw, hell! You're scared of her an' you overrate what Hildrith did for you once. Thet's all. This was the time for me to give you a hunch. I won't shoot off my chin again."

"An' the town's all het-up over the horse-thief raid?"

"You bet it is. Common talk runs thet there's some slick hombre here who's in with the hoss thieves. This Salmon Valley has lost nigh on to a thousand head in three years. An' every one of the big raids comes at a time when the thieves had to be tipped off."

"All big horse-thief gangs work that way," replied Dale ponderingly. Wesley was trying to tell him that suspicion had fallen upon his head. He dropped his eyes as he inquired about his friend Leale Hildrith.

"Humph! In town yesterday, roarin' louder than anybody about the raid. Swore this stealin' had to be stopped. Talked of offerin' ten thousand dollars' reward—that he'd set an outfit of riders after the thieves. You know how Leale raves. He's in town this mornin', too."

"So long, Wes," said Dale soberly, and was about to ride on when a commotion broke the ring of bystanders to admit Leale Hildrith himself.

Dale was not surprised to see the golden-bearded, booted, and spurred partner of Watrous, but he did feel a surprise at a fleeting and vanishing look in Hildrith's steel-blue eyes. It was a flash of hot murderous amazement at Dale there with Edith Watrous's thoroughbreds. Dale understood it perfectly, but betrayed no sign.

"Dale! You son-of-a-gun!" burst out Hildrith in boisterous gladness as he leaped to seize Dale's hand and pumped it violently. His apparent warmth left Dale cold, and bitterly sad for his friend. "Fetched Edith's favorites back! How on earth did you do it, Dale? She'll sure reward you handsomely. And Jim will throw a fit. . . . Where and how did you get back the horses?"

"They were stolen out of the pasture yesterday mornin' about daylight," replied Dale curtly. "I trailed the thieves. Found their camp last night. Three men, callin' themselves Ben, Alec, an' Steve. They were fightin' among themselves. Ben tricked them, the other two said. An' one of them shot him. . . . They caught me listenen' and forced me to kill them."

"You killed them!" queried Hildrith hoarsely, his face turning pale. His eyes held a peculiar oscillating question.

"Yes. An' I didn't feel over-bad about it, Leale," rejoined Dale with sarcasm. "Then I wrangled the horses an' rode down."

"Where was this?"

"Up on the mountain, over in Montana somewhere. After nightfall I sure got lost. But I hit the stage road. . . . I'll be movin' along, Leale."

"I'll come right out to the ranch," replied Hildrith, and hurried through the crowd.

"Open up, there," called Dale to the staring crowd. "Let me through."

As he parted the circle and left it behind, a taunting voice cut the silence. "Cute of you, Dale, fetchin' the high-steppers back. Haw! Haw!"

Dale rode on as if he had not heard, though he could have shot the owner of that mocking voice. He had been implicated in this horse stealing. Salmon was full of shifty-eyed, hard-lipped men who would have had trouble in proving honest occupations. Dale had clashed with some of them, and he was hated and feared. He rode on through town and out into the country. He put the horses to a brisk trot, as he wanted to reach the Watrous ranch ahead of Hildrith.

Dale stood appalled at the dual character of the man to whom he considered himself so deeply indebted, whom he had looked on as a friend and loved so much. It was almost impossible to believe. Almost every man in the valley liked Leale Hildrith and called him friend. The women loved him, and Dale felt sure, despite Wesley's blunt talk, that Edith Watrous was one of them. And if she did love him, she was on the way to disgrace and misery. Leale, the gay handsome blade, not yet thirty, so good-natured and kindly, bighearted and openhanded, was secretly nothing but a low-down horse thief. Dale had hoped against hope that when he saw Hildrith the disclosures of the three horse thieves would somehow be disproved. But that had not happened. Hildrith's eyes, in only a flash, had betrayed him. Dale suffered the degradation of his own disillusion. Yet the thought of Edith's unhappiness hurt him even more.

He had not gotten anywhere in his perplexed and bewildered state of mind when the bronze-and-gold hills of the Watrous ranch loomed before him. From the day he had ridden up to it, Dale had loved this great ranch, with its big old weather-beaten house nestling among the trees up from the river, its smooth shining hills bare to the gray rocks and timberline, its huge fields of corn and alfalfa green as emerald, its level range spreading away from the river gateway to the mountains. From that very day, too, Dale had loved the lithe, free-stepping, rouguish-eyed daughter of Jim Watrous, a melancholy and disturbing fact that he strove to banish from his consciousness. Her teasing and tormenting, her fits of cold indifference and her resentment that she could not make him bend to her like her other admirers, her flirting before his eyes plainly to make him jealous— all these weaknesses of Edith's did not equal in sum her kindness to him, and the strange inexplicable fact that when she was in trouble she always came to him.

As Dale rode around the grove into the green square where the gray ranch house stood on its slope, he was glad to see that Hildrith had not arrived. Three saddled horses standing on the porch, and they had sighted him. Crowding to the high steps, they could be heard exclaiming. Then gray-haired Jim Watrous, stalwart of build and ruddy of face, descended down a step to call lustily, "Edith! Rustle out here. Quick!"

Dale halted on the green below the porch. It was going to be a hard moment. Watrous and his visitors could not disturb him. But Edith! . . . Dale heard the swift patter of light feet—then a little scream, sweet, high-pitched, that raised a turbulent commotion in his breast.

"Oh, Dad! . . . My horses!" she exclaimed in ecstasy, and she clasped her hands.

"They sure are, lass," replied Watrous gruffly.

"Ha! Queer, Brittenham should fetch them," added a man back of Watrous.

In two leaps Edith came down the high steps, supple as a cat, and bounded at Dale, her bright hair flying, her dark eyes shining.

"Dale! Dale!" she cried rapturously, and ran to clasp both hands around his arm. "You old wild-horse hunter! You darling!"

"Well, I'll stand for the first," said Dale, smiling down at her.

"You'll stand for that . . . and hugs . . . and kisses when I get you alone, Dale Brittenham. . . . You've brought back my horses! My heart was broken. I was crazy. I couldn't eat or sleep. . . . Oh, it's too good to be true! Oh, Dale, I can never thank you enough."

She left him to throw her arms around Prince's dusty neck and to cry over him. Watrous came slowly down the steps, followed by his three visitors, two of whom Dale knew by sight. He bent the eyes of a hawk upon Dale.

"Howdy, Brittenham. What have you got to say for yourself?"

"Horses talk, Mr. Watrous, same as money," replied Dale coolly. He sensed the old horse trader's doubt and dismay.

"They sure do, young man. There's ten thousand dollars' worth of horseflesh. To Edith they're priceless. What's your story?"

Dale told it briefly, omitting the description of the horse-thief trail and the meeting upon it with the raided stock from the valley. He chose to save these details until he had had more time to ponder over them.

"Brittenham, you can prove those three horse thieves are dead—an' that you made away with two of them?" queried Watrous tensely.

"Prove!" ejaculated Dale, sorely nettled. "I could prove it—certainly, sir, unless their pards came along to pack them away. . . . But my word should be proof enough, Mr. Watrous."

"I reckon it would be, for me, Brittenham," returned the rancher hastily. "But this whole deal has a queer look. . . . This gang of horse thieves has an accomplice—maybe more than one—right here in Salmon."

"Mr. Watrous, I had the same thought," said Dale shortly.

"Last night, Brittenham, your name was whispered around in this connection."

"That doesn't surprise me. Salmon is full of crooked men. I've clashed with some. I've only a few friends, an'—"

Edith whirled to confront her father with pale face and blazing eyes.

"Dad! Did I hear right? What did you say?"

"I'm sorry, lass. I told Brittenham he was suspected of bein' the go-between for this horse-thief gang."

"For shame, Father! It's a lie. Dale Brittenham would not steal, let alone be a cowardly informer."

"Edith, I didn't say I believed it," rejoined Watrous, plainly upset. "But it's bein' said about town. It'll fly over the range. An' I thought Brittenham should know."

"You're right, Mr. Watrous," said Dale. "Thank you for tellin' me."

The girl turned to Dale, evidently striving for composure.

"Come, Dale. Let us take the horses out."

She led them across the green toward the lane. Dale had no choice but to follow, though he desperately wanted to flee. Before the men were out of range of his acute hearing, one of them exclaimed to Watrous. "Jim, he didn't deny it!"

"Huh! Did you see his eyes?" returned the rancher shortly. "I'd not want to be in the boots of the man who accuses him to his face."

"Here comes Hildrith, drivin' as if the devil was after him."

Dale heard the clattering buckboard, but he did not look. Neither did Edith. She walked with her head down, deep in thought. Dale dared to watch her, conscious of inexplicable feelings.

The stable boy, Joe, ran out to meet them, with a face that was a study in inexpressible wonder and delight. Edith did not relinquish the halters until she had led the horses up the incline into the wide barn.

"Joe, water them first," she said. "Then wash and rub them down. Take a look at their hoofs. Feed them a little alfalfa. And watch them every minute till the boys get back."

"Yes, Miss Edith, I shore will," he replied eagerly. "We done had words they'll be hyar by dark."

Dale dismounted and removed saddle and bridle from his tired horse.

"Let Joe watch your horse, Dale. I want to talk to you."

Dale leaned against some bales of hay, not wholly from weariness. He had often been alone with Edith Watrous, but never like this.

"Reckon I ought to . . . to clean up," he stammered, removing his sombrero. "I . . . I must look a mess."

"You're grimy and worn, yes. But you look pretty proven and good to me, Dale Brittenham. . . . What's that hole in your hat?"

"By thunder! I forgot about that. It's a bullet hole."

"Oh—so close. . . . Who shot it there, Dale?"

"One of the horse thieves."

"It was self-defense, then?"

"You bet it was."

"I've hated your shooting scrapes, Dale," she rejoined earnestly. "But here I see I'm squeamish—and unreasonable. . . . Only the reputation you have—your readiness to shoot—that's all I never liked about it."

"I'm sorry. But I can't help that," replied Dale, turning his sombrero round and round with restless hands.

"You needn't be sorry this time. . . . Dale, look me straight in the eye."

Thus so earnestly urged, Dale had to comply. Edith appeared pale of face and laboring under suppressed emotion. Her dark eyes had held many expressions for him, mostly roguish and coquettish, and sometimes blazing, but at this moment they were beautiful with a light, a depth he had never seen in them before. And it challenged him with a truth he had always driven from his consciousness—that he loved this bright-haired girl.

"Dale, I was ashamed of Dad," she said. "I detest that John Stafford. He is the one who brought the gossip from town—that you were implicated in this raid. I don't believe it."

"Thanks, Edith. It's good of you."

"Why didn't you say something?" she asked spiritedly. "You should have cussed Dad roundly."

"I was sort of flabbergasted."

"Dale, if this whole range believed you were a horse thief, I wouldn't. Even if your faithful Nalook believed it—though he never would."

"No. I reckon that Indian wouldn't believe bad of me."

"Nalook thinks heaps of you, Dale . . . and . . . and that's one reason why I do too."

"Heaps?"

"Yes, heaps."

"I'd never have suspected it."

"Evidently you never did. But it's true. And despite your . . . your rudeness . . . your avoidance of me, now is the time to tell it."

Dale dropped his eyes again, sorely perturbed and fearful that he might betray himself. Edith was not bent on conquest now. She appeared roused to championship of him, and there was something strange and soft about her that was new and bewildering.

"I never was rude," he denied stoutly.

"We won't argue about that now," she went on hurriedly. "Never mind about me and my petty vanity. . . . I'm worried about this gossip. It's serious, Dale. You'll get into trouble and go gunning for somebody—unless I keep you from it. I'm going to try. . . . Will you take a job riding for me—taking care of my horses?"

"Edith! . . . I'm sure obliged to you for that offer. But Watrous wouldn't see it."

"I'll make him see it."

"Hildrith? . . . He wouldn't like that idea now."

"Leale will like anything I want him to."

"Not this time."

"Dale, *will* you ride for me?" she queried impatiently.

"I'd like to . . . if . . . if . . . Well, I'll consider it."

"If you would, that'd stop this gossip more than anything I can think of. . . . I'd like it very much, Dale. I'll never feel safe about my horses again. Not until these thieves are rounded up. If you worked for me, I could keep you here—out of that rotten Salmon. And you wouldn't be going on those long wild-horse hunts."

"Edith, you're most amazin'—kind an' . . . an' thoughtful all of a sudden." Dale could not quite keep a little bitter surprise out of his voice.

She blushed vividly. "I might have been all that long ago—if you had let me," she responded.

"Who am I to aspire to your kindness?" he said almost coldly. "But even if I wasn't a poor wild-horse hunter, I'd never run after you like these . . . these—"

"Maybe that's one reason why . . . Well, never mind," she interrupted, with a hint of her old roguishness. "Dale, I'm terribly grateful to you for bringing back my horses. I know you won't take money. I'm afraid you'll refuse the job I offered. . . . So, Mr. Wild-Horse Hunter, I'm going to pay you as I said I would back at the house."

"No!" he cried, suddenly weak. "Edith, you wouldn't be so silly . . . so . . . Aw, it's just the devil in you."

"I'm going to, Dale."

Her voice drew him as well as her intent; and forced to look up, he was paralyzed to see her bending to him, her face aglow, her eyes alight. Her hands flashed upon his shoulders—slipped back—and suddenly pressed like bands of steel. Dale somehow recovered strength to stand up and break her hold.

"Edith, you're out of . . . your head," he said huskily.

"I don't care if I am. I always wanted to, Dale Brittenham. This was a good excuse . . . and I'll never get another."

The girl's face was scarlet as she drew back from Dale, but it paled before she concluded her strange speech.

"You're playin' with me—you darned flirt," he blurted out.

"Not this time, Dale," she replied soberly, and then Dale

grasped that something deeper and hitherto unguessed had followed hard on her real desire to reward him for his service.

"It'll be now or never, Dale. . . . For this morning at breakfast, I gave in at last to Dad's nagging . . . and consented to marry Leale Hildrith."

"Then it'll be never, my strange girl," replied Dale hoarsely, shot through with anguish for Edith and his treacherous friend. "I . . . I reckoned this was the case. . . . You love Leale?"

"I think . . . I do," replied Edith somewhat hesitantly. "He's handsome and gay. Everybody loves Leale. You do. All the girls are mad about him, I . . . I love him, I guess. . . . But it's mostly Dad. He hasn't given me any peace for a year. He's set on Hildrith. Then he thinks I ought to settle down . . . that I flirt . . . that I have all his riders at odds with each other on my account. . . . Oh, it made me furious."

"Edith, I hope you will be happy."

"A lot *you* care, Dale Brittenham."

"I cared too much. That was the trouble."

"*Dale!* . . . So that was why you avoided me?"

"Yes, that was why, Edith."

"But you are as good as any man."

"You're a rich rancher's daughter. I'm a poor wild-horse hunter."

"Oh! As if that made any difference between friends."

"Edith, it does," he replied sadly. "An' now they're accusin' me of being a horse thief . . . I'll have to kill again."

"No! You mustn't fight," she cried wildly. "You might be shot. Dale, promise me you'll not go gunning for anyone."

"That's easy, Edith. I promise."

"Thanks, Dale. . . . Oh, I don't know what's come over me." She dropped her head on his shoulder. "I'm glad you told me. It hurts—but it helps somehow. I . . . I must think."

"You should think that you must not be seen . . . like this," he said gently.

"I don't care," she flashed, suddenly aroused. Edith's propensity to change was one of her bewildering charms. Dale realized he had said the wrong thing and he shook in her tightening grasp. "You've cheated me, Dale, of a real friendship. And I'm going to punish you. I'm going to keep my word, no matter what comes of it. . . . Oh, you'll believe me a flirt—like Dad and all of these old fools that think I've kissed these beaux of mine. But I haven't—well, not since I was a kid. Not even Leale! . . . Dale, you might have kissed me if you'd had any sense."

"Edith, have *you* lost all sense of . . . of . . ." he choked out.

"Of modesty?. . . . I'm not in the least ashamed." But her face flamed as she tightened her arms around him and pressed sweet cool lips to his cheek. Dale was almost unable to resist crushing her in his arms. He tried, weakly, to put her back. But she was strong, and evidently in the grip of some emotion she had not calculated upon. For her lips sought his and their coolness turned to sweet fire. Her eyelids fell heavily. Dale awoke to spend his hunger for love and his renunciation in passionate response.

That broke the spell which had moved Edith.

"Oh, Dale!" she whispered as she wrenched her lips free. "I shouldn't have . . . Forgive me. . . . I was beside myself."

Her arms were sliding from his neck when quick footfalls and the ring of spurs sounded in the doorway. Dale looked up to see Hildrith, livid under his golden beard, with eyes flaring, halting at the threshold.

"What the hell!" he burst out incredulously.

Dale's first sensation was one of blank dismay, and as Edith, with arms dropping, drew back, crimson of face, he sank against the pile of bales like a guilty man caught in some unexplainable act.

"Edith, what did I see?" demanded Hildrith in jealous wrath.

"Not very much! You were too late. Why do you slip up on people like that?" the girl returned with a tantalizing laugh. She faced him, her blush and confusion vanishing. His strident voice no doubt roused her imperious spirit.

"You had your arms around Dale?"

"I'm afraid I had."

"You kissed him?"

"Once. . . . No, twice, counting a little one," returned this amazing creature. Dale suffered some kind of torture, only part of which was shame.

"Well, by heaven!" shouted Hildrith furiously. "I'll beat him half to death for that."

Edith intercepted him and got between him and Dale. She pushed him back with no little force. "Don't be a fool, Leale. It'd be dangerous to strike Dale. Listen . . ."

"I'll call him out," shouted her lover.

"And get shot for your pains. Dale has killed half a dozen men. . . . Let me explain."

"You can't explain a thing like this."

"Yes, I can. I admit it looks bad, but it really isn't . . . . When Dale brought my horses back, I was so crazy with joy that I wanted to hug and kiss him. I told him so. But I couldn't before Dad and all those men. When we came out here I . . . I tried to, but Dale repulsed me—"

"Edith! Do you expect me to believe that?" queried Hildrith.

"Yes. It's true. . . . But the second time, I succeeded— and you almost caught me in the act."

"You damned little flirt!"

"Leale, I wasn't flirting. I wanted to kiss Dale; I was in rapture about my horses. And before that, Dad and those men hinted Dale was hand and glove with these horse thieves. I hated that. It excited me. Perhaps I was out of my head. Dale said I was. But you shall not blame him. It was my fault."

"Oh, hell!" fumed Hildrith in despair. "Do you deny the poor beggar is in love with you?"

"I certainly do deny that," she retorted, and her gold-tan cheeks flamed red.

"Well, he is. Anybody could see that."

"I didn't. And if it's true, he never told me."

Hildrith began to pace the barn. "Good God! Engaged to marry me for half a day, and you do a brazen thing like that. . . . Watrous is sure right. You need to be tied down. Playing fast and loose with every rider on the range! Coaxing your Dad to set our marriage day three months off! . . . Oh, you drive me mad. I'll tell you, young woman, when you *are* my wife—"

"Don't insult me, Mr. Hildrith," interrupted Edith coldly. "I'm not your wife yet. I was honest with you because I felt sure you'd understand. I'm sorry I told you the truth, and I don't care whether you believe me or not."

With her bright head erect, she walked past Hildrith, avoiding him as he reached for her, and she was deaf to his entreaties.

"Edith, I'll take it all back," he cried after her. But so far as Dale could see or hear, she made no response. Hildrith turned away from the door, wringing his hands. It was plain that he worshiped the girl, that he did not trust her, that he was inordinately suspicious, that for an accepted lover he appeared the most wretched of men. Dale watched him, seeing him more clearly in the revelation of his dual nature. Just how far Hildrith had gone with this horse-stealing gang, Dale did not want to know. Dale did see that his friend's redemption was possible—that if he could marry this girl, and if he could be terribly frightened with possible exposure, he might be weaned from whatever association he had with Mason, and go honest and make Edith happy. It was not a stable conviction, but it gripped Dale. He had his debt to pay to Hildrith, and a glimmering of a possible way to do it formed in his mind. Even at that moment, though, he felt the ax of disillusion and reality at the roots of his love for this man. Hildrith was not what he had believed him. But that would not deter Dale from paying his debt a thousand-fold. Lastly, if Edith Watrous loved this man, Dale felt that he must save him.

Hildrith whirled upon Dale. "So this is how you appreciate what I've done for you, Dale. You made love to my girl. You damned handsome ragamuffin—you worked on Edith's sympathy! You've got me into a hell of a fix."

"Leale, you sure are in a hell of a fix," replied Dale with dark significance.

"What do you mean?" queried Hildrith sharply, with a quick uplift of head.

"You're one of Big Bill Mason's gang," rejoined Dale deliberately.

Hildrith gave a spasmodic start, as if a blade had pierced his side. His jaw dropped and his face blanched to an ashen hue under his blond beard. He tried to speak, but no words came.

"I sneaked up on the camp of those three horse thieves. I listened. Those low-down thieves—Ben, Alec, Steve— spoke familiarly of you. Alec an' Steve were concerned over what you'd do about the theft of the Watrous horses. Ben made light of it. He didn't care. They talked about Big Bill. An' that talk betrayed you to me. . . . Leale, you're the range scout for Mason. You're the man who sets the time for these big horse raids."

"You know! . . . Oh, my God!" cried Hildrith abjectly.

"Yes, I know that an' more. I know the trail to Mason's secret rendezvous. I was on that trail an' saw this last big drove of stolen horses pass by. I figured out how Mason's gang operates. Pretty foxy. I'll say. But it was too good, too easy, too profitable. It couldn't last."

"For God's sake, Dale, don't squeal on me!" besought Hildrith, bending over Dale with haggard, clammy face. "I've money. I'll pay you well—anything . . ."

"Shut up! Don't try to buy me off, or I'll despise you for a yellow cur. . . . I didn't say I'd squeal on you. But I do say you're a madman to think you can work long at such a low-down game."

"Dale, I swear to God this was my last deal. Mason forced me to one more, a big raid which was to be his last in this valley. He had a hold on me. We were partners in a cattle business over in Montana. He roped me into a rustling deal before I knew what it actually was. That was three years ago, over in Kalispel. Then he found a hiding place, a box canyon known only to the Indians, and that gave him the idea of raiding both Montana and Idaho ranges at the same time—driving to the canyon and there changing outfits and stolen horses. While a raid was on over there, Mason made sure to be in Bannock or Kalispel, and he roared louder than anyone at the horse thieves. He had the confidence of all the ranchers over there. My job was the same here in the Salmon Valley. But I fell in love with Edith and have been trying to break away."

"Leale, you say you swear to God this was your last deal with Mason?"

"Yes, I swear it. I have been scared to death. I got to thinking it was too good to last. I'd be found out. Then I'd lose Edith."

"Man, you'd not only lose her. But you'd be shot—or worse, you'd be hanged. These ranchers are roused. Watrous is ory-eyed, so Wesley told me. They'll organize an' send a bunch of Wyomin' cowboys out on Mason's trail. I'll bet that's exactly what Watrous is talkin' over now with these visitors."

"Then it's too late. They'll find me out. God! Why didn't I have some sense?"

"They won't find you out if you quit. Absolutely quit! I'm the only man outside the Mason gang who knows. If some of them are captured an' try to implicate you, it wouldn't be believed. I'll not give you away."

"Dale, by heaven, that's good of you," said Hildrith hoarsely. "I did you an injustice. Forgive me. . . . Dale, tell me what to do. I'm in your hands. I'll do anything. Only save me. I wasn't cut out for a horse thief. It's galled me. I've been sick after every raid. I haven't the guts. I've learned an awful lesson."

"Have you any idea how Edith would despise you if she knew?"

"That's what makes me sweat blood. I worship the very ground she walks on."

"Does she love you?"

"Oh, Lord, I don't know now. I thought so. She said she did. But she wouldn't . . . She promised to marry me. Watrous wants her settled. If she will marry me, I know I can make her love me."

"Never if you continued to be a two-faced, dirty, lousy, yellow dog of a horse thief," cried Dale forcefully. "You've got to perform a miracle. You've got to change. That's the price of my silence."

"Dale, I'm torn apart. . . . What use to swear? You know I'll quit—and go straight all my life. For Edith! What man wouldn't? You would if she gave herself . . . any man would. Don't you see?"

"Yes, I see that, an' I believe you," replied Dale, convinced of the truth in Hildrith's agony. "I'll keep your secret, an' find a way to save you if any unforseen thing crops up. . . . An' that squares me with you, Leale Hildrith."

Swift light footsteps that scattered the gravel cut short Hildrith's impassioned gratitude. Edith startled Dale by appearing before them, her hand at her breast, her face white as a sheet, her eyes blazing.

Hildrith met her on the incline, exclaiming, "Why, Edith! Running back like that! What's wrong?"

She paid no heed to him, but ran to Dale, out of breath and visibly shaking.

"Oh . . . Dale . . ." she panted. "Stafford sent . . . for the sheriff! . . . They're going to . . . arrest you."

"Stafford? Who's he? That man in the black coat?"

"Yes. He's lately got in with Dad. . . . Cattle. It's his outfit of cowboys coming. . . . He's hard as nails."

"Are they here?"

"Will be directly. I tore loose from Dad . . . and ran all the way. . . . Oh, Dale, what will you do?" She was unconscious of her emotion—and she put an appealing hand upon Dale's arm. Dale had never seen her like that, nor had Hildrith. They were deeply struck, each according to his reception of her white-faced, earnest demeanor.

"Edith, you can bet I won't run," declared Dale grimly. "Thank you, girl, all the same. . . . Don't take this so . . . so strangely. Why, you're all upset. They can't arrest me."

Hildrith drew back from the wide door. He appeared no less alarmed and excited than Edith. "They're coming, Dale," he said thickly. "Bayne and Stafford in the lead. . . . That sheriff has it in for you, Dale. Only last night I heard him swear he'd jail you if you came back. . . . It's ticklish business. What'll you do?"

"I'm sure I don't know," returned Dale with a laugh.

Edith besought him, "Oh, Dale, don't kill Bayne! . . . For my sake!"

"If you brace up, I reckon maybe I can avoid that."

Dale led his horse out of the barn, down the runway into the open. Then he stepped aside to face the advancing men, now nearly across the wide court. The dark-garbed Stafford was talking and gesticulating vehemently to a stalwart booted man. This was the one officer that Salmon supported, and it had been said of him that he knew which side of the law to be on. Watrous and three other men brought up the rear. They made no bones about sheering off to the side. Stafford, however, a swarthy and pompous man, evidently accustomed to authority, remained beside Bayne.

"Hey, you," called out Dale, far from civilly. "If you want to talk with me, that's close enough."

Hildrith, to Dale's surprise, came down in the incline and took up a stand beside Dale.

"What you mean by this turkey-strutting?" he demanded, and his simulation of resentment would have deceived anyone but Dale.

"Hildrith, we got business with Brittenham," declared Bayne harshly.

"Well, he's my friend, and that concerns me."

"Thanks, Leale," interposed Dale. "But let me handle this. Bayne, are you looking for me?"

"I sure am."

"At whose instigation?"

"Mr. Stafford, here. He sent for me, an' he orders you arrested."

Watrous broke in to say nervously, "Brittenham, I adivsed

against this. I have nothing to do with it. I don't approve of resorting to law on the strength of gossip. If you'll deny any association with horse thieves, that will do for me. If your word is good to Edith, it ought to be for me."

"Jim Watrous, you're a fool," rasped out Stafford. "Your daughter is apparently infatuated with this . . . this—"

"Careful!" cut in Dale. "You might say the wrong thing. An' leave Miss Edith's name out of this deal. . . . Stafford, what's your charge against me?"

"I think you're one of this horse-raiding gang," declared Stafford stoutly, though he turned pale.

"On what grounds?"

"I wasn't influenced by gossip, sir. I base my suspicion on your fetching back those thoroughbred horses. They must have been driven off by mistake. Any horse thief would know they couldn't be ridden or sold in Montana or Idaho. They'd be recognized. So you fetched them back because it was good business. Besides, it'd put you in better with Watrous, and especially his—"

"Shut up! If you speak of that girl again, I'll shoot your leg off," interrupted Dale. "An' you can gamble on this, Stafford: if I don't shoot you anyhow, it'll be the only peg on which you can hang a doubt of my honesty."

"You insolent ruffian!" ejaculated Stafford, enraged and intimidated. "Arrest him, sheriff."

"Brittenham, you'll have to come with me," spoke up Bayne with an uneasy cough. "You appear to be a talker. You'll get a chance to talk in court at Twin Falls."

"You're tryin' to go through with it?" asked Dale derisively.

"I say you're under arrest."

"What's *your* charge?"

"Same as Mr. Stafford's."

"But that's ridiculous, Bayne. You can't arrest a man for bringing back stolen horses. There's not the slightest case against me. Stafford has heard gossip in town—where half the population is crooked. How do I know an' how do you know that Stafford himself is not the big hand in this horse-stealin' gang? There's some big respectable rancher on this range who stands in with the thieves. Why do you pick on a poor wild-horse hunter? A ragamuffin, as he has called me. Look at my boots! Look at my saddle! If I was the go-between, wouldn't I have better equipment? You're not very bright, Bayne."

"Aw, that's all bluff. Part of your game. An' you've sure pulled it clever around here for three years."

While Dale had prolonged this argument, his mind had been conceiving and fixing upon a part he wanted to play. It would have been far easier but for Edith's inexplicable importunity. She had awakened to something strange and hitherto unrevealed. It must have been pity, and real sincerity and regret come too late. Then, the girl had always been fair in judging something between others. If Dale had had an inkling it was anything else, he never could have made the sacrifice, not even to save Hildrith. But she loved Hildrith; she would become his wife, and that surely meant his salvation. Dale felt that ignominy, a bad name thrust upon him, and acknowledged by his actions, could not make much difference to him. He was only a wild-horse hunter. He could ride away to Arizona and never be heard of again. Still, he hated the thing he felt driven to do.

Then Edith stepped into the foreground, no longer the distraught girl who had arrived there a few moments ago to warn Dale. Had she read his mind? That suspicion affected him more stirringly than anything yet that had happened.

"Sheriff Bayne, you must not try to arrest Dale without proof," she said earnestly.

"I'm sorry, lady. It's my duty. He'll get a fair trial."

"Fair!" she exclaimed scornfully. "When this arrest is so unfair! Bayne, there's something wrong—something dishonest here—and it's not in Dale."

"Edith, don't say more," interposed her father. "You're overwrought."

Hildrith strode to her side, hurried in manner, dark and strained of face.

"Leale, why don't you speak up for Dale?" she queried, and her eyes blazed upon him with a marvelously penetrating and strange look.

"Bayne, let Dale off," Hildrith said huskily. "Don't make a mistake here. You've no proof—and you can't arrest him."

"Can't! Why the hell can't I?" rejoined the sheriff.

"Because he won't let you. Good God, man, haven't you any mind?"

"Humph! I've got mind enough to see there's somethin' damn funny here. But it ain't in me. . . . Brittenham, you're under arrest. Come on, now, no buckin'."

As he made a step forward, Dale's gun gleamed blue and menacing.

"Look out, Bayne! If you move a hand, I'll kill you," he warned.

He backed cautiously down the court, leading his horse to one side.

"I see what I'm up against here, an' I'm slopin'," went on Dale. "Stafford, you had it figured. Watrous, I engineered that raid. . . . Edith, I fetched your horses back because I was in love with you." A strange laugh followed his words.

Dale backed across the square to the lane, where he leaped into his saddle and spurred swiftly out of sight.

2

Dale's campfire that night was on a bend of the brook near where he had surprised the three horse thieves and had recovered the Watrous thoroughbreds.

Upon riding away from the Watrous ranch, he had halted in Salmon long enough to buy supplies; then he had proceeded down the river to a lonely place where he had rested his horse and slept. By dawn he was climbing the mountain into Montana, and by sundown that night he was far down the horse-thief trail.

Notwithstanding the fact that Dale had branded himself by shouldering Hildrith's guilt, he had determined to find Big Bill Mason's rendezvous and evolve a plan to break up the horse-thief band. Born of his passion at riding away from the Watrous ranch a fugitive, leaving Edith to regret her faith in him, this plan seemed to loom as gigantic and impossible after the long hours of riding and thinking. But he would not abandon it.

"Stafford and Bayne will send a big outfit after me," he muttered as he sat before his little campfire. "An' I'll lead them to Mason's hiding place. Failin' that, I'll go down on the range below Bannock an' get the ranchers there to raise a big posse of cowboys. One way or another I'm goin' to break up Mason's gang."

Dale had not thought of that in the hour of his sacrifice for Hildrith and Edith. He had meant to take his friend's ignominy and ride away from Idaho forever. But two things had operated against this—first, the astounding and disturbing fact that Edith Watrous, in her stress of feeling, had betrayed not only faith in him but also more real friendship than she had ever shown; and secondly, his riding away in disgrace would leave the Mason gang intact, free to carry on their nefarious trade. He was the man for the job. If he broke up the gang, it would remove the stain from his name. Not that he would ever want to or dare to go back to the Watrous ranch! But there was a tremendous force in the thought that he might stand clean and fine again in Edith Watrous's sight. How strangely she had reacted to that situation when her father and the others had confronted him! What could she have meant when she said there was something wrong, something dishonest there in that climax? Could she have had a glimmering of the truth? This thought was so disturbing that it made Dale catch his breath. Edith was a resourceful, strong-minded girl, once she became aroused. On reflection, however, he eased away that doubt, and also the humanly weak joy at a possible indestructible faith in him. No! He felt sure Hildrith would be safe. Once the Mason outfit was broken up, with the principals killed and the others run out of the country, Hildrith would be safe, and Edith's happiness would be assured.

In hours past, Dale had, in the excitement of his flight, believed that he could kill his love for Edith Watrous and forget her. This proved to be an illusion, the recognition of which came to him beside his lonely campfire. He would love her more, because his act had been something big and for her sake, and in his secret heart he would know that if she could be told the truth, she would see her faith justified, and whatever feeling she had for him would be intensified.

He saw her dark proud eyes and her white face in the opal glow of his fire. And having succumbed to that, he could not help but remember her boldness to reward him, her arms and her kiss, and, most poignant of all, the way she had been betrayed by her impulse, how that kiss had trapped her into emotion she had not intended. Was it possible that he had had this chance for Edith Watrous and had never divined it? The thought was torture, and he put it from him, assuring himself that the girl's actions had been the result of her gratitude and joy at the return of her beloved horses.

The fire died down to ruddy coals; the night wind began to seep through the grass and brush; four-footed prowlers commenced their questing. Standing erect, Dale listened. He heard his horse cropping the grass. A brooding solitude lay upon the forest.

He made his bed close under the side of a fallen pine, using his saddle for a pillow. So many nights of his life he had lain down to look up at the open dark sky with its trains of stars. But this night the stars appeared closer and they seemed to talk to him. He was conscious that his stern task, and the circumstances which had brought it about, had heightened all his faculties to a superlative degree. He seemed a vastly different man, and he conceived that it might develop that he would revel in what fate had set him to do.

At last he fell asleep. During the night he awoke several times, and the last time, which was near dawn and nippingly cold, he got up and kindled a fire. All about him rose dark gray forest wall, except in the east, where a pale brightening betokened dawn.

It was Dale's custom to cook and eat a hearty breakfast, so that he could go long on this meal if he had to. His last task before saddling was to obliterate signs of his camp. Then, with light enough to see clearly, he mounted and was off on his perilous quest.

All the way, Dale had kept off the main trail. It would take an Indian or a wild-horse hunter to track him. He traveled some few paces off the horse-thief trail, but kept it in sight. And every mile or so he would halt, dismount, and walk a few steps away from his horse to listen. In that silent forest he could have heard a sound at a considerable distance.

By sunrise he was down out of the heavy timber belt and riding out upon a big country of scaly rock and immense thickets of evergreen and cedar, with only an occasional large pine. The brook disappeared—probably dried up, or sunk into the earth. The trail led on straight as a beeline for a while.

The sun rose high, and grew hot. With the morning half spent, he figured that he had traveled fifteen miles from his last camp. Occasionally he had glimpses of the lower range, gray and vast and dim below. The trail turned west, into more rugged plateaus and away from the descent. But presently, beyond a long fringe of evergreen thicket, he saw the peculiar emptiness that proclaimed the presence of a void.

Dale knew before he reached it that he had come upon the hole in the ground where Big Bill Mason had his hideout. Leaving the proximity of the trail, Dale rode to a little higher ground, where a gray stone eminence, less thickly overgrown, seemed to offer easy access to the place. Here he dismounted and pushed his way through the evergreens. At once he emerged upon a point, suddenly to stand rooted to the spot.

"What a wonderful place," he exclaimed as he grasped the fact that his sight commanded. He stood upon the rim of a deep gorge a mile long and half as wide. On all sides, the walls sheered down a thousand feet, gray and craggy, broken and caverned, lined by green benches, and apparently unscalable. Of course trails led in and out of this hole, but Dale could not see where. The whole vast level bottomland was as green as an emerald. At each end, where the gorge narrowed, glistened a lake. All around the rims stood up a thick border of evergreens, which screened the gorge from every side. Hunters and riders could pass near there without ever guessing the presence of such a concealed pocket in the mountain plateau.

"Ahuh. No wonder Mason can steal horses wholesale," soliloquized Dale. "All he had to do was to hide his tracks just after he made a raid."

Dale reflected that the thieves had succeeded in this up to present time. However, any good tracker could sooner or later find this rendezvous for resting and shifting droves of horses. Dale was convinced that Stafford and Watrous would send out a large outfit of riders as soon as they were available.

It struck Dale singularly that he could not see an animal or a cabin in the gorge below. But undoubtedly there were points not visible to him from this particular location. Returning to his horse, he decided to ride around the gorge to look for another trail.

He found, after riding for a while, that although the gorge was hardly more than three or four miles in circumference, to circle it on horseback or even on foot, a man would have to travel three times that far. There were canyon offshoots from the main valley, and these had to be headed.

At the west side Dale found one almost as long as the gorge itself. But it was narrow. Here he discovered the first sign of a trail since he had left the main one. And this was small, and had never been traveled by a drove of horses. It led off to the south toward Bannock. Dale deliberated a moment. If he were to risk going down to investigate this trail, about halfway between the lakes at each end should be the one for him to take. Certainly it did not show much usage. At length he rode down, impelled by a force that seemed to hold less of reason than of presagement.

It grew steep in the notch, and shady, following a precipitous watercourse. He had to get off and lead his horse. Soon trees and brush obstructed his view. The trail was so steep that he could only proceed slowly, and before he surmised that he was halfway down, he emerged into the open to see a beautiful narrow valley, richly green, enclosed by timbered slopes. A new cabin of peeled logs stood in the lea of the north side. He saw cattle, horses and finally a man engaged in building a fence. If Dale had encountered an individual laboring this way in any other locality he would have thought him a homesteader. It was indeed the most desirable place to homestead and ranch on a small scale that Dale had ever seen in his hunting trips.

The man saw Dale just about as quickly as Dale had seen him. Riding by the cabin, where a buxom woman and some children peeped out fearfully, Dale approached the man. He appeared to be a sturdy, thickset farmer, bearded and sharp-eyed. He walked forward a few steps and stopped significantly near a shiny rifle leaning against the fence. When Dale got close enough, he recognized him.

"Well, Rogers, you son-of-a-gun! What're you doin' down here?"

"Brittenham! By all thet's strange. I might ask you the same," was the hearty reply, as he offered a horny hand. Two years before, Dale had made the acquaintance of Rogers back in the Sawtooth range.

"When'd you leave Camus Creek?" he asked.

"This spring, fine place thet. But too cold. I was snowed in all winter. Sold out to a Mormon."

"How'd you happen to locate in here?"

"Just by accident. I went to Bannock, an' from there to Halsey. Liked thet range country. But I wanted to be high, where I could hunt an' trap as well as homestead. One day I hit the trail leadin' in here. An' you bet I located pronto."

"Before ridin' out in the big valley?"

"Yes. But I saw it. What a range! This was big enough for me. If I'm not run out, I'll get rich here in five years."

"Then you located before you found out you had neighbors?"

"What do you know about them?" queried Rogers, giving Dale a speculative glance.

"I know enough."

"Brittenham, I hope to heaven you're not in thet outfit."

"No. An' I hope the same of you. Have you got wise yet to Mason's way of operatin'?"

"Mason! You don't mean the rancher an' horse trader Bill Mason?"

"So help me! Big Bill—the biggest horse thief in this country."

"If thet's true, who can a man trust?"

"It's true, Rogers, as you can find out for yourself by watchin'. Mason runs a big outfit. They split. One operates in Idaho, the other in Montana. They drive the stolen horses up here an' switch men an' herds. They sell the Montana stock over in Idaho an' the Idaho stock over on the Montana ranges."

"Hell you say! Big idee an' sure a bold one. I savvy now why these men politely told me to pull up stakes an' leave. But I had my cabin up an' my family here before they found out I'd located. Then I refused to budge. Reed, the boss of the outfit, rode down again last week. Offered to buy me out. I thought thet strange. But he didn't offer much, so I refused to sell. He said his boss didn't want any home-steaders in here."

"Rogers, they'll drive you out or kill you," said Dale.

"I don't believe it. They're bluffin'. If they murdered me, it'd bring attention to this place. Nobody knows of it. I haven't told about it yet. My wife would, though, if they harmed me."

"This gang wouldn't hesitate to put you all out of the way. They just don't take you seriously yet. Think they can scare you out."

"Not me! Brittenham, how'd you come to know about this horse stealin' an' to find this hole?"

Dale told him about the theft of the Watrous thorough-breds, how he had trailed the robbers up the mountain, what happened there and lastly about the big raid that followed hard the same day.

"I'll tell you, Rogers. I got blamed for bein' the scout member of Mason's outfit. It made me sore. I left Salmon in a hurry, believe me. My aim in findin' this hole is to organize a big posse of cowboys an' break up Mason's gang."

"Humph! You ain't aimin' to do much atall."

"It'll be a job. There's no tellin' how many outfits Mason runs. It's a good bet that his ranch outfit is honest an' don't suspect he's a horse thief. I'll bet he steals his own horses. If I can raise a hard-fightin' bunch an' corral Mason's gang all here in this hole . . . To catch them here—that's the trick. I'd reckon they'll be stragglin' in soon. It doesn't take long to sell a bunch of good horses. Then they'd hide here, gamblin' an' livin' fat until time for another raid. . . . Rogers, breakin' up this outfit is important to you. How'd you like to help me?"

"What could I do? Remember I'm handicapped with a wife an' two kids."

"No fightin' an' no risk for you. I'd plan for you to watch the valley, and have some kind of signs I could see from the rim to tell me when the gang is here."

"Get down an' come in," replied the homesteader soberly. "We'll talk it over."

"I'll stop a little while. But I mustn't lose time."

"Come set on the porch. Meet the wife an' have a bite to eat. . . . Brittenham, I think I'll agree to help you. As for signs . . . There. It's the only place on the rim from which you can see my valley an' cabin. I've a big white cowhide thet I could throw over the fence. You could see it much farther than thet. If you did see it, you'd know the gang was here." ·

"Just the trick, Rogers. An' no risk to you," replied Dale with satisfaction. He unsaddled Hoofs and let him free on the rich grass. Then he accompanied Rogers to the cabin, where he spent a restful hour. When he left, Rogers walked with him to the trail. They understood one another and were in accord on the plan to break up Mason's band. Dale climbed on foot to the rim, his horse following, and then rode east to the point designated by the homesteader. Rogers watched for him and waved.

Across the canyon Dale located a curve in the wall which partly enclosed a large area black with horses. He saw cattle, too, and extensive gardens, and far up among the trees yellow cabins amidst the green. He rode back to Rogers's trail and headed for Bannock, keen and grim over his project.

The trail zigzagged gradually down toward lower country. Dale was always vigilant. No moving object escaped him. But there was a singular dearth of life along this scantily timbered eastern mountain slope. Toward late afternoon he found himself in broken country again, where the trail wound between foothills. It was dark when he rode into Bannock.

This town, like Salmon, was in the heyday of its productivity. And it was considerably larger. Gold and silver mining were its main assets, but there was some cattle trade, and extensive business in horses, and the providing of supplies for the many camps in the hills. Gambling halls of the period, with all their manifest and hidden evils, flourished flagrantly.

A miner directed Dale to a stable, where he left his horse. Here he inquired about his Indian friend Nalook. Then he went uptown to find a restaurant. He did not expect to meet anyone who knew him unless it was the Indian. Later that contingency would have to be reckoned with. Dale soon found a place to eat. Next to him at the lunch counter sat a red-faced cowboy who answered his greeting civilly.

"How's the hash here?" asked Dale.

"Fair to middlin'. . . . Stranger hereabouts, eh?"

"Yep. I hail from the Snake River country."

"I see you're a range rider, but no cowman."

"You're a good guesser. My job is horses."

"Bronco buster, I'll bet."

"Nope. But I can an' do break wild horses."

"Reckon you're on your way to Halsey. There's a big sale of Idaho stock there tomorrow."

"Idaho horses. You don't say?" ejaculated Dale, pretending surprise. "I hadn't heard of it."

"Wal, I reckon it wasn't advertised over your way," replied the cowboy with a short laugh. "An' when you buy fine horses at half their value, you don't ask questions."

"Cowboy, you said a lot. I'm goin' to have a look at that bunch. How far to Halsey?"

"Two hours for you, if you stretch leather. It takes a buckboard four."

Dale then attended to the business of eating, but that did not keep his mind from functioning actively. It staggered him to think that it was possible Mason had the brazen nerve to sell stolen Idaho horses not a hundred miles across the line.

"How about buckin' the tiger?" asked Dale's acquaintance as they went out into the street.

"No gamblin' for me, cowboy. I like to look on, though, when there's some big bettin'."

"I seen a game today. Poker. Big Bill Mason won ten thousand at Steen's. You should have heard him roar. 'Thet pays up for the bunch of hosses stole from me the other day.'"

"Who's Big Bill Mason?" asked Dale innocently.

"Wal, he's about the whole cheese down Halsey way. Got his hand in most everythin'. I rode for him a spell."

"Does he deal much in horses?"

"Not so much as with cattle. But he always runs four or five hundred haid on his ranch."

Presently Dale parted from the cowboy and strolled along the dimly lighted street, peering into the noisy saloons, halting near groups of men, and listening. He spent a couple of hours that way, here and there picking up bits of talk. No mention of the big steal of Idaho horses came to Dale's ears. Still, with a daily stagecoach between the towns it was hardly conceivable that some news had not sifted through to Bannock.

Before leaving town, Dale bought a new shirt and a scarf. He slept that night in the barn where he had his horse put up. A pile of hay made a better bed than Dale was used to. But for a disturbing dream about Edith Watrous, in which she visited him in jail, he slept well. Next morning he shaved and donned his new garments, after which he went into the town for breakfast. He was wary this morning. Early though the hour, the street was dotted with vehicles, and a motley string of pedestrians passed to and fro on the sidewalks.

Dale had a leisurely and ample breakfast, after which he strolled in the street to the largest store and entered, trying to remember what it was that he had wanted to purchase.

"Dale!" A voice transfixed him. He looked up to be confronted by Edith Watrous.

A red-cheeked, comely young woman accompanied Edith, and looked at Dale with bright, curious eyes. He stammered confusedly in answer to Edith's greeting.

"Susan, this is my friend Dale Brittenham." Edith introduced him hurriedly. "Dale . . . Miss Bradford. . . . I came over here to visit Susan."

"Glad to meet you, Miss," returned Dale, doffing his sombrero awkwardly.

"I've heard about you," said the girl, smiling at Dale. But evidently she saw something was amiss, for she turned to Edith and said, "You'll want to talk, I'll do my buying."

"Yes, I want to talk to my friend Dale Brittenham," agreed Edith seriously. Her desire to emphasize the word "friend" could not be mistaken. She drew him away from the entrance of the store to a more secluded space. Then: "Dale!" Her voice was low and full of suppressed emotion. Pale, and with eyes dark with scorn and sorrow, she faced him.

"How'd you come over here?" he queried, regaining his coolness.

"Nalook drove me in the buckboard. He returned to the ranch after you left. We got here last night."

"I'm sorry you had the bad luck to run into me."

"Not bad luck, Dale. I followed you. I was certain you'd come here. There's no other town to go to."

"Followed me? Edith, what for?"

"Oh, I don't know yet. . . . After you left, I had a quarrel with Leale and Dad. I upbraided them for not standing by you. I swore you couldn't be a horse thief. I declared you were furious—that in your bitterness you just helped them to think badly of you."

"How could they help that when I admitted my . . . my guilt?"

"They couldn't—but *I* could. . . . Dale, I know you. If you had been a real thief, you'd never . . . never have told me you . . . you loved me that last terrible moment. You couldn't. You wanted me to know. You looked bitter . . . hard . . . wretched. There was nothing low-down or treacherous about you."

"Edith, there you're wrong," returned Dale hoarsely. "For there is."

"Dale, don't kill my faith in you. . . . Don't kill something I'm . . . I'm afraid—"

"It's true—to my shame an' regret."

"Oh! . . . So that's why you never made love to me like the other boys? You were man enough for that, at least. I'm indebted to you. But I'll tell you what I've found out. If you had been the splendid fellow I thought you—and if you'd had sense enough to tell me sooner that you loved me—well . . . there was no one I liked better, Dale Brittenham."

"My God! Edith, don't—I beg you—don't say that now," implored Dale in passionate sadness.

"I care a great deal for Leale Hildrith. But it was Dad's match. I told Leale so. I would probably have come to it of my own accord in time. Yesterday we had a quarrel. He made an awful fuss about my leaving home, so I slipped away unseen. But I'll bet he's on the way here right now."

"I hope he comes after you," said Dale, bewildered and wrenched by this disclosure.

"He'd better not. . . . Never mind him, Dale. You've hurt me. Perhaps I deserved it. For I have been selfish and vain with my friends. To find out you're a . . . a thief . . . Oh, I hate you for making me believe it! It's just sickening. But you can't—you simply can't have become callous. You always had queer notions about range horses being free. There are no fences in parts of Idaho . . . Oh, see how I make excuses for you! Dale, promise me you will never help to steal another horse so long as you live."

Dale longed to fall upon his knees to her and tell her the truth. She was betraying more than she knew. He had seen her audacious and winning innumerable times, and often angry, and once eloquent, but never so tragic and beautiful as now. It almost broke down his will. He had to pull his hand from hers—to force a hateful stand utterly foreign to his nature.

"Edith, I won't lie to you—"

"I'm not sure of that," she retorted, her eyes piercing him. They had an intense transparancy through which her thought, her doubt, shone like a gleam.

"Nope. I can't promise. My old wild-horse business is about played out. I've got to live."

"Dale, I'll give . . . lend you money, so you can go away far and begin all over again. Please, Dale?"

"Thanks, lady," he returned, trying to be laconic. "Sure I couldn't think of that."

"You're so strange—so different. You didn't used to be like this. . . . Dale, is it my fault you went to the bad?"

"Nonsense!" he exclaimed in sudden heat. "Reckon it was just in me."

"Swear you're not lying to me."

"All right, I swear."

"If I believed I was to blame, I'd follow you and make you honest. I ought to do it anyhow."

"Edith, I'm sure glad you needn't go to such extremes. You can't save a bad egg."

"Oh . . . Dale . . ." She was about to yield further to her poignant mood when her friend returned.

"Edie, I'd have stayed away longer," said Susan, her eyes upon them. "Only if we're going to Halsey, we must rustle pronto."

"Edith, are you drivin' over there?" asked Dale quickly.

"Yes. Susan's brother is coming. There's a big horse sale on. I'm just curious to see if there will be any of Dad's horses there."

"I'm curious about that, too," admitted Dale soberly. "Good-by, Edith . . . Miss Bradford, glad to meet you, an' good-by."

Dale strode swiftly out of the store, though Edith's call acted upon him like a magnet. Once outside, with restraint gone, he fell in a torment. He could not think coherently, let alone reason. That madcap girl, fully aroused, might be capable of anything. Dale suffered anguish as he rushed down the street and to the outskirts of town, where he saddled his horse and rode away down the slope to the east.

There were both horsemen and vehicles going in the same direction, which he surmised was toward Halsey. Dale urged his mount ahead of them and then settled down to a steady sharp gait. He made no note of time, or the passing country. Long before noon, he rode into Halsey.

The town appeared to be deserted, except for clerks in stores, bartenders at the doors of saloons, and a few loungers. Only two vehicles showed down the length of the long street. Dale did not need to ask why, but he did ask to be directed to the horse fair. He was not surprised to find a couple of hundred people, mostly men, congregated at the edge of town, where in an open green field several score of horses, guarded by mounted riders, grazed and bunched in front of the spectators. Almost the first horse he looked at twice proved to be one wearing the Watrous brand.

Then Dale had a keen eye for that drove of horses and especially the horsemen. In a country where all men packed guns, their being armed did not mean anything to casual observers. Nevertheless, to Dale it was significant. They looked to him to be a seasoned outfit of hard riders. He hid Hoofs in the background and sauntered over toward the center of activities.

"Where's this stock from?" he asked one of a group of three men, evidently ranchers, who were bystanders like himself.

"Idaho. Snake River range."

"Sure some fine saddle hosses," went on Dale. "What they sellin' for?"

"None under a hundred dollars. An' goin' like hotcakes."

"Who's the hoss dealer?"

"Ed Reed. Hails from Twin Falls."

"Ahuh. Gentlemen, I'm a stranger in these parts," said Dale deliberately. "I hear there's no end of hoss business goin' on—hoss sellin', hoss buyin', hoss tradin' . . . and hoss stealin'."

"Wal, this is a hoss country," spoke up another of the trio dryly as he looked Dale up and down. Dale's cool speech had struck them significantly.

"You all got the earmarks of range men," Dale continued curtly. "I'd ask, without 'pearin' too inquisitive, if any one of you has lost stock lately?"

There followed a moment of silence, in which the three exchanged glances and instinctively edged close together.

"Wal, stranger. I reckon thet's a fair question," replied the eldest, a gray-haired, keen-eyed Westerner. "Some of us ranchers down in the range have been hit hard lately."

"By what? Fire, flood, blizzard, drought—or hoss thieves?"

"I'd reckon thet last, stranger. But don't forget you said it."

"Fine free country, this, where a range man can't talk right out," rejoined Dale caustically. "I'll tell you why. You don't know who the hoss thieves are. An' particular, their chief. He might be one of your respectable rancher neighbors."

"Stranger, you got as sharp a tongue as eye," returned the third member of the group. "What's your name an' what's your game?"

"Brittenham. I'm a wild-horse hunter from the Snake River Basin. My game is to get three or four tough cowboy outfits together."

"Wal, thet oughtn't be hard to do in this country, if you had reason," returned the rancher, his eyes narrowing. Dale knew he did not need to tell these men that the drove of horses before them had been stolen.

"I'll look you up after the sale," he concluded.

"My name's Strickland. We'll sure be on the lookout for you."

The three moved on toward the little crowd near the horses at that moment under inspection. "Jim, if we're goin' to buy some stock, we've got to hustle," remarked one.

Dale sauntered away to get a good look at the main drove of horses. When he recognized Dusty Dan, a superb bay that he had actually straddled himself, a bursting gush of hot blood burned through his veins. Deliberately he stepped closer, until he was halted by one of the mounted guards.

"Whar you goin', cowboy?" demanded this individual,

a powerful rider of mature years, clad in greasy leather chaps and dusty blouse. He had a bearded visage and deep-set eyes, gleaming under a black sombrero pulled well down.

"I'm lookin' for my hoss," replied Dale mildly.

The guard gave a slight start, barely perceptible.

"Wal, do you see him?" he queried insolently.

"Not yet."

"What kind of hoss, cowboy?"

"He's a black with white face. Wearin' a W brand like that bay there. He'd stand out in that bunch like a silver dollar in a fog."

"Wal, he ain't hyar, an' you can mosey back."

"Hell you say," retorted Dale, changing his demeanor in a flash. "These horses are on inspection . . . an' see here, Mr. Leather Pants, don't tell *me* to mosey anywhere."

Another guard, a lean, sallow-faced man, rode up to query, "Who's this guy, Jim?"

"Took him for a smart-alec cowboy."

"You took me wrong, you Montana buckaroos," interposed Dale, cool and caustic. "I'll mosey around an' see if I can pick out a big black hoss with the W brand."

Dale strode on, but he heard the guard called Jim mutter to his companion, "Tip Reed off." Presently Dale turned in time to see the rider bend from his saddle to speak in the ear of a tall dark man. Thus Dale identified Ed Reed, and without making his action marked, he retraced his steps. On his way he distinguished more W brands and recognized more Watrous horses.

Joining the group of buyers, Dale looked on from behind. After one survey of Big Bill Mason's right-hand man, Dale estimated him to be a keen, suave villain whose job was to talk, but who would shoot on the slightest provocation.

"Well, gentlemen, we won't haggle over a few dollars," Reed was saying blandly as he waved a hairy brown hand. "Step up and make your offers. These horses have got to go."

Then buying took on a brisk impetus. During the next quarter of an hour a dozen and more horses were bought and led away, among them Dusty Dan. That left only seven animals, one of which was the white-faced black Dale had spoken about to the guard, but had not actually seen.

"Gentlemen, here's the pick of the bunch," spoke up Reed. "Eight years old. Sound as a rock. His sire was blooded stock. I forget the name. What'll you offer?"

"Two hundred fifty," replied a young man eagerly.

"That's a start. Bid up, gentlemen. This black is gentle, fast, wonderful gait. A single-footer. You see how he stacks up."

"Three hundred," called Dale, who meant to outbid any other buyers, take the horse and refuse to pay.

"Come on. Don't you Montana men know horseflesh when—"

Reed halted with a violent start and the flare of his eyes indicated newcomers. Dale wheeled with a guess that he verified in the sight of Edith Watrous and Leale Hildrith, with another couple behind them. He also saw Nalook, the Indian, at the driver's seat of the buckboard. Hildrith's face betrayed excessive emotion under control. He tried to hold Edith back. But, resolute and pale, she repelled him and came on. Dale turned swiftly so as not to escape Reed's reaction to this no-doubt-astounding and dangerous interruption. Dale was treated to an extraordinary expression of fury and jealousy. It passed from Reed's dark glance and dark face as swiftly as it had come.

Dale disliked the situation that he saw imminent. There were ten in Reed's gang—somber, dark-browed men, whom it was only necessary for Dale to scrutinize once to gauge their status. On the other hand, the majority of spectators and buyers were not armed. Dale realized that he had to change his mind, now that Edith was there. To start a fight would be foolhardy and precarious.

The girl had fire in her eyes as she addressed the little group.

"Who's boss here?" she asked.

"I am, Miss. . . . Ed Reed, at your service." Removing his sombrero, he made her a gallant bow, his face strong and not unhandsome in a bold way. Certainly his gaze was one of unconcealed admiration.

"Mr. Reed, that black horse with the white face belongs to me," declared Edith imperiously.

"Indeed?" replied Reed, exhibiting apparently genuine surprise. "And who're you, may I ask?"

"Edith Watrous. Jim Watrous is my father."

"Pleased to meet you. . . . You'll excuse me, Miss Watrous, if I ask for proof that this black is yours."

Edith came around so that the horse could see her, and she spoke to him. "Dick, old boy, don't you know me?"

The black pounded the ground, and with a snort jerked the halter from the man who held him. Whinnying, he came to Edith, his fine eyes soft, and he pressed his nose into her hands.

"There! . . . Isn't that sufficient?" asked Edith.

Reed had looked on with feigned amusement. Dale gauged him as deep and resourceful.

"Sam, fetch my hoss. I'm tired standing and I reckon this lady has queered us for other buyers."

"Mr. Reed, I'm taking my horse whether you like it or not," declared Edith forcefully.

"But, Miss Watrous, you can't do that. You haven't proved to me he belongs to you. I've seen many fine horses that'd come to a woman."

"Where did you get Dick?"

"I bought him along with the other W-brand horses."

"From whom?" queried Edith derisively.

"John Williams. He's a big breeder in horses. His ranch is on the Snake River. I daresay your father knows him."

Dale stepped out in front. "Reed, there's no horse breeder on the Snake River," he said.

The horse thief coolly mounted a superb bay that had been led up, and then gazed sardonically from Edith to Dale.

"Where do you come in?"

"My name is Brittenham. I'm a wild-horse hunter. I know every foot of range in the Snake between the falls an' the foothills."

"Williams's ranch is way up in the foothills," rejoined Reed easily. He had not exactly made a perceptible sign to his men, but they had closed in, and two of them slipped out of their saddles. Dale could not watch them and Reed at the same time. He grew uneasy. These thieves, with their crafty and bold leader, were masters of the situation.

"Lady, I hate to be rude, but you must let go that halter," said Reed with an edge on his voice.

"I won't."

"Then I'll have to be rude. Sam, take that rope away from her."

"Leale, say something, can't you? What kind of a man are you, anyway?" cried Edith, turning in angry amazement to her fiancé.

"What can I say?" asked Hildrith, spreading wide his hands, as if helpless. His visage at the moment was not prepossessing.

"What! Why, tell him you know this is my horse."

Reed let out a laugh that had bitter satisfaction as well as irony in it. Dale had to admit that the predicament for Hildrith looked extremely serious.

"Reed, if Miss Watrous says it's her horse, you can rely on her word," replied the pallid Hildrith.

"I'd take no woman's word," returned the leader.

"Dale, you know it's my horse. You've ridden him. If you're not a liar, Mr. Reed knows you as well as you know me."

"Excuse me, lady," interposed Reed. "I never saw your wild-horse-hunter champion in my life. If he claims to know me, he is a liar."

"Dale!" Edith transfixed him with soul-searching eyes.

"I reckon you forget, Reed. Or you just won't own up to knowin' me. That's no matter. . . . But the horse belongs to Miss Watrous. I've ridden him. I've seen him at the Watrous ranch every day or so for years."

"Brittenham. Is that what you call yourself? I'd lie for her, too. She's one grand girl. But she can't rob me of this horse."

"Rob! That's funny, Mr. Reed," exclaimed Edith hotly. "You're the robber! I'll bet Dick against two bits that *you're* the leader of this horse-thief gang."

"Well, I can't shoot a girl, much less such a pretty and

tantalizing one as you. But don't sat that again. I might forget my manners."

"You brazen fellow!" cried Edith, probably as much incensed by his undisguised and bold gaze as by his threat. "I not only think you're a horse thief, but I call you one!"

"All right. You can't be bluffed, Edith," he returned grimly. "You've sure got nerve. But you'll be sorry, if it's the last trick I pull on this range."

"Edith, get away from here," ordered Hildrith huskily, and he plucked at her with shaking hands. "Let go that halter."

"No!" cried Edith, fight in every line of her face and form, and as she backed away from Hildrith, she inadvertently drew nearer to Reed.

"But you don't realize who . . . what this man—"

"Do you?" she flashed piercingly.

Dale groaned in spirit. This was the end of Leale Hildrith. The girl was as keen as a whip, and bristling with suspicion. The unfortunate man almost cringed before her. Then Reed rasped out, *"Rustle, there!"*

At the instant that Reed's ally Sam jerked the halter out of Edith's hand, Dale felt the hard prod of a gun against his back. "Put 'em up, Britty," called a surly voice. Dale lost no time getting his hands above his head, and he cursed under his breath for his haste and impetuosity. He was relieved of his gun. Then the pressure on his back ceased.

Reed reached down to lay a powerful left hand on Edith's arm.

"Let go!" the girl burst our angrily, and she struggled to free herself. "Oh . . . you hurt me! Stop, you ruffian."

"Stand still, girl!" ordered Reed, trying to hold her and the spirited horse. "He'll step on you—crush your foot."

"Ah-h!" screamed Edith in agony, and she ceased her violent exertion to stand limp, holding up one foot. The red receded from her face.

"Take your hand off her," shouted Hildrith, reaching for a gun that was not there.

"Is that your stand, Hildrith?" queried Reed, cold and hard.

"What do you . . . mean?"

"It's a showdown. This jig is up. Show yellow . . . or come out with the truth before these men. Don't leave it to me."

"Are you drunk . . . or crazy?" screamed Hildrith, beside himself. He did not grasp Reed's deadly intent, whatever his scheme was. He thought his one hope was to play his accustomed part. Yet he suspected a move that made him frantic. "Let her go! . . . Damn your black hide—let her go!"

"Black, but not yellow, you traitor!" wrung out Reed as he leveled a gun at Hildrith. "We'll see what the boss says to this. . . . Rustle, or I'll kill you. I'd like to do it. But you're not my man. . . . Get over there quick. Put him on a horse, men, and get going. Sam, up with her!"

Before Dale could have moved, even if he had been able to accomplish anything, unarmed as he was, the man seized Edith and threw her up on Reed's horse, where despite her struggles and cries he jammed her down in the saddle in front of Reed.

As Reed wheeled away, looking back with menacing gun, the spectators burst into a loud roar. Sam dragged the black far enough to be able to leap astride his own horse and spur away, pulling his captive into his stride. The other men, ahead of Reed, drove the unsaddled horses out in front. The swiftness and precision of the whole gang left the crowd stunned. They raced out across the open range, headed for the foothills. Edith's pealing cry came floating back.

3

Dale was the first to recover from the swift raw shock of the situation. All around him milled an excited crowd. Most of them did not grasp the significance of the sudden exodus of the horse dealers until they were out of sight. Dale, nearly frantic, lost no time in finding Strickland.

"Reckon I needn't waste time now convincin' you there are some horse thieves in this neck of the woods," he spat out sarcastically.

"Brittenham, I'm plumb beat," replied the rancher, and he looked it. "In my ten years on this range I never saw the like of that. . . . My Gawd! What an impudent rascal! To grab the Watrous girl right under our noses! Not a shot fired!"

"Don't rub it in," growled Dale. "I had to watch Reed. His man got the drop on me. A lot of slick hombres. An' that's not sayin' half."

"We'll hang every damn one of them," shouted Strickland harshly.

"Yes. After we save the girl. . . . Step aside here with me. Fetch those men you had. . . . Come, both of you . . . . Now, Strickland, this is stern business. We've not a minute to waste. I want a bunch of hard-ridin' cowboys here *pronto*. Figure quick now, while I get my horse an' find that Indian."

Dale ran into the lithe, dark, buckskin-clad Nalook as he raced for his horse. This Indian had no equal as a tracker in Idaho.

"Boss, you go me," Nalook said in his low voice, with a jerk of his thumb toward the foothills. Apparently the Indian had witnessed the whole action.

"Rustle, Nalook. Borrow a horse an' guns. I've got grub."

Dale hurried back, leading Hoofs. Reaching Strickland and his friends, he halted with them and waited, meanwhile taking his extra guns out of his pack.

"I can have a posse right here in thirty minutes," declared the rancher.

"Good. But I won't wait. The Indian here will go with me. We'll leave a trail they can follow on the run. Tracks an' broken brush."

"I can get thirty or more cowboys here in six hours."

"Better. Tell them the same."

Nalook appeared at his elbow. "Boss, me no find hoss."

"Strickland, borrow a horse for this Indian. I'll need him."

"Joe, go with the Indian," said Strickland. "Get him horse and outfit if you have to buy it."

"You men listen and hold your breath," whispered Dale. "This Reed outfit is only one of several. Their boss is Big Bill Mason."

The ranchers were beyond surprise or shock. Strickland snapped his fingers.

"That accounts. Dale, I'll tell you something. Mason got back to Halsey last night from Bannock, he said. He was not himself. This morning he sold his ranch—gave it away, almost—to Jeff Wheaton. He told Wheaton he was leaving Montana."

"Where is he now?"

"Must have left early. You can bet something was up for him to miss a horse sale."

"When did Reed's outfit arrive?"

"Just before noon."

"Here's what has happened," Dale calculated audibly. "Mason must have learned that Stafford an' Watrous was sendin' a big posse out on the trail of Mason's Idaho outfit."

"Brittenham, if this Ed Reed didn't call Hildrith to show his hand for or against that outfit, then I'm plumb deaf."

"It looked like it," admitted Dale gloomily.

"I thought he was going to kill Hildrith."

"So did I. There's bad blood between them."

"Hildrith has had dealings of some kind with Reed. Remember how Reed spit out, 'We'll see what the boss says about this. . . . I'd like to kill you'? Brittenham, I'd say Hildrith has fooled Watrous and his daughter, and this Mason outfit also."

Dale was saved from a reply by the approach of Nalook, mounted on a doughty mustang. He carried a carbine and wore a brass-studded belt with two guns.

"We're off, Strickland," cried Dale, kicking his stirrup straight and mounting. "Hurry your posse an' outfits. Pack light, an' rustle's the word."

Once out of the circle of curious onlookers, Dale told Nalook to take the horse thieves' trail and travel. The Indian pointed toward the foothills.

"Me know trail. Big hole. Indian live there long time. Nalook's people know hoss thieves."

"I've been there, Nalook. Did you know Bill Mason was chief of that outfit?"

"No sure. See him sometime. Like beaver. Hard see."

"We'd better not shortcut. Sure Reed will make for the hideout hole. But he'll camp on the way."

"No far. Be there sundown."

"Is it that close from this side? . . . All the better. Lead on, Nalook. When we hit the brush, we want to be close on Reed's heels."

The Indian followed Reed's tracks at a lope. They led off the grassy lowland toward the hills. Ten miles or more

down on the range to the east Dale spied a ranch, which
Nalook said was Mason's. At that distance it did not look
pretentious. A flat-topped ranch house, a few sheds and
corrals, and a few cattle dotting the grassy range inclined
Dale to the conviction that this place of Mason's had served
as a blind to his real activities.

Soon Nalook led off the rangeland into the foothills.
Reed's trail could have been followed in the dark. It wound
through ravines and hollows between hills that soon grew
high and wooded on top. The dry wash gave place to pools
of water here and there, and at last a running brook, lined
by grass and willows growing green and luxuriant.

At length a mountain slope confronted the trackers. Here
the trail left the watercourse and took a slant up the long
incline. Dale sighted no old hoofmarks and concluded that
Reed was making a shortcut to the rendezvous. At intervals
Dale broke branches on the willows and brush he passed,
and let them hang down, plainly visible to a keen eye. Rocks
and brush, cactus and scrub oak, grew increasingly manifest, and led to the cedars, which in turn yielded to the
evergreens.

It was about midafternoon when they surmounted the
first bench of the mountain. With a posse from Halsey
possibly only a half-hour behind, Dale slowed up the Indian.
Reed's tracks were fresh in the red bare ground. Far across
the plateau the belt of pines showed black, and the gray
rock ridges stood up. Somewhere in that big rough country
hid the thieves' stronghold.

"Foller more no good," said Nalook, and left Reed's
tracks for the first time.

Dale made no comment. But he fell to hard pondering.
Reed, bold outlaw that he was, would this time expect
pursuit and fight, if he stayed in the country. His abducting
the girl had been a desperate unconsidered impulse, prompted
by her beauty, or by desire for revenge on Hildrith, or
possibly to hold her for ransom, or all of these together.
No doubt he knew this easy game was up for Mason. He
had said as much to Hildrith. It was not conceivable to Dale

that Reed would stay in the country if Mason was leaving. They had made their big stake.

Nalook waited for Dale on the summit of a ridge. "Ugh!" he said, and pointed.

They had emerged near the head of a valley that bisected the foothills and opened out upon the range, dim and hazy below. Dale heard running water. He saw the white flags of deer in the green brush. It was a wild and quiet scene.

"Mason trail come here," said the Indian, with an expressive gesture downward.

Then he led on, keeping to the height of slope; and once over that, entered rough and thicketed land that impeded their progress. In many places the soft red and yellow earth gave way to stone, worn to every conceivable shape. There were hollows and upstanding grotesque slabs and cones, and long flat stretches, worn uneven by erosion. Evergreens and sage and dwarf cedars found lodgment in holes. When they crossed this area to climb higher and reach a plateau, the sun was setting gold over the black mountain heights. Dale recognized the same conformation of earth and rock that he had found on the south side of the robbers' gorge. Nalook's slow progress and caution brought the tight cold stretch to Dale's skin. They were nearing their objective.

At length the Indian got off his horse and tied it behind a clump of evergreens. Dale followed suit. They drew their rifles.

"We look—see. Mebbe come back," whispered Nalook. He glided on without the slightest sound or movement of foliage, Dale endeavoring to follow his example. After traversing half a mile in a circuitous route, he halted and put a finger to his nose. "Smell smoke. Tobac."

But Dale could not catch the scent. Not long afterward, however, he made out the peculiar emptiness behind a line of evergreens, and this marked the void they were seeking. They kept on at a snail's pace.

Suddenly Nalook halted and put a hand back to stop Dale. He could not crouch much lower. Warily he pointed over the fringe of low evergreens to a pile of gray rocks.

On the summit sat a man with his back to the trackers. He was gazing intently in the opposite direction. This surely was a guard stationed there to spy any pursuers, presumably approaching on the trail.

"Me shoot him," whispered Nalook.

"I don't know," whispered Dale in reply, perplexed. "How far to their camp?"

"No hear gun."

"But there might be another man on watch."

"Me see."

The Indian glided away like a snake. How invaluable he was in a perilous enterprise like this! Dale sat down to watch and wait. The sun sank and shadows gathered under the evergreens. The scout on duty seemed not very vigilant. He never turned once to look back. But suddenly he stood up guardedly and thrust his rifle forward. He took aim and appeared about to fire. Then he stiffened strangly, and jerked up as if powerfully propelled. Immediately there followed the crack of a rifle. Then the guard swayed and fell backward out of sight. Dale heard a low crash and a rattle of rocks. Then all was still. He waited. After what seemed a long anxious time, the thud of hoofs broke the silence. He sank down, clutching his rifle. But it was Nalook coming with the horses.

"We go quick. Soon night," said the Indian, and led the way toward the jumble of rocks. Presently Dale saw a trail as wide as a road. It led down. Next he got a glimpse of the gorge. From this end it was more wonderful to gaze down into, a magnificent hole, with sunset gilding the opposite wall, and purple shadows mantling the caverns, and the lake shining black.

Viewed from this angle, Mason's rendezvous presented a different and more striking spectacle. This north end where Dale stood was a great deal lower than the south end, or at least the walls were lower and the whole zigzag oval of rims sloped toward him, so that he was looking up at the southern escarpments. Yet the floor of the gorge appeared level. From this vantage point the caverns and cracks in the walls stood out darkly and mysteriously, suggesting hidden places and perhaps unseen exits from this magnificent burrow. The deep indentation of the eastern side, where Mason had his camp, was not visible from any other point. At that sunset hour a mantle of gold and purple hung over the chasm. All about it seemed silent and secretive, a wild niche of nature, hollowed out for the protection of men as wild as the place. It brooded under the gathering twilight. The walls gleamed dark with a forbidding menace.

Nalook started down, leading his mustang. Then Dale noted that he had a gun belt and long silver spurs hung over the pommel of his saddle. He had taken time to remove these from the guard he had shot. This trail was open and from its zigzag corners Dale caught glimpses of the gorge, and of droves of horses. Suddenly he remembered that he had forgotten to break brush and otherwise mark their path after they had sheered off Reed's tracks.

"Hist!" he whispered. The Indian waited. "It's gettin' dark. Strickland's posse can't trail us."

"Ugh. They foller Reed. Big moon. All same day."

Thus reassured, Dale followed on, grimly fortifying himself to some issue near at hand.

When they came out into the open valley below, dusk had fallen. Nalook had been in that hole before, Dale made certain. He led away from the lake along a brook, and let his horse drink. Then he drank himself, and motioned Dale to do likewise. He went on then in among scrub-oak trees to a grassy open spot, where he halted.

"Mebbe long fight," he whispered. "I rope hoss." Dale removed saddle and bridle from Hoofs and tied him on a long halter.

"What do?" asked Nalook.

"Sneak up on them."

By this time it was dark down in the canyon, though still light above. Nalook led out of the trees and, skirting them, kept to the north wall. Presently he turned and motioned Dale to lift his feet, one after the other, to remove his spurs. The Indian hung them in the crotch of a bush. Scattered trees of larger size began to loom up on this higher ground. The great black wall stood up rimmed with white stars. Dim

lights glimmered through the foliage and gradually grew
brighter. Nalook might have been a shadow for all the sound
he made. Intensely keen and vigilant as Dale was, he could
not keep from swishing the grass or making an occasional
rustle in the brush. Evidently the Indian did not want to
lose time, but he kept cautioning Dale with an expressive
backward gesture.

Nalook left the line of timber under the wall and took
out into the grove. He now advanced more cautiously than
ever. Dale thought this guide must have the eyes of a night
hawk. They passed a dark shack which was open in front
and had a projecting roof. Two campfires were blazing a
hundred yards farther on. And a lamp shone through what
must have been a window of a cabin.

Presently the Indian halted. He pointed. Then Dale saw
horses and men, and he heard gruff voices and the sound
of flopping saddles. Some outfit had just arrived. Dale wondered if it was Reed's. If so, he had tarried some little time
after getting down into the gorge.

"We go look—see," whispered Nalook in Dale's ear.
The Indian seemed devoid of fear. He seemed actuated by
more than friendship for Dale and gratitude to Edith Watrous. He hated someone in that horse-thief gang.

Dale followed him, growing stern and hard. He could
form no idea of what to do except get the lay of the land,
ascertain if possible what Reed was up to, and then go back
to the head of the trail and wait for the posse. But he well
realized the precarious nature of spying on these desperate
men. He feared, too, that Edith Watrous was in vastly more
danger of harm than of being held for ransom.

The campfires lighted up two separate circles, both in
front of the open-faced shacks. Around the farther one, men
were cooking a meal. Dale smelled ham and coffee. The
second fire had just been kindled and its bright blaze showed
riders moving about still with chaps on, unsaddling and
unpacking. Dale pierced the gloom for sight of Edith but
failed to locate her.

The Indian sheered away to the right so that a cabin hid
the campfires. This structure was a real log cabin of some

pretensions. Again a lamp shone through a square window. Faint streaks of light, too, came from chinks between the logs. Dale tried to see through the window, but Nalook led him at a wrong angle. Soon they reached the cabin. Dale felt the rough peeled logs. Nalook had an ear against the log wall. No sound within! Then the Indian, moving with extreme stealth, slipped very slowly along the wall until he came to one of the open chinks. Dale suppressed his eagerness. He must absolutely move without a sound. But that was easy. Thick grass grew beside the cabin. In another tense movement Dale came up with Nalook, who clutched his arm and pulled him down.

There was an aperture between the logs where the mud filling had fallen out. Dale applied his eyes to the small crack. His blood leaped at sight of a big man sitting at a table. Black-browed, scant-bearded, leonine Bill Mason! A lamp with a white globe shed a bright light. Dale saw a gun on the corner of the table, some buckskin sacks, probably containing gold, in front of Mason, and some stacks of greenbacks. An open canvas pack sat on the floor beside the table. Another pack, half full, and surrounded by articles of clothing added to Dale's conviction that the horse-thief leader was preparing to leave this rendezvous. The dark frown on Mason's brow appeared to cast its shadow over his strong visage.

A woman's voice, high-pitched and sweet, coming through the open door of the cabin, rang stingingly on Dale's ears.

". . . I told you . . . keep your horsy hands off me. I can walk."

Mason started up in surprise. "A woman! Now, what in hell?"

Then Edith Watrous, pale and worn, her hair disheveled and her dress so ripped that she had to hold it together, entered the cabin to fix dark and angry eyes upon the dual-sided rancher. Behind her, cool and sardonic, master of the situation, appeared Reed, blocking the door as if to keep anyone else out.

"Mr. Mason, I am Edith . . . Watrous," panted the girl.

"You needn't tell me that. I know you. . . . What in the world are you doing here?" rejoined Mason slowly, as he arose to his commanding height. He exhibited dismay, but he was courteous.

"I've been . . . treated to an . . . outrage. I was in Halsey . . . visiting friends. There was a horse sale . . . I went out. I found my horse Dick—and saw other Watrous horses in the bunch. . . . I promptly told this man Reed it was my horse. He argued with me. . . . Then Hildrith came up . . . and that precipitated trouble. Reed put something up to Hildrith—I didn't get just what. But it looks bad. I thought he was going to kill Hildrith. But he didn't. He cursed Hildrith and said he'd see what the boss would do about it. . . . They threw me on Reed's horse . . . made me straddle his saddle in front . . . and I had to endure a long ride . . . with my dress up to my head . . . my legs exposed to brush . . . and, what was more, to . . . to the eyes of Reed and his louts. . . . It was terrible . . . I'm so perfectly furious that . . . that . . ."

She choked in her impassioned utterance.

"Miss Watrous, I don't blame you," said Mason. "Please understand this is not my doing." Then he fastened his black angry eyes upon his subordinate. "Fool! What's your game?"

"Boss, I didn't have any," returned Reed coolly. "I just saw red. It popped into my head to make off with this stuck-up Watrous woman. And here we are."

"Reed, you're lying. You've got some deep game . . . . Jim Watrous was a friend of mine. I can't stand for such an outrage to his daughter."

"You'll have to stand it, Mason. You and I split, you know, over this last deal. It's just as I gambled would happen. You've ruined us. We're through."

"Ha! I can tell you as much."

"There was a wild-horse hunter down at Halsey—Dale Brittenham. I know about him. He's the man who trailed Ben, Alec and Steve—killed them. He's onto us. I saw that. He'll have a hundred gunners on our trail by sunup."

"Ed, that's not half we're up against," replied the chief gloomily. "This homesteader Rogers, with his trail to Bannock—that settled our hash. Stafford and Watrous have a big outfit after us. I heard it at Bannock. That's why I sold out. I'm leaving here as soon as I can pack."

"Fine. That's like you. Engineered all the jobs and let us do the stealing while you hobnobbed with the ranchers you robbed. Now you'll leave us to fight. . . . Mason, I'm getting out too—and I'm taking the girl."

"Good God! Ed, it's bad enough to be a horse thief like this. . . . Why, man, it's madness! What for, I ask you?"

"That's my business."

"You want to make Watrous pay to get her back. He'd do it, of course. But he'd tear Montana to pieces, and hang you."

"I might take his money—later. But I confess to a weakness for the young lady. . . . And I'll get even with Hildrith."

"Revenge, eh? You always hated Leale. But what's he got to do with your game?"

"He's crazy in love with her. Engaged to marry her."

"He *was* engaged to me, Mr. Mason," interposed Edith scornfully. "I thought I cared for him. But I really didn't. I despise him now. I wouldn't marry him if he was the last man on earth."

"Reed, does she know?" asked Mason significantly.

"Well, she's not dumb, and I reckon she's got a hunch."

"I'll be. . . .!" Whatever Mason's profanity was, he did not give it utterance. "Hildrith! But we had plans to pull stakes and leave this country. Did he intend to marry Miss Watrous and bring her with us? . . . That's not conceivable."

"Boss, he cheated you. He never meant to leave."

Mason made a passionate gesture, and as if to strike deep and hard, his big eyes rolled in a fierce glare. It was plain now to the watching Dale why Reed had wanted Hildrith to face his chief.

"Where's Hildrith?" growled Mason.

"Out by the fire under guard."

"Call him in." Reed went out.

Then Edith turned wonderingly and fearfully to Mason.

"Hildrith is *your* man!" she affirmed rather than queried.

"Yes, Miss Watrous, he was."

"Then *he* is the spy, the scout—the traitor who acted as go-between for you."

"Miss Watrous, he certainly has been my right-hand man for eight years. . . . And I'm afraid Reed and you are right about his being a traitor."

At that juncture Hildrith lunged into the cabin as if propelled viciously from behind. He was ashen-hued under his beard. Reed stamped in after him, forceful and malignant, sure of the issue. But just as Mason, after a steady hard look at his lieutenant, was about to address him, Edith flung herself in front of Hildrith.

"It's all told, Leale Hildrith," she cried with a fury of passion. "Reed gave you away. Mason corroborated him. . . . *You* are the tool of these men. *You* were the snake in the grass. *You*, the liar who ingratiated himself into my father's confidence. Made love to me! Nagged me until I was beside myself! . . . But your wrong to me— your betrayal of Dad—these fall before your treachery to Dale Brittenham. . . . You let *him* take on your guilt. . . . Oh, I see it all now. It's ghastly. That man loved you. . . . You despicable . . . despicable . . . "

Edith broke off, unable to find further words. With tears running down her colorless cheeks, her eyes magnificent with piercing fire, she manifestly enthralled Reed with her beauty and passion. She profoundly impressed Mason and she struck deep into what manhood the stricken Hildrith had left.

"All true, Bill, I'm sorry to confess," he said, his voice steady. "I'm offering no excuse. But look at her, man . . . look at her! And then you'll understand."

"What's that, Miss, about Dale Brittenham?" queried Mason.

"Brittenham is a wild-horse hunter," answered Edith, catching her breath. "Hildrith befriended him once. Dale loved Hildrith. . . . When Stafford came to see Dad— after the last raid—he accused Dale of being the spy who kept your gang posted. The go-between. He had the sheriff come to arrest Dale. . . . Oh, I see it all now. Dale *knew* Hildrith was the traitor. He sacrificed himself for Hildrith— to pay his debt . . . or because he thought I loved the man. For us both! . . . He drew a gun on Bayne—said Stafford was right—that *he* was the horse-thief spy. . . . Then he rode away."

It was a poignant moment. No man could have been unaffected by the girl's tragic story. Mason paced to and fro, then halted behind the table.

"Boss, that's not all," interposed Reed triumphantly. "Down at Halsey, Hildrith showed his color—and what meant most to him. Brittenham was there, as I've told you. And *he* was onto us. I saw the jig was up. I told Hildrith. I put it up to him. To declare himself. Every man there had waked up to the fact that we were horse thieves. I asked Hildrith to make his stand—for or against us. He failed us, boss."

"Reed, that was a queer thing for you to insist on," declared Mason in stern doubt. "Hildrith's cue was the same as mine. Respectability. Could you expect him to betray himself there—before all, Halsey and his sweetheart, too?"

"I knew he wouldn't. But I meant it."

"You wanted to show him up, before them all, especially her?"

"I certainly did."

"Well, you're low-down yourself, Reed, when it comes to one you hate."

"All's fair in love and war," replied the other with a flippant laugh.

The chief turned to Hildrith. "I'm not concerned with the bad blood between you and Reed. But . . . is he lying?"

"No. But down at Halsey I didn't understand he meant me to give myself away," replied Hildrith with the calmness of bitter resignation. He had played a great game, for a great stake, and he had lost. Friendship, loyalty, treachery, were nothing compared to his love for this girl.

"Would you have done so if you had understood Reed?"

"No. Why should I? There was no disloyalty in that. If I'd guessed that, I'd have shot him."

"You didn't think quick and right. That'd have been your game. Too late, Hildrith. I've a hunch it's too late for all of us. . . . You meant to marry Miss Watrous if she'd have you?"

"Why ask that?"

"Well, it was unnecessary. . . . And you really let this Brittenham sacrifice himself for you?"

"Yes, I'd have sacrificed anyone—my own brother."

"I see. That was dirty, Leale. . . . But after all these things, don't . . . You've been a faithful pard for many years. God knows, a woman—"

"Boss, he betrayed *you*," interrupted Reed stridently. "All the rest doesn't count. He split with you. He absolutely was not going to leave the country with you."

"I get that—hard as it is to believe," rasped Mason, and he took up the big gun from the table and deliberately cocked it.

Edith cried out low and falteringly, "Oh . . . don't kill him! If it was for me, spare him!"

Reed let out that sardonic laugh. "Bah! He'll deny . . . he'll lie with his last breath."

"That wouldn't save you, Leale, but . . ." Mason halted, the dark embodiment of honor among thieves.

"Hell! I deny nothing," rang out Hildrith, with something grand in his defiance. "It's all true. I broke over the girl. I was through with you, Mason—you and your raids, you and your lousy sneak here, you and your low-down—"

The leveled gun boomed to cut short Hildrith's wild denunciation. Shot through the heart, he swayed a second, his distorted visage fixing, and then, with a single explosion of gasping breath, he fell backward through the door.

4

A heavy cloud of smoke obscured Dale's sight of the center of the cabin. As he leaned there near the window, strung like a quivering wire, he heard the thump of Mason's gun on the table. It made the gold coins jingle in their sacks. The thud of boots and hoarse shouts arose on the far side of the cabin. Then the smoke drifted away to expose Mason hunched back against the table, peering through the door into the blackness. Reed knelt on the floor where Edith had sunk in a faint.

Other members of the gang arrived outside the cabin. "Hyar! It's Hildrith. Reckon the boss croaked him."

"Mebbe Reed did it. He sure was hankerin' to."

"How air you, chief?" called a third man, presenting a swarthy face in the lamplight.

"I'm . . . all right," replied Mason huskily. "Hildrith betrayed us. I bored him. . . . Drag him away. . . . You can divide what you find on him."

"Hey, I'm in on that," called Reed as the swarthy man backed away from the door. "Lay hold, fellers."

Slow, labored footfalls died away. Mason opened his gun to eject the discharged shell and to replace it with one from his belt.

"She keeled over," said Reed as he lifted the girl's head.

"So I see. . . . Sudden and raw for a tenderfoot. I'm damn glad she hated him. . . . Did you see him feeling for his gun?"

"No. It's just as well I took that away from him on the way up. Nothing yellow about Hildrith at the finish."

"Queer what a woman can do to a man! Reed, haven't you lost your head over this one?"

"Hell yes!" exploded the other.

"Better turn her loose. She'll handicap you. This hole will be swarming with posses tomorrow."

"You're sloping tonight?"

"I am. . . . How many horses did you sell?"

"Eighty-odd. None under a hundred dollars. And we drove back the best."

"Keep it. Pay your outfit. We're square. My advice is to let this Watrous girl go, and make tracks away from here."

"Thanks. . . . But I won't leave my tracks," returned Reed constrainedly. "She's coming too."

"Pack her out of here. . . . Reed, I wouldn't be in your boots for a million."

"And just why, boss?"

"Women always were your weakness. Your only one. You'll hang on to the Watrous girl."

"You bet your life I will."

"Don't bet my life on it. You're gambling your own. And you'l lose it."

Reed picked up the reviving Edith and took her through the door, turning sidewise to keep from striking her head. Dale's last glimpse of his gloating expression, as he gazed down into her face, nerved him to instant and reckless action. Reed had turned to the left outside the door, which gave Dale the impression that he did not intend to carry the girl toward the campfires.

Nalook touched Dale and silently indicated that he would go around his end of the cabin. Dale turned to the left. At the corner he waited to peer out. He saw a dark form cross the campfire light. Reed! He was turning away from his comrades, now engaged in a heated hubbub, no doubt over money and valuables they had found on Hildrith.

Dale had to fight his overwhelming eagerness. He stole out to follow Reed. The man made directly for the shack that Dale and Nalook had passed on their stalk to the cabin. Dale did not stop to see if the Indian followed, though he expected him to do so. Dale held himself to an absolutely noiseless stealth. The deep grass made that possible.

Edith let out a faint cry, scarcely audible. It seemed to loose springs of fire in Dale's muscles. He glided on, gaining upon the outlaw with his burden. They drew away from the vicinity of the campfires. Soon Dale grew sufficiently accustomed to the starlight to keep track of Reed. The girl was speaking incoherently. Dale would rather have had her still unconscious. She might scream and draw Reed's comrades in that direction.

Under the trees, between the bunches of scrub oak, Reed hurried. His panting breath grew quite audible. Edith was no slight burden, especially as she had begun to struggle in his arms.

"Where? . . . Who? . . . Let me down," she cried, but weakly.

"Shut up, or I'll bat you one," he panted.

The low shack loomed up blacker than the shadows. A horse, tethered in the gloom, snorted at Reed's approach. Dale, now only a few paces behind the outlaw, gathered all his forces for a spring.

"Let me go. . . . Let me go. . . . I'll scream—"

"Shut up, I tell you. If you scream I'll choke you. If you fight, I'll beat you."

"But, Reed . . . for God's sake! . . . You're not drunk. You must be mad—if you mean . . ."

"Girl, I didn't know what I meant when I grabbed you down there," he panted passionately, "but I know now

. . . . I'm taking you away . . . Edith Watrous . . .
out of Montana. . . . But tonight, by heaven!"

Dale closed in swiftly and silently. With relentless strength
he crushed a strangling hold around Reed's neck. The man
snorted as his head went back. The girl dropped with a
sudden gasp. Then Dale, the fingers of his left hand buried
in Reed's throat, released his right hand to grasp his gun.
He did not dare to shoot, but he swung the weapon to try
to stun Reed. He succeeded in landing only a glancing blow.

"Aggh!" gasped Reed, and for an instant his body appeared to sink.

Dale tried to strike again. Because of Reed's sudden grip
on his arm he could not exert enough power. The gun stuck.
Dale felt it catch in the man's coat. Reed let out a strangled
yell, which Dale succeeded in choking off again.

Suddenly the outlaw let go Dale's right hand and reached
for his gun. He got to it, but could not draw, due to Dale's
constricting arm. Dale pressed with all his might. They
staggered, swayed, bound together as with bands of steel.
Dale saw that if his hold loosened on either Reed's throat
or gun hand, the issue would be terribly perilous. Reed was
the larger and more powerful, though now at a disadvantage.
Dale hung on like the grim death he meant to mete out to
that man.

Suddenly, with a tremendous surge, Reed broke Dale's
hold and bent him back. Then Dale saw he would be forced
to shoot. But even as he struggled with the gun, Reed, quick
as a cat, intercepted it, and with irresistible strength turned
the weapon away while he drew his own. Dale was swift
to grasp that with his left hand. A terrific struggle ensued,
during which the grim and silent combatants both lost hold
of their guns.

Reed succeeded in drawing a knife, which he swung
aloft. Dale caught his wrist and jerked down on it with such
tremendous force that he caused the outlaw to stab himself
in the side. Then Dale grappled him round the waist, pinning
both arms to Reed's sides, so that he was unable to withdraw
the knife. Not only that, but soon Dale's inexorable pressure

sank the blade in to the hilt. A horrible panting sound escaped Reed's lips.

Any moment Nalook might come to end this desperate struggle. The knife stuck in Reed's side, clear to the hilt. Dale had the thought that he must hold on until Reed collapsed. Then he would have to run with Edith and try to get up the trail. He could not hope to find the horses in that gloomy shadow.

Reed grew stronger in his frenzy. He whirled so irresistibly that he partly broke Dale's hold. They plunged down, with Dale on the top and Reed under him. Dale had his wind almost shut off. Another moment . . . But Reed rolled like a bear. Dale, now underneath, wound his left arm around Reed. Over and over they rolled, against the cabin, back against a tree, and then over a bank. The shock broke both Dale's holds. Reed essayed to yell, but only a hoarse sound came forth. Suddenly he had weakened. Dale beat at him with his right fist. Then he reached for the knife in Reed's side, found the haft, and wrenched so terrifically that he cracked Reed's ribs. The man suddenly relaxed. Dale tore the knife out and buried it in Reed's breast.

That ended the fight. Reed sank shudderingly into a limp state. Dale slowly got up, drawing the knife with him. He had sustained no injury that he could ascertain at the moment. He was wet with sweat or blood, probably both. He slipped the knife in his belt and untied his scarf to wipe his hands and face. Then he climbed up the bank, expecting to see Edith's white blouse in the darkness.

But he did not see it. Nor was Nalook there. He called low. No answer! He began to search around on the ground. He found his gun. Then he went into the shack. Edith was gone and Nalook had not come. Possibly he might have come while the fight was going on down over the bank and, seeing the chance to save Edith, had made off with her to the horses.

Dale listened. The crickets were in loud voice. He could see the campfires, and heard nothing except the thud of the hoofs. They seemed fairly close. He retraced his steps back to the shack. Reed's horse was gone. Dale strove for control over his whirling thoughts. He feared that Edith, in her terror, had run off at random, to be captured again by some of the outlaws. After a moment's consideration, he dismissed that as untenable. She had fled, unquestionably, but without a cry, which augured well. Dale searched the black rim for the notch that marked the trail. Then he set off.

Reaching the belt of brush under the rim, he followed it until he came to an opening he thought he recognized. A stamp of hoofs electrified him. He hurried toward it and presently emerged into a glade less gloomy. First his keen sight distinguished Edith's white blouse. She was either sitting or lying on the ground. Then he saw the horses. As he hurried forward, Nalook met him.

"Nalook! Is she all right?" he whispered eagerly.

"All same okay. No hurt."

"What'd you do?"

"Me foller. See girl run. Me ketch."

"Go back to that shack and search Reed. He must have a lot of money on him. . . . We rolled over a bank."

"Ugh!" The Indian glided away.

Dale went on to find Edith sitting propped against a stone. He could not distinguish her features, but her posture was eloquent of spent force.

"Edith," he called gently.

"Oh . . . Dale! . . . Are you . . . ?"

"I'm all right," he replied hastily. .

"You . . . you killed him?"

"Of course. I had to. Are you hurt?"

"Only bruised. That ride! . . . Then he handled me . . . Oh, the brute! I'm glad you killed . . . I saw you bend him back—hit him. I knew you would. But it was awful. . . . And seeing Leale murdered, so suddenly— right before my eyes—that was worse."

"Put all that out of your mind. . . . Let me help you up. We can't stay here long. Your hands are like ice," he whispered as he got her up.

"I'm freezing to death," she replied. "This thin waist. I left my coat in the buckboard."

"Here. Slip into mine." Dale helped her into his coat, and then began to rub her cold hands between his.

"Dale, I wasn't afraid of Reed—at first. I scorned him. I saw how his men liked that. I kept telling him that you would kill him for this outrage to me. That if *you* didn't, Dad would hang him. But there in Mason's cabin—there I realized my danger. . . . You must have been close."

"Yes. Nalook and I watched between the logs. I saw it all. But I tell you to forget it."

"Oh, will I ever? . . . Dale, you saved me from God only knows what," she whispered, and putting her arms around his neck, she leaned upon his breast, and looked up. Out of her pale face great midnight eyes that reflected the starlight transfixed him with their mystery and passion. "You liar. You fool!" she went on, her soft voice belying the hard words. "You poor misguided man! To dishonor your name for Hildrith's sake! To tell Stafford he was right! To let Dad hear you say you were a horse thief! . . . Oh, I shall never forgive you."

"My dear. I did it for Leale—and perhaps more for your sake," replied Dale unsteadily. "I thought you loved him. That was a chance to reform. He would have done it, too if—"

"I don't care what he would have done. I imagined I loved him. But I didn't. I was a vain, silly, headstrong girl. And I was influenced. I don't believe I ever could have married him—after you brought back my horses. I didn't realize then. But when I kissed you . . . Oh, Dale! Something tore through my heart. I know now. It was love. Even then, what I needed was this horrible experience. It has awakened me. . . . Oh, Dale, if I loved you then, what do you think it is now?"

"I can't think . . . dearest," whispered Dale huskily, as he drew her closer, and bent over her to lay his face against her hair. "Only, if you're not out of your mind, I'm the luckiest man that ever breathed."

"Dale, I'm distraught, yes, and my heart is bursting. But I know I love you . . . love you . . . love you! Oh, with all my mind and soul!"

Dale heard in a tumultuous exaltation, and he stood holding her with an intensely vivid sense of the place and moment. The ragged rim loomed above them, dark and forbidding, as if to warn; the incessant chirp of crickets, the murmur of running water, the rustle of the wind in the brush, proved that he was alive and awake, living the most poignant moment of his life.

Then Nalook glided silently into the glade. Dale released Edith, and stepped back to meet the Indian. Nalook thrust into his hands a heavy bundle tied up in a scarf.

"Me keep gun," he said, and bent over his saddle.

"What'll we do, Nalook?" asked Dale.

"Me stay—watch trail. You take girl Halsey."

"Dale, I couldn't ride it. I'm exhausted. I can hardly stand," interposed Edith.

"Reckon I'd get lost in the dark," returned Dale thoughtfully. "I've a better plan. There's a homesteader in this valley. Man named Rogers. I knew him over in the mountains. An' I ran across his cabin a day or so ago. It's not far. I'll take you there. Then tomorrow I'll go with you to Bannock, or send you with him."

"Send me!"

"Yes. I've got to be here. Strickland agreed to send a posse after me in half an hour—an' later a big outfit of cowboys."

"But you've rescued me. Need you stay? Nalook can guide these men."

"I reckon I want to help clean out these horse thieves."

"Bayne is on your trail with a posse."

"Probably he's with Stafford's outfit."

"That won't clear you of Stafford's accusation."

"No. But Strickland an' his outfit will clear me. I must be here when that fight comes off. If it comes. You heard Mason say he was leavin' tonight. I reckon they'll all get out pronto."

"Dale! You . . . you might get shot—or even . . . Oh, these are wicked, hard men!" exclaimed Edith as she fastened persuasive hands on his coatless arms.

"That's the chance I must run to clear my name, Edith," he rejoined gravely.

"You took a fearful chance with Reed."

"Yes. But he had you in his power."

"My life and more were at stake then," she said earnestly. "It's still my love and my happiness."

"Edith, I'll have Nalook beside me an' we'll fight like Indians. I swear I'll come out of it alive."

"Then . . . go ahead . . . anyway . . ." she whispered almost inaudibly, and let her nerveless hands drop from him.

"Nalook, you watch the trail," ordered Dale. "Stop any man climbing out. When Strickland's posse comes, hold them till the cowboys get here. If I hear shots this way, I'll come pronto."

The Indian grunted and, taking up his rifle, stole away. Dale untied and led his horse up to where his saddle lay. Soon he had him saddled and bridled. Then he put on his spurs, which the Indian had remembered to get.

"Come," said Dale, reaching for Edith. When he lifted her, it came home to him why Reed had not found it easy to carry her.

"That's comfortable, if I can stay on," she said, settling herself.

"Hoofs, old boy," whispered Dale to his horse. "No actin' up. This'll be the most precious load you ever carried."

Then Dale, rifle in hand, took the bridle and led the horse out into the open. The lake gleamed like a black starlit mirror. Turning to the right, Dale slowly chose the ground and walked a hundred steps or more before he halted to listen. He went on and soon crossed the trail. Beyond that he breathed easier, and did not stop again until he had half circled the lake. He saw lights across the water up among the trees, but heard no alarming sound.

"How're you ridin'?" he whispered to Edith.

"I can stick on if it's not too far."

"Half a mile more."

As he proceeded, less fearful of being heard, he began to calculate about where he should look for Rogers's canyon. He had carefully marked it almost halfway between the two lakes and directly across from the highest point of the rim. When Dale got abreast of this he headed to the right, and was soon under the west wall. Then despite the timber on the rim and the shadowed background, he located a gap which he made certain marked the canyon.

But he could not find any trail leading into it. Therefore he began to work a cautious way through the thickets. The gurgle and splash of running water guided him. It was so pitch black that he had to feel his way. The watercourse turned out to be rocky, and he abandoned that. When he began to fear he was headed wrong, a dark tunnel led him out into the open canyon. He went on and turned a corner to catch the gleam of a light. Then he rejoiced at his good fortune. In a few minutes more he arrived at the cabin. The door was open. Dale heard voices.

"Hey, Rogers, are you home?" he called.

An exclamation and thud of bootless feet attested to the homesteader's presence. The next instant he appeared in the door.

"Who's thar?"

"Brittenham," replied Dale, and lifting Edith off the saddle, he carried her up on the porch into the light. Rogers came out in amazement. His wife cried from the door, "For land's sake!"

"Wal, a girl! Aw, don't say she's hurt," burst out the homesteader.

"You bet it's a girl. An' thank heaven she's sound! Jim Watrous's daughter, Rogers. She was kidnapped by Reed at the Halsey horse sale. That happened this afternoon. I just got her back. Now, Mrs. Rogers, will you take her in for tonight? Hide her someplace."

"That I will. She can sleep in the loft. . . . Come in, my dear child. You're white as a sheet."

"Thank you. I've had enough to make me green," replied Edith, limping into the cabin.

Dale led Rogers out of earshot. "Hell will bust loose here about tomorrow," he said, and briefly told about the several posses en route for the horse thieves' stronghold, and the events relating to the capture and rescue of Edith.

"By gad! Thet's all good," ejaculated the homesteader. "But it's not so good—all of us hyar if they have a big fight."

"Maybe the gang will slope. Mason is leavin'. I heard him tell Reed. An' Reed meant to take the girl. I don't know about the rest of them."

"Wal, these fellers ain't likely to rustle in the dark. They've been too secure. An' they figger they can't be surprised at night."

"If Mason leaves by the lower trail, he'll get shot. My Indian pard is watchin' there."

"Gosh, I hope he tries it."

"Mason had his table loaded with bags of coin an' stacks of bills. We sure ought to get that an' pay back the people he's robbed."

"It's a good bet Mason won't take the upper trail. . . . Brittenham, you look fagged. Better have some grub an' drink. An' sleep a little."

"Sure. But I'm a bloody mess, an' don't want the women to see me. Fetch me somethin' out here."

Later Dale and Rogers walked down to the valley. They did not see any lights or hear any sounds. Both ends of the gorge, where the trails led up, were dark and silent. They returned, and Dale lay down on the porch on some sheepskins. He did not expect to sleep. His mind was too full. Only the imminence of a battle could have kept his mind off the wondrous and incomprehensible fact of Edith's avowal. After pondering over the facts and probabilities, Dale decided a fight was inevitable. Mason and Reed had both impressed him as men at the end of their ropes. The others would, no doubt, leave, though not so hurriedly, and most probably would be met on the way out.

Long after Rogers's cabin was dark and its inmates wrapped in slumber, Dale lay awake, listening, thinking, revolving plans to get Edith safely away and still not seem to shirk his share of the fight. But at least, worn out by strenuous activity and undue call on his emotions, Dale fell asleep.

A step on the porch aroused him. It was broad daylight. Rogers was coming in with an armload of firewood.

"All serene, Brittenham," he said with satisfaction.

"Good. I'll wash an' slip down to get a look at the valley."

"Wal, I'd say if these outfits of cowboys was on hand, they'd be down long ago."

"Me too." Dale did not go clear out into the gateway of the valley. He climbed to a ruddy eminence and surveyed the gorge from the lookout. Sweeping the gray-green valley with eager gaze, he failed to see a moving object. Both upper and lower ends of the gorge appeared as vacant as they were silent. But at length he quickened sharply to columns of blue smoke rising above the timber up from the lower lake. He watched for a good hour. The sun rose over the gap at the east rim. Concluding that posses and cowboys had yet to arrive, Dale descended the bluff and retraced his steps toward the cabin.

He considered sending Edith out in charge of Rogers, to conduct her as far as Bannock. This idea he at once conveyed to Rogers.

"Don't think much of it," returned the homesteader forcibly. "Better hide her an' my family in a cave. I know where they'll be safe until this fracas is over."

"Well! I reckon that is better."

"Come in an' eat. Then we'll go scoutin'. An' if we see any riders, we'll rustle back to hide the women an' kids."

Dale had about finished a substantial breakfast when he thought he heard a horse neigh somewhere at a distance. He ran out on the porch and was suddenly shocked to a standstill. Scarcely ten paces out stood a man with leveled rifle.

"Hands up, Britt," he ordered with a hissing breath. Two other men, just behind him, leaped forward to present guns, and one of them yelled, "Hyar he is, Bayne."

"Rustle! Up with 'em!"

Then Dale, realizing the cold bitter fact of an unlooked-for situation, shot up his arms just as Rogers came stamping out.

"What the hell? *Who . . ."*

Six or eight more men, guns in hands, appeared at the right, led by the red-faced sheriff of Salmon. He appeared to be bursting with importance and vicious triumph. Dale surveyed the advancing group, among whom he recognized old enemies, and then his gaze flashed back to the first man with the leveled rifle. This was none other than Pickens, a crooked young horse trader who had all the reason in the world to gloat over rounding up Dale in this way.

"Guess I didn't have a hunch up thar, fellers, when we crossed this trail," declared Bayne in loud voice. "Guess I didn't measure his hoss tracks down at Watrous's for nothin'!"

"Bayne, you got the drop," spoke up Dale coolly, "and I'm not fool enough to draw in the face of that."

"You did draw on me once, though, didn't you, wild-hoss hunter?" called Bayne derisively.

"Yes."

"An' you told Stafford he was right, didn't you?"

"Yes, but—"

"No buts. You admitted you was a hoss thief, didn't you?"

"Rogers here can explain that, if you won't listen to me."

"Wal, Brittenham, your homesteadin' pard can explain thet after we hang you!"

Rogers stalked off the porch in the very face of the menacing guns and confronted Bayne in angry expostulation.

"See here, Mr. Bayne, you're on the wrong track."

"We want no advice from you," shouted Bayne. "An' you'd better look out or we'll give you the same dose."

"Boss, he's shore one of this hoss-thief gang," spoke up a lean, weathered member of the posse.

"My name's Rogers. I'm a homesteader. I have a wife

an' two children. There are men in Bannock who'll vouch
for my honesty," protested Rogers.

"Reckon so. But they ain't here. You stay out of
this. . . . Hold him up, men."

Two of them prodded the homesteader with cocked rifles,
a reckless and brutal act that would have made the bravest
man turn gray. Rogers put up shaking hands.

"Friend Rogers, don't interfere," warned Dale, who had
grasped the deadly nature of Bayne's procedure. The sheriff
believed Dale was one of the mysterious band of thieves
that had been harassing the ranchers of Salmon River Valley
for a long time. It had galled him, no doubt, to fail to bring
a single thief to justice. Added to that was an animosity
toward Dale and a mean leaning to exercise his office. He
wanted no trial. He would brook no opposition. Dale stood
there a self-confessed criminal.

"Rope Brittenham," ordered Bayne. "Tie his hands behind his back. Bore him if he as much as winks."

Two of the posse dragged Dale off the porch, and in a
moment had bound him securely. Then Dale realized too
late that he should have leaped while he was free to snatch
a gun from one of his captors, and fought it out. He had
not taken seriously Bayne's threat to hang him. But he saw
now that unless a miracle came to pass, he was doomed.
The thought was so appalling that it clamped him momen-
tarily in an icy terror. Edith was at the back of that emotion.
He had faced death before without flinching, but to be
hanged while Edith was there, possibly a witness—that
would be too horrible. Yet he read it in the hard visages of
Bayne and his men. By a tremendous effort he succeeded
in getting hold of himself.

"Bayne, this job is not law," he expostulated. "It's revenge. When my innocence is proved, you'll be in a tight
fix."

"Innocence! Hell, man, didn't you confess your guilt?"
ejaculated Bayne. "Stafford heard you, same as Watrous
an' his friends."

"All the same, that was a lie."

"Aw, it was? My Gawd, man, but you take chances with your life! An' what'd you lie for?"

"I lied for Edith Watrous."

Bayne stared incredulously and then he guffawed. He turned to his men.

"Reckon we better shet off his wind. The man's plumb loco."

From behind Dale a noose, thrown by a lanky cowboy, sailed and widened to encircle his head, and to be drawn tight. The hard knot came just under Dale's chin and shut off the hoarse cry that formed involuntarily.

"Over thet limb, fellers," called out Bayne briskly, pointing to a spreading branch of a piñon tree some few yards farther out. Dale was dragged under it. The loose end of the rope was thrown over the branch, to fall into eager hands.

"Dirty business, Bayne, you—!" shouted Rogers, shaken by horror and wrath. "So help me Gawd, you'll rue it!"

Bayne leaped malignantly, plainly in the grip of passion too strong for reason.

"Thar's five thousand dollars' reward wrapped up in this wild-hoss hunter's hide, an' I ain't takin' any chance of losin' it."

Dale forced a strangled utterance. "Bayne . . . I'll double that . . . if you'll arrest me . . . give . . . fair trial."

"Haw! Haw! Wal, listen to our ragged hoss thief talk big money."

"Boss, he ain't got two bits. . . . We're wastin' time."

"Swing him, fellers!"

Four or five men stretched the rope and had lifted Dale to his toes when a piercing shriek from the cabin startled them so violently that they let him down again. Edith Watrous came flying out, half-dressed, her hair down, her face blanched. Her white blouse fluttered in her hand as she ran, barefooted, across the grass.

"Merciful heaven! Dale! That rope!" she screamed, and as the shock of realization came, she dropped her blouse to the ground and stood stricken before the staring men, her bare round arms and lovely shoulders shining white in the sunlight. Her eyes darkened, dilated, enlarged as her consciousness grasped the significance here, and then fixed in terror.

Dale's ghastly sense of death faded. This girl would save him. A dozen Baynes could not contend with Edith Watrous, once she was roused.

"Edith, they were about . . . to hang me."

"Hang you?" she cried, suddenly galvanized. "These men?. . . . *Bayne?"*

Leaping red blood burned out the pallor of her face. It swept away in a wave, leaving her whiter than before, and with eyes like coals of living fire.

"Miss Watrous. What you . . . doin' here?" queried Bayne, halting, confused by this apparition.

"I'm here—not quite too late," she replied, as if to herself, and a ring of certainty in her voice followed hard on the tremulous evidence of her thought.

"Kinda queer—meetin' you up here in this outlaw den," went on Bayne with a nervous cough.

"Bayne . . . I remember," she said ponderingly, ignoring his statement. "The gossip linking Dale's name with this horse-thief outfit . . . Stafford! . . . Your intent to arrest Dale! . . . His drawing on you! His strange acceptance of Stafford's accusation!"

"Nothin' strange about thet, Miss," rejoined Bayne brusquely. "Brittenham was caught in a trap. An' like a wolf, he bit back."

"That confession had to do with me, Mr. Bayne," she retorted.

"So he said. But I ain't disregardin' same."

"You are not arresting him," she asserted swiftly.

"Nope, I ain't."

"But didn't you let him explain?" she queried.

"I didn't want no cock-an'-bull explainin' from him or this doubtful pard of his here, Rogers. . . . I'll just hang Brittenham an' let Rogers talk afterwards. Reckon he'll not have much to say then."

"So, that's your plan, you miserable thick-headed skunk of a sheriff?" she exclaimed in lashing scorn. She swept her flaming eyes from Bayne to his posse, all of whom appeared uneasy over this interruption. "Pickens! . . . Hall . . . Jason . . . Pike! And some more hard nuts from Salmon. Why, if you were honest yourself, you'd arrest them. My father could put Pickens in jail. . . . Bayne, your crew of a posse reflects suspiciously on you."

"Wal, I ain't carin' for what you think. It's plain to me you've took powerful with this hoss thief an' I reckon thet reflects suspicions on you, Miss," rejoined Bayne, galled to recrimination.

A scarlet blush wiped out the whiteness of Edith's neck and face. She burned with shame and fury. That seemed to remind her of herself, of her hlf-dressed state, and she bent to pick up her blouse. When she rose to slip her arms through the garment, she was pale again. She forgot to button it.

"You dare not hang Brittenham."

"Wal, lady, I just do," he declared, but he was weakening somehow.

"You shall not!"

"Better go indoors, Miss. It ain't pleasant to see a man hang an' kick an' swell an' grow black in the face."

Bayne had no conception of the passion and courage of a woman. He blundered into the very speeches that made Edith a lioness.

"Take that rope off his neck," she commanded, as a queen might have to slaves.

The members of the posse shifted from one foot to the other, and betrayed that they would have looked to their leader had they been able to remove their fascinated gaze from this girl. Pickens, the nearest to her, moved back a step, holding his rifle muzzle up. The freckles stood out awkwardly on his dirty white face.

"Give me that rifle," she cried hotly, and she leaped to snatch at it. Pickens held on, his visage a study in consternation and alarm. Edith let go with one hand and struck him a staggering blow with her fist. Then she fought him for the weapon. Bang! It belched fire and smoke up into the tree. She jerked it away from him, and leaping back, she worked the lever with a swift precision that proved her familiarity with firearms. Without aiming, she shot at Pickens's feet. Dale saw the bullet strike up dust between them. Pickens leaped with a wild yell and fled.

Edith whirled upon Bayne. She was magnificent in her rage. Such a thing as fear of these men was as far from her as if she had never experienced such an emotion. Again she worked the action of the rifle. She held it low at Bayne and pulled the trigger. Bang! The bullet sped between his legs, and burned the left one, which flinched as the man called, "Hyar! Stop thet, you fool woman. You'll kill somebody!"

"Bayne, I'll kill *you* if you try to hang Brittenham," she replied, her voice ringing high-keyed but level and cold. "Take that noose off his neck!"

The frightened sheriff made haste to comply.

"Now untie him!"

"Help me hyar—somebody," snarled Bayne, turning Dale around to tear at the rope. "My Gawd, what's this range comin' to when wild women bust loose? . . . The luck! We can't shoot her! We can't rope Jim Watrous's girl!"

"Boss, I reckon it may be jist as well," replied the lean gray man who was helping him, "'cause it wasn't regular."

"You men! Put away your guns," ordered Edith. "I wouldn't hesitate to shoot any one of you. . . . Now, listen, all of you. . . . Brittenham is no horse thief. He is a man who sacrificed his name . . . his honor, for his friend— and because he thought I loved that friend. Leale Hildrith! *He* was the treacherous spy—the go-between, the liar who deceived my father and me. Dale took his guilt. I never believed it. I followed Dale to Halsey. Hildrith followed me. There we found Ed Reed and his outfit selling Watrous horses. I recognized my own horse, Dick, and I accused Reed. He betrayed Hildrith right there and kidnapped us both, and rode to his hole. . . . We got here last night. Reed took me before Bill Mason. Big Bill, who is leader of this band. They sent for Hildrith. And Mason shot him. Reed made off with me, intending to leave. But Dale had trailed us, and he killed Reed. Then he fetched me here to this cabin. . . . You have my word. I swear this is the truth."

"Wal, I'll be . . .!" ejaculated Bayne, who had grown so obsessed by Edith's story that he had forgotten to untie Dale.

"Boss! Hosses comin' hell bent!" shouted one of Bayne's men, running in.

"Whar?"

A ringing trample of swift hoofs on the hard trail drowned further shouts. Dale saw a line of riders sweep round the corner and race right down upon the cabin. They began to shoot into Bayne's posse. There were six riders, all shooting as hard as they were riding, and some of them had two guns leveled. Hoarse yells rose about the banging volley of shots.

The horsemen sped on past, still shooting. Bullets thudded into the cabin. The riders vanished in a cloud of dust and the clatter of hoofs died away.

Dale frantically unwound the rope which Bayne had suddenly let go at the onslaught of the riders. Freeing himself, Dale leaped to Edith, who had dropped the rifle and stood unsteadily, her eyes wild.

"Did they hit you?" gasped Dale, seizing her.

Rogers rushed up to join them, holding a hand to a bloody shoulder. "Some of Mason's outfit," he boomed, and he gazed around with rolling eyes. Pickens lay dead, his bloody head against the tree. Bayne had been shot through the middle. A spreading splotch of red on his shirt under his clutching hands attested to a mortal wound. Three other men lay either groaning or cursing. That left four apparently unscratched, only one of whom, a lean oldish man, showed any inclination to help his comrades.

"Lemme see how bad you're hit," he was growling over one of them.

"Aw, it ain't bad, but it hurts like hell."

"Edith, come, I'll take you in," said Dale, putting his arm around the weakening girl.

"Britt, I've a better idee," put in Rogers. "I'll take her an' my family to the cave, where they'll be safe."

"Good! That outfit must have been chased."

"We'd have heard shots. I reckon they were rustlin' away and jest piled into us."

The two reached the cabin, where Dale said, "Brace up, Edith. It sure was tough. It'll be all right now."

"Oh, I'm sick," she whispered, as she leaned against him.

Rogers went in, calling to his wife. Dale heard him rummaging around. Soon he appeared in the door and handed a tin box and a bundle of linen to Dale.

"Those hombres out there can take care of their own wounded."

Dale pressed Edith's limp hand and begged earnestly, "Don't weaken now, dear. Good Lord, how wonderful an' terrible you were! . . . Edith, I'll bear a charmed life after this. . . . Go with Rogers. An' don't worry, darlin'. . . . The Mason gang is on the run, that's sure."

"I'll be all right," she replied with a pale smile: "Go— do what's best . . . but don't stay long away from me."

Hurrying out, Dale found all save one of the wounded on their feet.

"Wal, thet's decent of you," said the lean, hawk-faced man, as he received the bandages and medicine from Dale. "Bayne jist croaked an' he can stay croaked right there for all I care. I'm sorry he made the mistake takin' you for a hoss thief."

"He paid for it," rejoined Dale grimly. "You must bury him and Pickens. I'll fetch you some tools. But move them away from here."

Dale searched around until he found a spade and mattock, which he brought back. Meanwhile the spokesman of Bayne's posse and Jason Pike had about concluded a hasty binding of the injured men.

"Brittenham, we come down this trail from Bannock. Are there any other ways to get in an' out of this hole?"

"Look here," replied Dale, and squatted down to draw an oval in the dust. "This represents the valley. It runs almost directly north an' south. There's a trail at each end. This trail of Rogers's leads out of here, almost due west, an' leads to Bannock. There might be, an' very probably is, another trail on the east side, perhaps back of Mason's camp. But Nalook didn't tell me there was."

"Thet outfit who rid by here to smoke us up—they must have been chased or at least scared."

"Chased, I figure that, though no cowboys appear to be comin' along. You know Stafford an' Watrous were sendin' a big outfit of cowboys up from Salmon. They'll come down the south trail. An' I'm responsible for two more, raised by a rancher named Strickland over at Halsey. They are due an' they'll come in at the lower end of the hole. The north end."

"Wal, I'd like to be in on that round-up. What say, Jason?"

"Hell, yes. But, Tom, you'd better send Jerry an' hike out with our cripples. They'd just handicap us."

"Reckon so. Now let's rustle to put these stiffs under the sod an' the dew. Strip them of valuables. Funny about Bayne. He was sure rarin' to spend that five thousand Stafford offered for Brittenham alive or dead."

"Bayne had some faults. He was some previous on this job. . . . Hyar, fellars, give us a hand."

"I'll rustle my horse," said Dale, and strode off. He had left Hoofs to graze at will, but the sturdy bay was nowhere in sight. Finally Dale found him in Rogers's corral with two other horses. He led Hoofs back to the cabin, and was saddling him when he saw Rogers crossing the brook into the open. Evidently he had taken the women and children somewhere in that direction. Dale's keen eye approved of the dense thicket of brush and trees leading up to a great wall of cliffs and caverns and splintered sections. They would be safely hidden in there.

Then Dale bethought himself of his gun, which Pickens had taken from him. He found it under the tree with the weapons, belts and spurs of the slain men. Dale took up the carbine that Pickens had held, and which Edith had wrenched out of his hands. He decided he would like to keep it, and carried it to the cabin.

Tom and Pike, with the third man, returned from their gruesome task somewhere below. The next move was to send the four cripples, one of whom lurched in his saddle, up the trail to Bannock with their escort.

When Dale turned from a dubious gaze after them, he sighted Nalook riding up from the valley. The Indian appeared to be approaching warily. Dale hallooed and strode out to meet him.

The Indian pointed with dark hand at the hoof tracks in the trail.

"Me come slow—look see."

"Nalook, those tracks were made by six of Mason's outfit who rode through, hell bent for election."

"Me hear shots."

"They killed Bayne an' one of his posse, an' crippled four more."

"Ugh! Bayne jail Injun no more!" Nalook ejaculated with satisfaction.

"I should smile not. But, Nalook, what's doin' down in the hole?"

"Ten paleface, three my people come sunup. No cowboy."

"Well! That's odd. Strickland guaranteed a big outfit. I wonder . . . No sign of Stafford's cowboys on the other trail?"

"Me look long, no come."

"Where's that outfit from Halsey?"

The Indian indicated by gesture that he had detained these men at the rim.

"You watch trail all night?"

Nalook nodded, and his inscrutable eyes directed Dale's to the back of his saddle. A dark coat of heavy material, and evidently covering a bundle, had been bound behind the cantle. Dale put a curious hand on the coat. He felt something hard inside, and that caused him to note how securely and rightly the coat had been tied on. Suddenly a dark red spot gave him a shock. Blood! He touched it, to find it a smear glazed over and dry. Dale looked into the bronzed visage and somber eyes of the Indian with a cold sense of certainty.

"Mason?"

The Indian nodded. "Me watch long. Big Bill he come.

Two paleface foller. Top trail. Me watch. Big powwow. They want gold. Mason no give. Cuss like hell. They shoot. Me kill um."

"Nalook, you just beat hell!" ejaculated Dale, at once thrilled and overcome at the singular way things were working out. He had not forgotten the sacks of gold and pile of greenbacks on Mason's table. To let the robber chief make off with that had been no easy surrender.

"Me beat hoss thief," replied the Indian, taking Dale literally. "Big Bill no good. He take Palouse girl away."

"Aha! So that's why you've been so soft and gentle with these horse thieves. . . . Nalook, I don't want anyone, not even Rogers, to see this coat an' what's in it."

"Me savvy. Where hide?"

"Go to the barn. Hide it in the loft under the hay."

Nalook rode on by the cabin. Dale sat down on the porch to wait for his return and the others. He found himself trembling with the significance of the moment. He had possession of a large amount of money, probably more than enough to reimburse all the ranchers from whom cattle and horses had been stolen. Moreover, the losses of any poor ranchers over on the Palouse range would have to be made good. That, however, could hardly make much of a hole in the fortune Mason had no doubt been accumulating for years.

The Indian came back from the barn, leading his horse. He sat down beside Dale and laid a heavy hand on his arm.

"No look! . . . Me see man watchin' on the rock," he said.

"Where?" asked Dale, checking a start.

Nalook let go of Dale and curved a thumb that indicated the bare point on the west rim, in fact the only lookout on that side, and the one from which he had planned to get Rogers's signal. On the moment, Rogers returned.

"Rogers, stand pat now," said Dale. "The Indian sighted someone watchin' us. From the bare point you know, where I was to come for our signal."

"Wal, thet ain't so good," growled the homesteader with

concern. "Must be them cusses who busted through here, shootin'. By thunder, I'd like to get a crack at the feller who gave me this cut in the shoulder."

"I forgot, Rogers. Is it serious?"

"Not atall. But it's sore an' makes me sore. I was fool enough to show it to my wife. But I couldn't tie it up myself. Blood always sickens wimmen."

"What do?" asked the Indian.

"We won't let on we know we're bein' watched . . . . Rogers, could any scout on that point see where you took your wife an' Edith?"

"I reckon not. Fact is, I'm sure not."

"Well, you stay here. It's reasonable to figure these horse thieves won't come back. An' if any others came out of the valley, they'll be stretchin' leather. You keep hid. I'll take Nalook an' these men, an' see what's up out there."

"Couldn't do no better. But you want to come back by dark, 'cause that girl begged me to tell you," replied Rogers earnestly. "Gosh, I never saw such eyes in a human's face. You be . . . careful, Britt. Thet girl is jist livin' for you."

"Rogers, I'm liable to be so careful that I'll be yellow," rejoined Dale soberly.

Soon Dale was jogging down the trail at the head of the quartet. In the brush cover at the outlet of the canyon they had to ride single file. Once out in the valley, Nalook was the first to call attention to horses scattered here and there all over the green. They evidently had broken out of the pasture or had been freed. Dale viewed them and calculated their number with satisfaction. Not a rider in sight!

Dale led a brisk trot. It did not take long to reach the lower trail. Here he sent Nalook up to fetch down the ten white men and four Indians that Strickland had been able to get together. After an interval of keen survey of the valley, Dale voiced his surprise to Tom and Jason.

"Queer, all right," agreed the older man. "Kinda feels like a lull before the storm."

"I wonder what happened to Stafford's outfit. They've had hours more time than needed. They've missed the trail."

The Indian was clever. He sent the men down on foot,

some distance apart. They made but little noise and raised scarcely any dust. Dale looked this posse over keenly. They appeared to be mostly miners, rough, bearded, matured men. There were, however, several cowboys, one of whom Dale had seen at the horse sale. The last two to descend the trail proved to be Strickland with the Indian.

"By Jove, you, Strickland!" ejaculated Dale in surprise.

"I couldn't keep out of it, Brittenham," returned the rancher dryly. "This sort of thing is my meat. Besides, I'm pretty curious and sore."

"How about your cowboys?"

"I'm sure I can't understand why those outfits haven't shown up. but I didn't send for my own. I've only a few now, and they're out on the range. Sanborn and Drew were to send theirs, with an outfit from the Circle Bar. Damn strange! This is stern range business that concerns the whole range."

"Maybe not so strange. If they were friends of Mason."

"Thick as hops!" exclaimed Strickland with a snort.

"We'll go slow an' wait for Stafford's cowboys," decided Dale ponderingly.

"Hoss thieves all get away mebbe," interposed Nalook, plainly not liking this idea of waiting.

"All right, Nalook. What's your advice?"

"Crawl like Injun," he replied, and spread wide his fingers. "Mebbe soon shoot heap much."

"Strickland, this Indian is simply great. We'll be wise to listen to him. Take your men an' follow him. Cowboy, you hide here at the foot of the trail an' give the alarm if any riders come down. We've reason to believe some of the gang are scoutin' along this west rim. I'll slip up on top an' have a look at Mason's camp."

Drawing his rifle from its saddle sheath, Dale removed his coat and spurs. Nalook was already leading his horse into the brush, and the Indians followed him. Strickland, with a caustic word of warning to Dale, waved his men after the Indian.

"Come with me. Throw your chaps an' spurs, cowboy," advised Dale, and addressed himself to the steep trail. Soon the long-legged cowboy caught up with him, but did not speak until they reached the rim. Dale observed that he also carried a rifle and had the look of a man who could use it.

"Brittenham, if I see any sneakin' along the rim, shall I smoke 'em up?" he queried.

"You bet, unless they're cowboys."

"Wal, I shore know thet breed."

They parted. Dale stole into the evergreens, walking on his toes. He wound in and out, keeping as close to the rim as possible, and did not halt until he had covered several hundred yards. Then he listened and tried to peer over the rim. But he heard nothing and could see only the far part of the valley. Another quarter of a mile ought to put him where he could view Mason's camp. But he had not gone quite so far when a thud of hoofs on soft ground brought him up tight-skinned and cold. A horse was approaching at some little distance from the rim. Dale glided out to meet it. Presently he saw a big sombrero, then a red youthful face, above some evergreens. In another moment horse and rider came into view. Leveling his rifle, Dale called him to halt. The rider was unmistakably a young cowboy, and as cool as he could be. He complied with some range profanity. Then at second glance he drawled, "Howdy, Brittenham."

"You've got the advantage of me, Mr. Cowboy," retorted Dale curtly.

"Damn if I can see thet," he rejoined, with a smile that eased Dale's grimness.

"You know me?" querried Dale.

"Shore, I recognized you. I've a pard, Jen Pierce, who's helped you chase wild hosses. My name's Al Cook. We both ride for Stafford."

"You belong to Stafford's outfit?" asked Dale, lowering his rifle.

"Yep. We got heah before sunup this mornin'."

"How many of you an' where are they?"

"About twenty, I figger. Didn't count. Jud Larken, our foreman, left five of us to watch thet far trail, up on top. He took the rest down."

"Where are they now?"

"I seen them just now. I can show them to you."

"Rustle. By gum, this is queer."

"You can gamble on it," returned Cook as he turned his horse. "We got tired waitin' for a showdown. I disobeyed orders an' rode around this side. Glad I did For I run plumb across a trail fresh with tracks of a lot of horses. All shod! Brittenham, them hoss thieves have climbed out."

"Another trail? Hell! If that's not tough. . . . Where is it?"

"Heads in thet deep notch back of them cabins."

"They had a back hole to their burrow. Nalook didn't know that."

"Heah we air," said the cowboy, sliding off. "Come out on the rim."

In another moment Dale was gazing down upon the grove of pines and the roofs of cabins. No men—no smoke! The campsite appeared deserted.

"Say, what the hell you make of thet?" ejaculated the cowboy, pointing. "Look! Up behind the thicket, makin' for the open grass! There's Larkin's outfit all strung out, crawlin' on their bellies like snakes!"

Dale saw, and in a flash he surmised that Stafford's men were crawling up on Strickland's. Each side would mistake the other for the horse thieves. And on the instant a clear crack of a rifle rang out. But it was up on the rim. Other shots, from heavy short guns, boomed. That cowboy had run into the spying outlaws. Again the sharp ring of the rifle.

"Look!" cried the cowboy, pointing down.

Dale saw puffs of blue smoke rise from the green level below. Then gunshots pealed up.

"My Gawd! The locoed idiots are fightin' each other. But at that, neither Nalook or Strickland would know Stafford's outfit."

"Bad! Let me ride down an' put them wise."

"I'll go. Lend me your horse, you follow along the rim to the trail. Come down."

Dale ran back to leap into the cowboy's saddle. The stirrups fit him. With a slap of the bridle and a kick he

urged the horse into a gallop. It did not take long to reach
the trail. Wheeling into it, he ran the horse out to the rim,
and then sent him down at a sliding plunge. He yelled to
the cowboy on guard. "Brittenham! Brittenham! Don't
shoot!" Then, as the horse sent gravel and dust sky-high,
and, reaching a level, sped by the cowboy, Dale added,
"Look out for our men above!"

Dale ran the fast horse along the edge of the timber and
then toward the thicket where he calculated Nalook would
lead Strickland. He crashed through one fringe of sage and
laurel, right upon the heels of men. Rifles cracked to left
and right. Dale heard the whistle of bullets that came from
Stafford's outfit.

"*Stop!*" he yelled at the top of his lungs. "Horse thieves
gone! You're fightin' our own men!"

Out upon the open grass level he rode, tearing loose his
scarf. He held this aloft in one hand and in the other his
rifle. A puff of white smoke rose from the deep grass ahead,
then another from a clump of brush to the right, and next,
one directly in front of him. The missile from the gun which
belched that smoke hissed close to Dale's ear. He yelled
with all his might and waved as no attacking enemy ever
would have done. But the shots multiplied. The cowboys
did not grasp the situation.

"No help for it!" muttered Dale with a dark premonition
of calamity. But he had his good name to regain. He raced
on right upon kneeling, lean-shaped cowboys.

"*Stop! Stop!* Horse thieves gone! You're fightin' friends!
My outfit! Brittenham! Britt—"

Dale felt the impact of a bullet on his body somewhere.
Then a terrible blinding shock.

When consciousness returned, Dale knew from a jolting
sensation that he was being moved. He was being propped
up in a saddle by a man riding on each side of his horse.
His head sagged, and when he opened his eyes to a blurred
and darkened sight, he saw the horn of his saddle and the
mane of his horse. His skull felt as if it had been split by
an ax.

His senses drifted close to oblivion again, then recovered a little more clearly. He heard voices and hoofbeats. Warm blood dripped down on his hands. That sensation started conscious thought. He had been shot, but surely not fatally, or he would not have been put astraddle a horse. His reaction to that was swift, and revivifying with happiness. A faintness, a dizziness seemed to lessen, but the pain in his head grew correspondingly more piercing.

Dale became aware then that a number of horsemen rode with him. They began to crash through brush out into the open again, where gray walls restricted the light. Then he felt strong hands lift him from the saddle and lay him on the grass. He opened his eyes. Anxious faces bent over him, one of which was Strickland's.

"My Gawd, men!" came to Dale in Rogers's deep voice. "It's Brittenham! Don't say he's—"

"Just knocked out temporarily," replied Strickland cheerfully. "Ugly scalp wound, but not dangerous. Another shot through the left shoulder. Fetch whiskey, bandages, hot water, and iodine if you have it."

"Aw!" let out Rogers, expelling a loud breath. He thumped away.

Dale lay with closed eyes, deeply grateful for having escaped serious injury. They forced him to swallow whiskey, and then they began to work over him.

"You're the homesteader, Rogers?" Strickland queried.

"Yes, Me an' Britt have been friends. Knew each other over in the Sawtooths. . . . Lord, I'm glad he ain't bad hurt. It'd just have killed thet Watrous girl."

"I'm Strickland," replied the other. "These fellows here are part of a posse I brought up from Halsey."

"Much of a fight? I heerd a lot of shootin'."

"It would have been one hell of a fight but for Brittenham. You see, the horse-thief gang had vamoosed last night. But we didn't know that. The Indian led us up on an outfit that had discovered us about the same time. We were crawling toward each other, through the thickets and high grass. The Indian began to shoot first. That betrayed our position, and a lively exchange of shots began. It grew hot. Brittenham had gone up on the rim to scout. He discovered our blunder and rode back hell bent for election right into our midst. He stopped us, but the other outfit kept on shooting. Brittenham went on, and rode into the very face of hard shooting. He got hit twice. Nervy thing to do! But it saved lives. I had two men wounded besides him. Stafford's outfit suffered some casualties, but fortunately no one killed."

"What become of the hoss thieves?"

"Gone! After Reed and Mason had been killed, the gang evidently split. Some left in the night, leaving all their property except light packs. Sam Hood, one of Strickland's boys, killed two of them up on the rim, just before our fight started below."

"Ha! Thet ought to bust the gang for keeps," declared Rogers, rubbing his big hands.

"It was the best night's work this range ever saw. And the credit goes to Brittenham."

"Wal, I'll go fetch the wimmin," concluded Rogers heartily.

When, a little later, Dale had been washed and bandaged, and was half sitting up receiving the plaudits of the riders, he saw Edith come running out from under the trees into the open. She ran most of the way; then, nearing the cabin, she broke into a hurried walk and held a hand over her heart. Even at a distance Dale saw her big dark eyes, intent and staring in her pale face. As she neared the spot where he lay surrounded by a half-circle of strange men, it was certain she saw no one but him. Reaching the spot where he lay, she knelt beside him.

"Dale!"

"Hello . . . Edith," he replied huskily. "I guess I didn't bear such a charmed life . . . after all. I sure got in the way of two bullets. But my luck held, Edith."

"Oh! You're not seriously injured?" she asked composedly, with a gentle hand on his. "But you are suffering."

"My head did hurt like h—sixty. It's sort of whirlin' now."

"Rogers told me, Dale. That was a wonderful and splendid thing for you to do," Edith said softly. "What will Dad say? And won't I have Mr. Stafford in a hole?"

Strickland interposed with a beaming smile, "You sure will, Miss Watrous. And I hope you make the most of it."

"Edith, I reckon we might leave for Bannock pronto," spoke up Dale eagerly. "I sent Nalook to tell your friends of your safety."

"Wal, Dale, mebbe I'll let you go tomorrow," chimed in Rogers.

"Don't go today," advised Strickland.

Next day Dale, despite his iron will and supreme eagerness to get home, suffered an ordeal that was almost too much for him. Toward the end of the ride to Bannock, members of Strickland's posse were supporting Dale on his horse. But to his relief and Edith's poignant joy, he made it. At Bannock, medical attention and a good night's sleep made it possible for him to arrange to go on to Salmon by stage.

The cowboy Cook, who had taken a strong fancy to Dale, and had hung close to him, came out of the inn carrying a canvas-covered pack that Dale had him carefully stow under the seat.

"Britt, you sure have been keen about that pack. What's in it?" inquired Strickland with shrewd curiosity.

"Wouldn't you like to know, old-timer?"

"I've got a hunch. Wal, I'll look you up over at the Watrous ranch in a couple of days. I want to go home first."

"Ahuh. You want to find out why those cowboy outfits didn't show up?"

"I confess to a little curiosity," replied the rancher dryly.

"Don't try to find out. Forget it," said Dale earnestly.

The stage, full of passengers, and driven by the jovial stage driver Bill Edmunds, rolled away to the cheers of a Bannock crowd.

"Dale, what *is* in this pack under the seat?" asked Edith.

"Guess."

"It looked heavy, and considering how fussy you've been about it, I'd say . . . *gold,*" she whispered.

Dale put his lips to her ear. "Edith, no wonder I'm fussy.

I'm wild with excitement. That gang is broken up. An' I have Reed's money in my coat here—an' Mason's fortune in that pack."

"Oh, how thrilling!" she whispered, and then on an afterthought she spoke out roguishly. "Well, in view of the . . . er . . . rather immediate surrender of your independence, I think I'd better take charge."

Darkness had settled down over the Salmon River Valley when the stage arrived at Salmon. Old Bill, the driver, said to Edith, "I reckon I'd better hustle you young folks out home before the town hears what Britt has done."

"Thad'd be good of you, Bill," replied Edith gratefully. "Dale is tired. And I'd be glad to get him home pronto."

They were the only passengers for the three miles out to the ranch. Dale did not speak, and Edith appeared content to hold his hand. They both gazed out at the shining river and the dark groves, and over the moonlit range. When they arrived at the ranch, Dale had Bill turn down the lane to the little cabin where he lived.

"Carry this pack in, Bill, an' don't ask questions, you son-of-a-gun, or you'll not get the twenty-dollar gold piece I owe you."

"Wal, if this hyar pack is full of gold, you won't miss thet double eagle, you doggone lucky wild-hoss hunter."

"Thank you, Bill," said Edith. "I'll walk the rest of the way."

Dale was left alone with Edith, who stood in the shadow of the maples with the moon lighting her lovely face. He could hear the low roar of rapids on the river.

"It's wonderful, gettin' back, this way," he said haltingly. "You must run in an' tell your dad."

"Dad can wait a moment longer. . . . Oh, Dale, I'm so proud—so happy—my heart is bursting."

"Mine feels queer, too. I hope this is not a dream, Edith."

"*What*, Dale?"

"Why, all that's happened—an' you standin' there safe again—an' so beautiful. You just don't appear real."

"I should think you could ascertain whether I'm real flesh and blood or not."

Dale fired to that. "You'll always be the same, Edith. Can't you see how serious this is for me?" He took her in his arms. "Darlin', I reckon I know how you feel. But no words can tell you my feelin's. . . . Kiss me, Edith—then I'll try."

She was in his arms, to grow responsive and loving in her eager return of his kisses.

"Oh . . . Dale!" she whispered, with eyes closed. "I have found my man at last."

"Edith, I love you . . . an' tomorrow I'll have the courage to ask your dad if I can have you."

"Dale, I'm yours—Dad or no Dad. But he'll be as easy as that," she replied, stirring in his arms and snapping her fingers. "I hate to leave you. But we have tomorrow—and forever. Oh, Dale! I don't deserve all this happiness. Kiss me good night. . . . I'll fetch your breakfast myself . . . . Kiss me once more. . . . *Another!* Oh, I am . . ."

She broke from him to run up the lane and disappear under the moonlit maples. Dale stood there a few moments alone in the silver-blanched gloom, trying to persuade himself that he was awake and in possession of his senses.

Next morning he got up early, to find the pain in his head much easier. But his shoulder was so stiff and sore that he could not use the arm on that side. Having only one hand available, he was sore beset by the difficulty of washing, shaving and making himself as presentable as possible. He did not get through any too soon, for Edith appeared up the lane accompanied by a servant carrying a tray. She saw him and waved, then came tripping on. Dale felt his heart swell and he moved about to hide his tremendous pride. He shoved a bench near the table under a canvas shelter that served for a porch. And when he could look up again, there she was, radiant in white.

"Mornin', Edith. Now I believe in fairies again."

"Oh, you look just fine. I'm having my breakfast with you. Do you feel as well as you look?"

"Okay, except for my arm. It's stiff. I had a devil of a time puttin' my best foot forward. You'll have to do with a one-armed beau today."

"I'd rather have your one arm than all the two arms on the range," she replied gaily.

They had breakfast together, which to Dale seemed like enchantment. Then she took him for a stroll under the cottonwoods out along the riverbank. And there, hanging on his good arm, she told him how her father had taken her story. Visitors from Salmon had come last night up to a late hour, and had begun to arrive already that morning. Stafford's outfit had returned driving a hundred recovered horses. Dale's feat was on the tip of every tongue.

"I didn't tell Dad about . . . about *us* till this morning," she added finally.

"Lord help me! What'd he say?" gulped Dale.

"I don't know whether it was flattering or not—to me," Edith replied dubiously. "He said, 'That wild-horse tamer? Thank God, your hash is settled at last!'"

"He sure flatters me if he thinks I can tame you. Wait till I tell him how you routed Bayne's outfit!"

"Oh, Dale, Dad was fine. He's going to ask you . . . But that'd be telling."

"Edith, if he accepts me, must I . . . will I have to wait very long for you?"

"*If!* Dad has accepted you, Dale. And honestly, he's happy over it. . . . And as for the other—just what do you mean, Mr. Brittenham?"

"Aw! Will you marry me soon?"

"How soon?"

"I . . . I don't know, darlin'."

"Dale, dearest, I couldn't marry you with your head bandaged like that—or your arm in a sling," she said tantalizingly, as her dark eyes shed soft warm light upon him.

"But Edith!" he burst out. "I could take them off pronto. In less than a week!"

"Very well. Just that pronto."

Watrous came out to meet them as they crossed the green. His face showed emotion and his eyes, at that moment, had something of the fire of Edith's. He wrung Dale's hand. But as befitted a Westerner, a little trace of his deep feeling pervaded his voice.

"Brittenham, I won't try to thank you," he said in simple heartiness.

"That suits me, Mr. Watrous. I'm kind of overwhelmed An' . . . so I'd better get somethin' out before I lose my nerve . . . I've loved Edith since I came here first, three years ago. Will you give her to me?"

"Dale, I will, and gladly, provided you live here with me. I'm getting on, and since Mother has been gone, Edith has been all to me."

"Dad, we will never leave you," replied Edith softly.

"Bless you, my children! And, Dale, there's a little matter I'd like to settle right now. I'll need a partner. Stafford has persuaded me to go in big for the cattle game. I see its possibilities. That, of course, means we'll have cattle stealing as we have had horse stealing. I'll need you pretty bad."

"Dad!" cried Edith in dismay. "You didn't tell me you'd want Dale to go chasing cattle thieves!"

"My dear, it might not come for years. Such developments come slowly. By that time Dale may have some grown cowboy sons to take his place."

"Oh!" exclaimed Edith, plunged into sudden confusion.

"Dale, do you accept?" added Watrous, extending his hand with an engaging smile.

"Yes, Mr. Watrous. An' I'll give Edith an' you the best that's in me."

"Settled! Oh, here comes Stafford. Lay into him, youngster, for he sure has been nasty."

As Stafford came slowly down the broad steps, Dale found himself unable to feel the resentment that had rankled in him.

"Brittenham," said the rancher as he advanced, "I've made blunders in my life, but never so stupid a one as that regarding you. I am ashamed and sorry. It'll be hard for me to live this injustice down unless you forgive me. Can I ask that of you?"

"Nothin' to forgive," declared Dale earnestly, won by Stafford's straightforwardness and remorse. He offered his hand and gripped the rancher's. "Suspicion pointed at me.

An' I took on Hildrith's guilt for reasons you know. Let's forget it an' be friends."

"You are indeed a man."

But when Stafford turned to Edith, he had a different proposition to face. She eyed him with disdainful scorn, and stood tapping a nervous foot on the path.

"Edith, you can do no less than he. Say you forgive me, too."

"Yes, of course, since Dale is so kind. But I think you are a rotten judge of men."

"Indeed I am, my dear."

"And you're a hard man when you're crossed."

"Yes. But I'm a loyal friend. After all, this was a misunderstanding. You believed it, didn't you?"

"I never did—not for a minute. That's why I followed Dale."

"Well, you found him and brought him back." Stafford took a colored slip of paper from his pocket. He looked at it, then held it out to Edith. "I offered five thousand dollars' reward for Brittenham, dead or alive. You brought him back alive—very much alive, as anyone with half an eye could see. And no wonder! It seems to me that this reward should go to you. Indeed, I insist upon your taking it."

"Reward! But, Mr. Stafford . . . you . . . I . . ." stammered Edith. "Five thousand dollars for *me?*"

"Surely. I imagine you will be able to spend it pronto. We all know your weakness for fine clothes and fine horses. Please accept it as a wedding present from a friend who loves you and who will never cease to regret that he mistook so splendid and noble a fellow as Dale Brittenham for a horse thief!"

The Saga of the
Ice Cream Kid

1

"Now, this here story," Ramblin' Red began, "is a story without one of them morals a story is supposed to have—'less you can dig out one for yourself, which I doubt very much if you sage-rabbits can. But that ain't the point—"

A figure emerged from the night and joined those grouped about the ruddy glow of the fire.

"—jest what is th' point, then?" demanded the newcomer gruffly. He sank to the ground and stretched out comfortably.

Ramblin' Red grinned and paused to roll a cigarette.

"You bin mixin' cactus in with your cookin', Chuck," he said. "This is a yarn about the Ice Cream Kid and it jest goes to show how a mess of troubles can corral a feller until they plumb bust his spirit—or else."

And this is the tale he told:

The history of the West, ever since the first white man decided to fight coyotes and cactus fer a living, has been a story of struggle and bloodshed (said Ramblin' Red).

And even so, one period of hard luck and heartache stands

out above all the rest—and that was when barb-wire and railroads started windin' their way over the West.

That brought farmers and squatters and promoters and a pack of people rushin' in on the land which the old-timers had fought to get and to hold. They kept on fightin' fer a while, as far as that goes, but it didn't do 'em any good. Folks kept crowdin' in jest the same.

Colonel Lawson had the Long L ranch down in Texas and it was as purty a spread of grazin' land as you'd ever hope to see. Plenty of long lush grass, running water which kept on running when it was needed most—and th' whole place stocked with fine cattle, thousands of 'em.

It seemed too good to last—and it was. Purty soon a whole flock of new cattle companies started edgin' in on the Colonel; squeezin' him here and jostlin' him there and bitin' off a bit of land some other place till the Long L wasn't but just another ranch.

It was all legal like, mind you. Colonel Lawson knew cattle and he knew how to raise 'em in spite of wolves, weather and high water—but he couldn't handle the law. Every time he came up against some legal question, somebody else knew the answer and wham went away another piece of the Long L.

Well, it didn't take the Colonel long to get a bellyful of that sort of doin's. He figgered that the law was a fine thing an' all that—but if it was goin' to carve down the ranch he had spent years buildin' up, he would jest move on to some'eres where there wasn't any law yet.

And that's what he did, with his family and his cowhands and his fine cattle. He split his cattle into two herds an' sent the first batch up Arizona way with half his cowhands and his son Bob. Sally Lawson, his daughter, went along with the first move, too.

Colonel Lawson hung around Texas for a while cleanin' up his affairs and then he and the rest of the hands started out with the remainin' cattle. It was durin' this drive that he ran across the hombre who finally came to be known as the Ice Cream Kid.

2

They were makin' the drive through hot, dry country when one day Slim Peters, one of the hands, came ridin' up to the Colonel at a dead gallop.

"Boss," he yelled, "drop on back here and see what we found!"

The Colonel wheeled his horse around and trailed Slim to the supply wagon. What he saw wasn't a very purty sight.

Two men were stretched out on a pile of blankets and they were limp and still. When the Colonel got closer he saw that they were more dead than alive, if they were at all. Alkali was caked over 'em from head to foot; their faces were swollen and burnt and blistered and their lips were all cracked open. Most of their clothes were just rags and one of 'em had wrapped part of his shirt around his boot, where the sole was torn away.

The Colonel sort of whistled.

"They're sure done up," he said. "How'd you come across 'em?"

"A steer broke away from the herd," Slim explained, "an' when I took out after it I durn near rode right over these men."

"All right," said the Colonel. "You found 'em, Slim— now see what you can do for 'em."

Slim was equal to the job and for the next few days he nursed the two strangers as if his own life depended on it. After a while they started to come around and at the end of a week they were well enough to talk and make sense. But even when they could talk they didn't much, except to thank Slim for what he had done.

Now, out in that country men minded their own business purty much and no questions asked. But there was no law against a man doin' a little figgerin' in the back of his head and more than one of the Long L boys began to wonder how come these strangers were out in the badlands—afoot and hard up.

The answer was easy. Nobody wandered out into country like that because they wanted to—they had to be drove into it. And one of the best drivers in those day was—the law! The strangers didn't talk enough to deny it.

By the time the cattle drive got near to the spot where the new Long L ranch was bein' staked out, the men had recovered and was helpin' ride the herd. And such a strange team you never saw.

The young one—the one called the Kid—was as likable a cuss as could be. It didn't take him long to make friends with all the Long L boys and Slim Peters in particular. He was strong and lean and he walked like a man who knew his own mind. His eyes were sort of slate color and real serious-lookin'—they could bore a hole right through a feller.

But Coyote McKee, his sidekick, was a mess fer fair. He was a stubborn, headstrong hombre, who never said much. His face was about the color of saddle leather and he had a frazzled, droopin' mustache that looked like prairie dogs had been chewin' on it. His eyes were jest narrow slits; they were as cold and beady-lookin' as a rattlesnake's and about half as friendly. He was a character, and a bad one.

How those two ever got hooked up together was a question, but it was easy to see that they had a past—and that the Kid was none too proud of it, either. It was after the drive reached the new Long L ranch that Colonel Lawson and Slim Peters began to get a line on them.

3

Colonel Lawson liked the Kid as the rest of the boys did and he took him on as a steady hand. The Kid knew ropin' and ridin' and he could hold his own with the best of 'em. Whatever his past had been, the Kid settled down to life on the range like he was made fer it.

The Colonel was leanin' against the corral one day when Slim Peters rode in.

"Slim," called the Colonel, "you come over here a minute."

Slim took care of his horse, then waddled over. It didn't take the Colonel long to spill what was on his mind.

"I'm wonderin' about the Kid," he began. "How do you make him out, Slim?"

Slim dragged out a big knife and opened it and started carvin' on the corral.

"Your guess is as good as mine," he said.

"All right—what is your guess?"

Slim snapped his knife shut.

"It's this. He started out on the wrong foot sometime or other and then he got tied up with that Coyote McKee, which didn't help him none. After that—well, they probably got in a scrape or two. But I'm willin' to bet that right now th' Kid is as straight as the best of us."

"So am I," the Colonel agreed. "At least, that's what I want to think. And I'm goin' to keep the Kid here on the Long L as long as I keep on seein' it that way."

But neither of them really knew what was goin' on deep down in the Kid's own heart.

As long as the Kid could remember, he had considered life something to be lived fast and dangerously—to a quick and sudden end. But that was before he got stranded in the desert, where a man's life held on and on until his last hot, choked breath. Where, with the blazin' sun overhead and his eyes swollen shut and his tongue black and dry, death dogged his footsteps and his past life kept paradin' before him.

That experience in the desert gave the Kid a new slant on life. He didn't have any hankerin' to go rip-tearin' around the country, an' he seemed purty satisfied with his forty a month and three squares a day.

It gave him a sort of a funny habit, too. Have any of you hombres ever been stranded out somewhere afoot and so almighty hungry you could eat saddle leather and like it? I mean more than hungry—I mean starvin', when your stomach seems to draw up in a tight knot and your strength slips away and all you can think of is food and more food—and the more you think of it the worse you get. After a spell like that, a man looks on food a little different. Every time he eats he thinks of that time he was stranded and hungry—and it tastes twice as good as it did before.

Well, the Kid got a queer twist like that, and it wasn't a bad one, either. When he was out there on the desert, with the hot dry sand sweepin' into his face and fillin' his mouth and his tongue parched and swollen and alkali chokin' in his throat, all he could think of was water. Nice cool sweet spring water, tricklin' from some shady spot. Cool water to bathe his hot, cracked lips and wash the desert dust

from his throat. Of all the things in the world, that's what
he wanted most. And even after Slim Peters found him and
Colonel Lawson gave him a job on the new Long L, the
Kid never got the picture of that cool, refreshin' water
entirely out of his mind. He even went it one better. Every
time he rode into town, which was purty often, he went in
the restaurant there and ordered a double order of ice cream.
Then he would take that big dish of ice cream to a table in
the coolest part of the place and sit down and dig into it.
When the cold, sweet flavor of the ice cream started meltin'
in his mouth, his eyes would become dreamy and thoughtful
and he would smile to himself real satisfied like. You see,
in his mind right then, he was back on the desert.

Some of the boys around town smiled and started callin'
him the Ice Cream Kid, but it wasn't till later that the name
stuck proper—an' then nobody smiled when they said it.

Well, affairs on the new Long L ran right smooth for a
while. Bob Lawson and Sally Lawson liked the Kid as well
as the Colonel did and it wasn't long until the Kid and Sally
began to spend a good deal of time together. That was all
right with the Colonel.

But Bob Lawson had the makin's of a wild young buck
and more than once some of the Long L hands had seen
him runnin' around town with bad hombres. Some of them
dropped a hint or two to the Colonel, but they didn't take.

Sally was closer to the boy than the Colonel was and she
saw how he was changin' for the worse. And she was
worried.

One day, as she was out ridin' with the Kid, she spoke
her mind.

"Some of the boys," she began, "have told me about
seeing Bob gambling in town, Kid."

"That's news to me," said the Kid truthfully.

"I hoped that it wasn't true. But I asked Bob and he
didn't deny it. He . . . he told me it wasn't any of my
business what he did!"

The Kid scowled.

"He needs a good spankin'!" he said angrily. "He shouldn't
talk to you like that."

"I don't care how he talks to me," said Sally, "if he only would straighten up and help Father around the ranch and quit associating with the wrong kind of men."

"Hmm!" said the Kid. "Who mostly?"

"I don't know for sure, but I heard him say something about 'Coyote.'"

"Hmmm!" said the Kid again.

"Can't you—won't you do something about it?" pleaded the girl.

"I can and I will," promised the Kid.

But the Kid was in no position to give orders to Coyote McKee—and he knew it. For Coyote knew the secret of his past and he never let the Kid forget that he knew it.

Once each month the Kid made a sad, slow ride into town and held a session with his former partner. Coyote received a part of the previous month's pay and agreed to remain silent until his next blackmail money was due. Thus did the Ice Cream Kid pay and pay for the secrecy of his past life to remain a secret.

He knew the chances were that Colonel Lawson and Slim and the rest of the boys of the Long L would continue to accept him as a friend despite what they might be told of his past—but Sally was another problem. Men of the West accepted other men according to their face value at the moment. But a woman could not so easily forgive and forget. The Kid was in a bad spot.

And Coyote was preparing to lead the Lawson boy over the same rough trail the Kid had ridden before!

Several days later, Sally stopped him as he was walking toward the corral.

"Bob hasn't been home for two days," she began abruptly. "One of the boys saw him in town with that Coyote person and tried to make him come home. But he wouldn't come."

"That's bad," said the Kid helplessly, knowing what was about to come.

"I told you it was bad," said Sally, "when we were out riding the other day. Oh, why don't you do something? They say you know this Coyote. Why don't you go talk to him?"

"What could I say?" asked the Kid.

"That's up to you!" flared the girl. "But if you don't help me as you promised—you need never to speak to me again!"

She turned and hurried toward the house.

"Now what?" groaned the Kid to himself. "If I leave things ride as they are, Sally won't have anything to do with me. If I go in town and have a showdown with Coyote, he'll come out here and spill the works to her—and she'll be through with me for good. No matter what I do, I lose!"

4

The next day was payday, and the Ice Cream Kid—remembering his sorrowful monthly duty to perform—rode into town. He knew where to look for Coyote and he found him talking to the bartender. He slumped down at a table, and Coyote, without needing to be asked, came over and joined him.

"A little slow comin' in, ain't you?" asked Coyote gruffly.

The Kid's eyes narrowed.

"I'm here, and that's what counts. Coyote, I'm gettin' sick and tired of shellin' out money to you."

"Now, ain't that jest too bad!" sneered Coyote sarcastically. "You'll hand me over the dough every month and like it—or else. And you know what that means."

"For a plugged two-bit piece," the Kid said slowly, "I'd tell you to go jump in the lake and let you do what you pleased about it. The boys out at the Long L wouldn't believe anything you told 'em anyway."

Coyote smiled crookedly.

"What I could tell the boys at the Long L, I could prove—and you know it. But I wouldn't care much if they believed me or not. But the girl, now—she would begin to do a heap of wonderin' if I spilled my trap."

"You talk to her," said the Ice Cream Kid coldly, "and I'll blast you down like I would any of the other coyotes around here."

Coyote McKee laughed harshly.

"No you won't. You woulda done that a long time ago, Kid, to get rid of me—if you thought you coulda got by with it. But the folks around here won't stand for murder."

"If they'll put up with you, they'll stand for almost anything," the Kid grumbled.

But Coyote was right, he knew. He was helpless.

"All right," the Kid said finally. "You'll get your money and you'll get it steady. But one peep out of you and I'll blow the lid off the whole thing, see?"

"Now, don't get all riled up," said Coyote. "Everything's dandy."

"No, it's not. There's another little matter I want to take up with you. From now on, you lay off the Lawson kid. Get someone else to help with your shady deals, but leave the Lawson boy alone."

"What Bob and I do is our business," said Coyote angrily. "If you want to get so plumb righteous that you can't help a old partner turn a trick or two, I got to get someone else to help me."

"Mebbe so," said the Kid, "but get someone else besides Bob Lawson."

Coyote McKee rose to his feet.

"You better go back out to the ranch and chappyroon the cows, Kid," he said. "Bob and me are stickin' together and we're doin' what we damn well please. You can take that and like it. Even so, I may give you a break. We got a big deal comin' off—and if it comes out all right, I may skip this part of the country and leave you be. How's that?"

The Kid's face paled uner its tan.

"No good. Sit down, Coyote."

Something in the Kid's voice made Coyote obey.

"Look here," began the Kid huskily, "I got a mighty good reason for not wantin' the Lawson boy mixed up in this deal or any other like it. You say you gotta have help—and that you'll skip out afterwards and leave me alone. How about me givin' you a hand on that big deal?"

Coyote stared.

"Are you on the level, Kid?"

"Did you ever see me when I wasn't?" the Kid demanded coldly.

"All right, it's a go. Come into town day after next, at dark, and meet me right here. It'll be like old times, Kid."

"Never mind the sob stuff," snapped the Kid. "I'll go through with it—but you have to count Bob Lawson out. Call him off right away. Send him home and tell him to stick there. Have you got that straight?"

"I'll count Bob out," said Coyote, "and you're in."

When the Kid got up and left the place, he was in a sort of a daze. In something less than a minute he had tied up with Coyote again and had started back for the old trail they rode together before.

He mounted and rode slowly back to the Long L ranch.

Every minute of the next day dragged like an hour. The Kid went about his work like he was doped, and once he almost fell out of the saddle, which, for the Ice Cream Kid, was very unusual. But his whole world was whirlin' around his head, and more than once that day he wished that he was right back in the desert, tortured and thirsty and half dead like when the Colonel picked him up, so he could start all over and leave the Long L and Sally Lawson out of it. That'll give you an idea of how he felt.

Sally met him twice that day and didn't even look at him, much less speak to him.

Late in the afternoon, Bob Lawson came ridin' in from town. He looked sort of funny and he took care of his horse and went into the house without sayin' a word.

"Well, that's that!" said the Kid to himself.

But he was a little sudden in congratulatin' himself. A

little past noon of the next day, which was the day the Kid has his appointment in town with Coyote, he was leanin' against the corral with Slim and talkin'.

"I sure wish I could get into town tonight," said Slim.

"Then why don't you go?" asked the Kid, natural-like.

"I was all set to go," Slim explained, "when Bob comes along and asks me would I mind ridin' the herd tonight in place of him. Seein' he's the boss's son, I said I'd be glad to."

"What's he goin' to do, then?" asked the Kid, suddenly alarmed.

Slim grinned and flipped away his cigarette.

"That's easy. He's goin' to town instead of me!"

But the Kid knew different. Bob Lawson was going in town to meet Coyote, for Coyote had not broken with him, as he promised the Kid to do. To the Ice Cream Kid, the story was an old one. Coyote was pulling his big deal and preparing to leave the country. With Bob and the Kid helping him, he would make his haul and leave Bob Lawson to take the blame.

A blind red rage swept over the Kid. He stalked away from the corral and went in search of Bob. One of the hands told him where Bob could be found. The Kid's first flare of anger died away and now he was cool and calculating.

"Bob," he said evenly, "I hear you're plannin' to go into town tonight. I think you better hang around the ranch instead."

The boy flushed.

"I don't care what you think," he answered hotly. "I'm goin' to town and it's my business why."

"You're goin' in to meet Coyote McKee," said the Kid, "and that makes it my business."

With that, the Kid swung and caught Bob square on the point of the jaw. The boy's head jerked back and he went down, but he came right up again. The Kid ducked an easy one and lashed out again. Bob slumped to the floor and stayed there.

"Sorry, boy," said the Kid softly.

Then he turned and ran for his horse.

Without explaining anything to anyone at the Long L, he galloped from the ranch and headed for town.

Although Coyote's double-cross was plain enough to him, he was a little puzzled about what to do next. But he wanted to have a talk with Coyote, that was sure.

When he reached town, he went to Coyote's hangout. His man wasn't there, nor did anyone know where he was. The Kid searched every dive in town and Coyote was in none of them.

By that time it was late afternoon, and the Kid decided to eat while he had the time. He went to the only restaurant in town and he sat at the last table in the room, facing the door. The Kid was taking no chances. As a customer started to leave, the Kid hailed him.

"Say, Pete," the Kid said. "If you see Coyote McKee around anywhere, tell him I'm in here, will you?"

"Shore thing, Kid," said Pete.

The Kid ordered and ate slowly. A dead silence hung over the place and an old clock, over in one corner, ticked monotonously.

He had finished his meal and was starting in on a huge plate of ice cream when the door of the place opened and the Kid looked up.

Sally Lawson and her brother stormed into the room. Sally's face was flushed with an intense anger and her eyes flashed fire. Bob sort of limped when he came in, and several bruises were darkening around a long cut on the side of his jaw. Sally spied the Kid at once and swept between the rows of tables toward him, knocking over a chair as she came.

"You . . . you . . . I said I'd never speak to you again," she began angrily, "but I'm going to tell you enough right now to last you a lifetime! What was the idea of fighting with Bob? What did he ever do to you?"

The Kid took a great spoonful of ice cream and lit a cigarette and leaned back in his chair.

"Will you listen to me?" shrilled Sally. "I asked you—why did you deliberately fight my brother and knock him down? First you—"

The Kid flipped away his cigarette and leaned forward to his ice cream again. His eyes had that faraway look in them—but they never wandered from the front door of the place. He took another spoonful.

"—first you refused when I asked you to help him, and then, without any reason, you beat him and ran away. Just wait till my father comes back and hears about this . . ."

The other people in the restaurant, listening interestedly to Sally's rage, saw the Kid's eyes finally widen and a strange look creep over his face. He held his ice cream spoon in his left hand now, and his right hand dropped carelessly beneath the table. But he was looking past Sally and Bob. He was looking at the door—for it had silently opened and Coyote McKee, his swarthy face distorted with anger, was walking into the place. His two guns swung heavily about his legs as he strode over to the counter. Then he turned his back to it and stared across the room at the Ice Cream Kid.

"So," said Coyote McKee, "you want a showdown, eh?"

"What are you talking about?" asked the Kid pleasantly.

"You know what I'm talkin' about," snarled Coyote. "You had to go and beat up young Lawson until he can hardly get around."

"I heard about that already," said the Kid. "But what's that to you, Coyote? I thought you counted the Lawson boy out."

"Yeah? Well, now I'm about to count you out!"

Coyote glanced toward Sally, who had stood speechless during the encounter.

"You think the Kid is just about the white-haired boy around here, eh?" he sneered. "Well, let me tell you somethin' you don't know about him! About what he was before your father found him!"

He turned to the Kid, who was taking a spoonful of ice cream and listening with great interest.

"I'll tell these people about the Fargo job—how'll that be for a starter?" leered Coyote.

The Kid took another bite of ice cream and said nothing.

"—or what happened along the Rio Grande!" continued Coyote, a bit louder than before.

The Kid dipped his spoon down to his desert.

"—or the—*Say, You—I'm Talkin' To You!*"

Coyote's nerve snapped under the terrible tension of the room. As his voice rose to a shriek, his hand swept downward toward his guns.

At that moment the Kid was raising a spoonful of ice cream to his lips. According to what the onlookers said later, the Kid—still holding the spoon—sprang to his feet and drew his gun with one swift motion. Its roar thundered through the restaurant and Coyote bent forward and buckled to the floor. It was a perfect case of self-defense, and it cleared up the Kid's problems for once and for all.

He stuck his gun back in his holster and finished his ice cream.

After that, when they called him the Ice Cream Kid, nobody ever smiled.

Ramblin' Red leaned forward and flicked his cigarette into the red eye of the campfire.

"And how about Sally and the Ice Cream Kid?" asked someone sleepily.

"Ain't you never satisfied?" demanded Ramblin' Red. "Well, when Sally found out that the Kid jumped her brother to keep him from gettin' mixed up with Coyote that night, everything was all right. And Bob Lawson, after he saw the cool nerve of the Kid, understood that it took more than the bluff and bluster of an hombre like Coyote to make a real man. So he forgot Coyote and took after the Kid. He even took a likin' to ice cream, they say. That's how it turned out."

"Say, Red," said a voice thoughtfully. "Fer jest tellin' the story, you seem to know a powerful lot of the details."

Ramblin' Red smiled in the darkness.

"Now, that is strange, ain't it?" he admitted.

And the men turned to their blankets.

Don: The Story
of a
Lion Dog

Don was part bloodhound—or at least this is how frontiersman Buffalo Jones described him. But he *looked* more intelligent and better kept than the nondescript packdogs that Jones had gathered to help him hunt and lasso wild lions in the Grand Canyon.

This is the true story of the expedition where my father accompanied Jones to the north rim of the Grand Canyon, where they were to do their hunting. Don seemed more aloof and reserved than did the other dogs, but my father soon made a friend of him. He was to find out later that Don's intelligence and courage were to result in one day saving his own life as well.

It has taken me years to realize the greatness of a dog; and often as I have told the story of Don—his love of freedom and hatred of men, how I saved his life and how he saved mine—it never was told as I feel it now.

I saw Don first at Flagstaff, Arizona, where arrangements had been made for me to cross the desert with Buffalo Jones and a Mormon caravan en route to Lee's Ferry on the Colorado River. Jones had brought a pack of nondescript dogs. Our purpose was to cross the river and skirt the Vermilion Cliffs, and finally work up through Buckskin Forest to the north rim of the Grand Canyon, where Jones expected to lasso mountain lions and capture them alive. The most important part of our outfit, of course, was the pack of hounds. Never had I seen such a motley assembly of canines. They did not even have names. Jones gave me the privilege of finding names for them.

Among them was a hound that seemed out of place because of his superb proportions, his sleek, dark, smooth skin, his noble head, and great, solemn black eyes. He had extraordinarily long ears, thick-veined and faintly tinged with brown. Here was a dog that looked to me like a thoroughbred. My friendly overtures to him were unnoticed. Jones said he was part bloodhound and had belonged to an old Mexican don in southern California. So I named him Don.

We were ten days crossing the Painted Desert, and protracted horseback-riding was then so new and hard for me that I had no enthusiasm left to scrape acquaintance with the dogs. Still, I did not forget and often felt sorry for them as they limped along, clinking their chains under the wagons. Even then I divined that horses and dogs were going to play a great part in my Western experience.

At Lee's Ferry we crossed the Colorado and I was introduced to the weird and wild canyon country, with its golden-red walls and purple depths. Here we parted with the caravan and went on with Jones's rangers, Jim and Emmet, who led our outfit into such a wonderful region as I had never dreamed of. We camped several days on the vast range where Jones let his buffalo herd run wild. One day the Arizonians put me astride a white mustang that apparently delighted in carrying a tenderfoot. I did not then know what I was soon to learn—that the buffalo always chased this mustang off the range. When I rode up on the herd, to my utter amazement and terror they took after me and . . . But I am digressing, and this is a dog story.

Once across the river, Jones had unchained the dogs and let them run on ahead or lag behind. Most of them lagged. Don for one, however, did not get sore feet. Beyond the buffalo range we entered the sage, and here Jones began to train the dogs in earnest. He carried on his saddle an old blunderbuss of a shotgun, about which I had wondered curiously. I had supposed he meant to use it to shoot small game.

Moze, our black-and-white dog, and the ugliest of the lot, gave chase to a jackrabbit.

"Hyar, you Moze, come back," bawled Jones in stentorian tones. But Moze paid no attention. Jones whipped out the old shotgun and before I could utter a protest he had fired. The distance was pretty far—seventy yards or more—but Moze howled piercingly and came sneaking and limping back. It was remarkable to see him almost crawl to Jones's feet.

"Thar, that'll teach you not to chase rabbits. You're a lion dog," shouted the old plainsman as if he were talking to a human.

At first I was so astounded and furious that I could not speak. But presently I voiced my feeling.

"Wal, it looks worse than it is," he said, with his keen gray-blue eyes on me. "I'm usin' fine birdshot an' it can't do any more than sting. You see, I've no time to train these dogs. It's necessary to make them see quick that they're not to trail or chase any varmints but lions."

There was nothing for me to do but hold my tongue, though my resentment appeared to be shared by Jim and Emmet. They made excuses for the old plainsman. Jim said: "He shore can make animals do what he wants. But I never seen the dog or hoss that cared two bits for him."

We rode on through the beautiful purple sageland, gradually uphill, toward a black-fringed horizon that was Buckskin Forest. Jack-rabbits, cottontails, coyotes and foxes, prairie dogs and pack rats infested the sage and engaged the attention of our assorted pack of hounds. All the dogs except Don fell victim to Jones's old blunderbuss; and surely stubborn Moze received a second peppering, this time at closer range. I espied drops of blood upon his dirty white skin. After this it relieved me greatly to see that not even Moze transgressed again. Jones's method was cruel, but effective. He had captured and subdued wild animals since his boyhood. In fact, that had been the driving passion of his life, but no sentiment entered into it.

"Reckon Don is too smart to let you ketch him," Jim once remarked to our leader.

"Wal, I don't know," responded Jones dubiously. "Mebbe he just wouldn't chase this sage trash. But wait till we jump some deer. Then we'll see. He's got bloodhound in him, and I'll bet he'll run deer. All hounds will, even the best ones trained on bear an' lion."

Not long after we entered the wonderful pine forest the reckoning of Don came as Jones had predicted. Several deer bounded out of a thicket and crossed ahead of us, soon disappearing in the green blur.

"Ahuh, now we'll see," ejaculated Jones, deliberately pulling out the old shotgun.

The hounds trotted alongside our horses, unaware of the danger ahead. Soon we reached the deer tracks. All the hounds showed excitement. Don let out a sharp yelp and shot away like a streak on the trail.

"Don, come hyar," yelled Jones, at the same time extending his gun. Don gave no sign he had heard. Then Jones pulled trigger and shot him. I saw the scattering of dust and pine needles all round Don. He doubled up and rolled. I feared he might be badly injured. But he got up and turned back. It seemed strange that he did not howl. Jones drew his plunging horse to a halt and bade us all stop.

"Don, come back hyar," he called in a loud, harsh, commanding voice.

The hound obeyed, not sneakingly or cringingly. He did not put his tail between his legs. But he was frightened and no doubt pretty badly hurt. When he reached us I saw that he was trembling all over and that drops of blood dripped from his long ears. What a somber, sullen gaze in his eyes.

"See hyar," bellowed Jones. "I knowed you was a deer-chaser. Wal, now you're a lion dog."

Later that day, when I had recovered sufficiently from my disapproval, I took Jones to task about this matter of shooting the dogs. I wanted to know how he expected the hounds to learn what he required of them.

"Wal, that's easy," he replied curtly. "When we strike a lion trail I'll put them on it—let them go. They'll soon learn."

It seemed plausible, but I was so incensed that I doubted the hounds would chase anything; and I resolved that if Jones shot Don again I would force the issue and end the hunt unless assured there would be no more of such drastic training methods.

Soon after this incident we made camp on the edge of a beautiful glade where a snowbank still lingered and a stream of water trickled down into a green swale. Before we got camp pitched a band of wild horses thudded by, thrilling me deeply. My first sight of wild horses. I knew I should never forget that splendid stallion, the leader, racing on under the trees, looking back at us over his shoulder.

At this camp I renewed my attempts to make friends with Don. He had been chained apart from the other dogs. He ate what I fetched him, but remained aloof. His dignity and distrust were such that I did not risk laying a hand on him then. But I resolved to win him if it were possible. His tragic eyes haunted me. There was a story in them I could not read. He always seemed to be looking afar. On this occasion I came to the conclusion that he hated Jones.

Buckskin Forest was well named. It appeared to be full of deer, the large black-tailed species known as mule deer. This species must be related to the elk. The size and beauty of them, the way they watched with long ears erect and then bounded off as if on springs, never failed to thrill me with delight.

As we traveled on, the forest grew wilder and more beautiful. In the parklike glades a bleached white grass waved in the wind and bluebells smiled wanly. Wild horses outnumbered the deer, and that meant there were some always in sight. A large gray grouse flew up now and then, and most striking of the forest creatures to fascinate me was a magnificent black squirrel, with a long bushy white tail, and tufted ears, and a red stripe down its glossy sides.

We rode for several days through this enchanting wilderness, gradually ascending, and one afternoon we came abruptly to a break in the forest. It was the north rim of the Grand Canyon. My astounded gaze tried to grasp an appalling abyss of purple and gold and red, a chasm too terrible and beautiful to understand all at once. The effect of that moment must have been tremendous, for I have never recovered from it. To this day the thing that fascinates me most is to stand upon a great height—canyon wall, or promontory, or peak—and gaze down into the mysterious colorful depths.

Our destination was Powell's Plateau, an isolated cape jutting out into the canyon void. Jones showed it to me—a distant gold-rimmed, black-fringed promontory, seemingly inaccessible and unscalable. The only trail leading to it was a wild-horse hunter's trail, seldom used, exceedingly dangerous. It took us two days over this canyon trail to the Saddle—a narrow strip of land dipping down from the Plateau and reaching up to the main rim. We camped under a vast looming golden wall, so wonderful that it kept me from sleeping. That night lions visited our camp. The hounds barked for hours. This was the first chance I had to hear Don. What a voice he had. Deep, ringing, wild, like the bay of a wolf.

Next morning we ascended the Saddle, from the notch of which I looked down into the chasm, still asleep in purple shadows; then we climbed a narrow deer trail to the summit of the Plateau. Here indeed was the grand, wild, isolated spot of my dreams. Indeed, I was in an all-satisfying trance of adventure. I wanted to make camp on the rim, but Jones laughed at me. We rode through the level, stately forest of pines until we came to a ravine on the north side of which lay a heavy bank of snow. This was very necessary, for there was no water on the Plateau. Jones rode off to scout while the rest of us pitched camp. Before we had completed our tasks a troop of deer appeared across the ravine, and motionless they stood watching us. There were big and little deer, blue-gray in color, sleek and graceful, so tame that to me it seemed brutal to shoot at them.

Don was the only one of the dogs that espied the deer. He stood up to gaze hard at them, but he did not bark or show any desire to chase them. Yet there seemed to me to be a strange yearning light in his dark eyes. I had never failed to approach Don whenever opportunity afforded, to continue my overtures of friendship. But now, as always, Don turned away from me. He was cold and somber. I had never seen him wag his tail or whine eagerly, as was common with most hounds.

Jones returned to camp jubilant and excited, as far as it was possible for the old plainsman to be. He had found lion trails and lion tracks, and he predicted a great hunt for us.

The Plateau resembled in shape the ace of clubs. It was perhaps six miles long and three or four wide. The body of it was covered with a heavy growth of pine, and the capes that sloped somewhat toward the canyon were thick with sage and cedar. This lower part, with its numerous swales and ravines and gorges, all leading down into the jungle of splintered crags and thicketed slopes of the Grand Canyon, turned out to be a paradise for deer and lion.

We found many lion trails leading down from the cedared broken rim to the slopes of yellow and red. These slopes really constituted a big country, and finally led to the sheer perpendicular precipices, three thousand feet lower.

Deer were numerous and as tame as cattle on a range. They grazed with our horses. Herds of a dozen or more were common. Once we saw a very larg band. Down in the sage and under the cedars and in ravines we found many remains of deer. Jones called these lion-kills. And he frankly stated that the number of deer killed yearly upon the Plateau would be incredible to anyone who had not seen the actual signs.

In two days we had three captive lions tied up to pine saplings near camp. They were two-year-olds. Don and I had treed the first lion; I had taken pictures of Jones lassoing him; I had jumped off a ledge into a cedar to escape another; I had helped Jones hold a third; I had scratches from lion claws on my chaps, and . . . But I keep forgetting that this is not a story about lions. Always before when I have told it, I have slighted Don.

One night, a week or more after we had settled in camp, we sat around a blazing red fire and talked over the hunt of the day. We all had our parts to tell. Jones and I had found where a lioness had jumped a deer. He showed me where the lioness had crouched upon a little brushy knoll, and how she had leaped thirty feet to the back of the deer. He showed me the tracks the deer had made—bounding, running, staggering with the lioness upon its back—and where, fully a hundred paces beyond, the big cat had downed its prey and killed it. There had been a fierce struggle. Then the lioness had dragged the carcass down the slope, through the sage, to the cedar tree where her four two-year-old cubs waited. All that we found of the deer were the ragged hide, some patches of hair, cracked bones, and two long ears. These were still warm.

Eventually we got the hounds on this trail and soon put up the lions. I found a craggy cliff under the rim and sat there watching and listening for hours. Jones rode to and fro above me, and at last dismounted to go down to join the other men. The hounds treed one of the lions. How that wild canyon slope rang with barks and bays and yells. Jones tied up this lion. Then the hounds worked up the ragged slope toward me, much to my gratification and excitement. Somewhere near me the lions had taken to cedars or crags, and I strained my eyes searching for them.

At last I located a lion on top of an isolated crag right beneath me. The hounds, with Don and Ranger leading, had been on the right track. My lusty yells brought the men. Then the lion stood up—a long, slender, yellowish cat— and spat at me. Next it leaped off that crag, fully fifty feet to the slope below, and bounded down, taking the direction from which the men had come. The hounds gave chase, yelping and baying. Jones bawled at them, trying to call them off—for what reason, I could not guess. But I was soon to learn. They found the lion Jones had captured and left lying tied under a cedar, and they killed it, then took the trail of the other. They treed it far down in the rough jumble of rocks and cedars.

One by one we had ridden back to camp that night, tired out. Jim was the last in and he told his story last. And what was my amazement and fright to learn that all the three hours I had sat upon the edge of the caverned wall, the lioness had crouched on a bench above me. Jim on his way up had seen her, and then located her tracks in the dust back of my position. When this fact burst upon me, I remembered how I had at first imagined I heard faint panting breaths near me somewhere. I had been too excited to trust my ears.

"Wal," said Jones, standing with the palms of his huge hands to the fire, "we had a poor day. If we had stuck to Don, there'd have been a different story. I haven't trusted him. He has faults, though. He's too fast. He outruns the other hounds, an' he's goin' to be killed because of that. Someday he'll beat the pack to a mean old Tom lion or a lioness with cubs, an' he'll get his everlastin'. Another fault is, he doesn't bark often. That's bad, too. You can't stick to him. He's got a grand bay, shore, but he saves his breath. Don wants to run an' trail an' fight alone. He's got more nerve than any hound I ever trained. He's too good for his own sake—an' it'll be his death."

Naturally I absorbed all that Buffalo Jones said about dogs, horses, lions, everything pertaining to the West, and I believed it as if it had been gospel. But I observed that the others, especially Jim, did not always agree with our chief in regard to the hounds. A little later, when Jones had left the fire, Jim spoke up with his slow Texas drawl.

"Wal, what does he know about dawgs? I'll tell you right heah, if he hadn't shot Don we'd had the best hound that ever put his nose to a track. Don is a wild, strange hound, shore enough. Mebbe he's like a lone wolf. But it's plain he's been mistreated by men. An' Jones has just made him wuss."

Emmet inclined to Jim's point of view. And I respected this giant Mormon who was famous on the desert for his kindness to men and animals. His ranch at Lee's Ferry was overrun with dogs, cats, mustangs, burros, sheep, and tamed wild animals that he had succored.

"Yes, Don hates Jones and, I reckon, all of us," said Emmet. "Don's not old, but he's too old to change. Still, you can never tell what kindness will do to animals. I'd like to take Don home with me and see. But Jones is right. That hound will be killed."

"Now, I wonder why Don doesn't run off from us?" inquired Jim.

"Perhaps he thinks he'd get shot again," I ventured.

"If he ever runs away, it'll not be here in the wilds," replied Emmet. "I take Don to be about as smart as any dog ever gets. And that's pretty close to human intelligence. People have to live lonely lives with dogs before they understand them. I reckon I understand Don. He's either loved one master once and lost him, or else he has always hated all men."

"Humph. That's shore an idee," ejaculated Jim dubiously. "Do you think a dog can feel like that?"

"Jim, I once saw a little Indian shepherd dog lie down on its master's grave and die," returned the Mormon sonorously.

"Wal, dog-gone me," exclaimed Jim in mild surprise.

One morning Jim galloped in, driving the horses pell-mell into camp. Any deviation from the Texan's usual leisurely manner of doing things always brought us up short with keen expectation.

"Saddle up," called Jim. "Shore thar's a chase on. I seen a big red lioness up heah. She must have come down out of the tree whar I hang my meat. Last night I had a haunch of venison. It's gone. . . . Say, she was a beauty. Red as a red fox."

In a very few moments we were mounted and riding up the ravine, with the eager hounds sniffing the air. Always overanxious in my excitement, I rode ahead of my comrades. The hounds trotted with me. The distance to Jim's meat tree was a short quarter of a mile. I knew well where it was and, as of course the lion trail would be fresh, I anticipated a fine opportunity to watch Don. The other hounds had come to regard him as their leader. When we neared the meat tree, which was a low-branched oak shaded by thick silver spruce, Don elevated his nose high in the air. He had caught a scent even at a distance. Jones had said more than once that Don had a wonderful nose. The other hounds, excited by Don, began to whine and yelp and run around with noses to the ground.

I had eyes only for Don. How imbued he was with life and fire. The hair on his neck stood up like bristles. Suddenly he let out a wild bark and bolted. He sped away from the pack and like a flash passed that oak tree, running with his head high. The hounds strung out after him and soon the woods seemed full of a baying chorus.

My horse, Black Bolly, well knew the meaning of that medley and did not need to be urged. He broke into a run and swiftly carried me up out of the hollow and through a brown-aisled pine-scented strip of forest to the canyon.

I rode along the edge of one of the deep indentations on the main rim. The hounds were bawling right under me at the base of a low cliff. They had jumped the lioness. I could not see them, but that was not necessary. They were running fast toward the head of this cove, and I had hard work to hold Black Bolly to a safe gait along that rocky rim. Suddenly she shied, and then reared, so that I fell out of the saddle as much as I dismounted. But I held the bridle, and then jerked my rifle from the saddle sheath. As I ran toward the rim I heard the yells of the men coming up behind. At the same instant, I was startled and halted by sight of something red and furry flashing up into a tree right in front of me. It was the red lioness. The dogs had chased her into a pine the middle branches of which were on a level with the rim.

My skin went tight and cold and my heart fluttered. The lioness looked enormous, but that was because she was so close. I could have touched her with a long fishing pole. I stood motionless for an instant, thrilling in every nerve, reveling in the beauty and wildness of that great cat. She did not see me. The hounds below engaged all her attention. But when I let out a yell, which I could not stifle, she jerked spasmodically to face me. Then I froze again. What a tigerish yellow flash of eyes and fangs. She hissed. She could have sprung from the tree to the rim and upon me in two bounds. But she leaped to a ledge below the rim, glided along that, and disappeared.

I ran ahead and with haste and violence clambered out upon a jutting point of the rim, from which I could command the situation. Jones and the others were riding and yelling back where I had left my horse. I called for them to come.

The hounds were baying along the base of the low cliff. No doubt they had seen the lioness leap out of the tree. My eyes roved everywhere. This cove was a shallow V-shaped gorge, a few hundred yards deep and as many across. Its slopes were steep, with patches of brush and rock.

All at once my quick eye caught a glimpse of something moving up the opposite slope. It was a long red pantherish shape. The lioness. I yelled with all my might. She ran up the slope and at the base of the low wall she turned to the right. At that moment Jones strode heavily over the rough loose rocks of the promontory toward me.

"Where's the cat?" he boomed, his gray eyes flashing. In a moment more I had pointed her out. "Ha. I see . . . . Don't like that place. The canyon boxes. She can't get out. She'll turn back."

The old hunter had been quick to grasp what had escaped me. The lioness could not find any break in the wall, and manifestly she would not go down into the gorge. She wheeled back along the base of this yellow cliff. There appeared to be a strip of bare clay or shale rock against which background her red shape stood out clearly. She glided along, slowing her pace, and she turned her gaze across the gorge.

Then Don's deep bay rang out from the slope to our left. I saw him running down. He leaped in long bounds. The other hounds heard him and broke for the brushy slope. In a moment they had struck the scent of their quarry and given tongue.

As they started down, Don burst out of the willow thicket at the bottom of the gorge and bounded up the opposite slope. He was five hundred yards ahead of the pack. He was swiftly climbing. He would run into the lioness.

Jones gripped my arm in his powerful hand.

"Look," he shouted. "Look at that fool hound . . . . Runnin' uphill to get to that lioness. She won't run. She's cornered. She'll meet him. She'll kill him . . . . Shoot her. Shoot her."

I scarcely needed Jones's command to stir me to save Don, but it was certain that the old plainsman's piercing voice made me tremble. I knelt and leveled my rifle. The lioness showed red against the gray—a fine target. She was gliding more and more slowly. She saw or heard Don. The gun sight wavered. I could not hold steady. But I had to hurry. My first bullet struck two yards below the beast, puffing the dust. She kept on. My second bullet hit behind her. Jones was yelling in my ear. I could see Don out of the tail of my eye. . . . Again I shot. Too high. But the lioness jumped and halted. She lashed with her tail. What a wild picture. I strained, clamped every muscle, and pulled trigger. My bullet struck right under the lioness, scattering a great puff of dust and gravel in her face. She bounded ahead a few yards and up into a cedar tree. An instant later Don flashed over the bare spot where she had waited to kill him, and in another his deep bay rang out under the cedar.

"Treed, by gosh," yelled Jones, joyfully pounding me on the back with his huge fist. "You saved that fool dog's life. She'd have killed him shore. . . . Wal, the pack will be there pronto, an' all we've got to do is go over an' tie her up. But it was a close shave for Don."

That night in camp Don was not in the least different from his usual somber self. He took no note of my proud proprietorship or my hovering near him while he ate the supper I provided, part of which came from my own plate. My interest and sympathy had augmented to love.

Don's attitude toward the captured and chained lions never ceased to be a source of delight and wonder to me. All the other hounds were upset by the presence of big cats. Moze, Sounder, Tige, Ranger would have fought these collared lions. Not so Don. For him they had ceased to exist. He would walk within ten feet of a hissing lioness without the slightest sign of having seen or heard her. He never joined in the howling chorus of the dogs. He would go to sleep close to where the lions clanked their chains, clawed the trees, whined and spat and squalled.

Several days after that incident of the red lioness we had a long and severe chase through the brushy cedar forest on the left wing of the Plateau. I did well to keep the hounds within earshot. When I arrived at the end of that run I was torn and blackened by the brush, wet with sweat, and hot as fire. Jones, lasso in hand, was walking round a large cedar under which the pack of hounds was clamoring. Jim and Emmet were seated on a stone, wiping their red faces.

"Wal, I'll rope him before he rests up," declared Jones.

"Wait till . . . I get my breath," panted Emmet.

"We shore oozed along this mawnin'," drawled Jim.

Dismounting, I untied my camera from the saddle and then began to peer up into the bushy cedar.

"It's a Tom lion," declared Jones. "Not very big, but he looks mean. I reckon he'll mess us up some."

"Haw, Haw," shouted Jim sarcastically. The old plainsman's imperturbability sometimes wore on our nerves.

I climbed a cedar next to the one in which the lion had taken refuge. From a topmost fork, swaying to and fro, I stood up to photograph our quarry. He was a good-sized animal, tawny in color, rather gray of face, and a fierce-looking brute. As the distance between us was not far, my situation was as uncomfortable as thrilling. He snarled at me and spat viciously. I was about to abandon my swinging limb when the lion turned away from me to peer down through the branches.

Jones was climbing into the cedar. Low and deep the lion growled. Jones held in one hand a long pole with a small fork at the end, upon which hung the noose of his lasso. Presently he got far enough up to reach the lion. Usually he climbed close enough to throw the rope, but evidently he regarded this beast as dangerous. He tried to slip the noose over the head of the lion. One sweep of a big paw sent pole and noose flying. Patiently Jones made ready and tried again, with similar result. Many times he tried. His patience and perseverance seemed incredible. One attribute of his great power to capture and train wild animals here asserted itself. Finally the lion grew careless or tired, on which instant Jones slipped the noose over its head.

Drawing the lasso tight, he threw his end over a thick branch and let it trail down to the men below. "Wait now," he yelled, and quickly backed down out of the cedar. The hounds were leaping eagerly.

"Pull him off that fork an' let him down easy so I can rope one of his paws."

It turned out, however, that the lion was hard to dislodge. I could see his muscles ridge and bulge. Dead branches cracked, the tree-top waved. Jones began to roar in anger. The men replied with strained hoarse voices. I saw the lion drawn from his perch, and, clawing the branches, springing convulsively, he disappeared from my sight.

Then followed a crash. The branch over which Jones was lowering the beast had broken. Wild yells greeted my startled ears, and a perfect din of yelps and howls. Pandemonium had broken loose down there. I fell, more than I descended, from that tree.

As I bounded erect, I espied the men scrambling out of the way of a huge furry wheel. Ten hounds and one lion comprised that brown whirling ball. Suddenly out of it a dog came hurtling. He rolled to my feet, staggered up.

It was Don. Blood was streaming from him. Swiftly I dragged him aside, out of harm's way. And I forgot the fight. My hands came away from Don wet and dripping with hot blood. It shocked me. Then I saw that his throat had been terribly torn. I thought his jugular vein had been severed. Don lay down and stretched out. He looked at me with those great somber eyes. Never would I forget. He was going to die right there before my eyes.

"Oh, Don. Don. What can I do?" I cried in horror.

As I sank beside Don, one of my hands came in contact with snow. It had snowed that morning and there were still white patches in shady places. Like a flash, I ripped off my scarf and bound it round Don's neck. Then I scraped up a double handful of snow and placed that in my bandanna handkerchief. This also I bound tightly round his neck. I could do no more. My hope left me then, and I had not the courage to sit there beside him until he died.

All the while I had been aware of a bedlam near at hand. When I looked I saw a spectacle for a hunter. Jones, yelling at the top of his stentorian voice, seized one hound after the other by the hind legs and, jerking him from the lion, threw him down the steep slope. Jim and Emmet were trying to help while at the same time they avoided close quarters with that threshing beast. At last they got the dogs off and the lion stretched out. Jones got up, shaking his shaggy head. Then he espied me and his hard face took on a look of alarm.

"Hyar . . . you're all . . . bloody," he panted plaintively, as if I had been exceedingly remiss.

Whereupon I told him briefly about Don. Then Jim and Emmet approached and we all stood looking down on the quiet dog and the patch of bloody snow.

"Well, I reckon he's a goner," said Jones, breathing hard. "Shore I knew he'd get his everlastin'."

"Looks powerful like the lion has aboot got his, too," added Jim.

Emmet knelt by Don and examined the bandage round his neck. "Bleeding yet," he muttered thoughtfully. "You did all that was possible. Too bad. . . . The kindest thing we can do is to leave him here."

I did not question this, but I hated to consent. Still, to move him would only bring on more hemorrhage, and to put him out of his agony would have been impossible for me. Moreover, while there was life there was hope. Scraping up a goodly ball of snow, I rolled it close to Don so that he could lick it if he chose. Then I turned aside and could not look again. But I knew that tomorrow or the following day I would find my way back to this wild spot.

The accident to Don and what seemed the inevitable issue weighed heavily upon my mind. Don's eyes haunted me. I very much feared that the hunt had reached an unhappy ending for me. Next day the weather was threatening and, as the hounds were pretty tired, we rested in camp, devoting ourselves to needful tasks. A hundred times I thought of Don, alone out there in the wild brakes. Perhaps merciful death had relieved him of suffering. I would surely find out on the morrow.

But the indefatigable Jones desired to hunt in another direction next day, and as I was by no means sure I could find the place where Don had been left, I had to defer that trip. We had a thrilling, hazardous, luckless chase, and I for one gave up before it ended.

Weary and dejected, I rode back. I could not get Don off my conscience. The pleasant woodland camp did not seem the same place. For the first time the hissing, spitting, chain-clinking, tail-lashing lions caused me irritation and resentment. I would have none of them. What was the capture of a lot of spiteful, vicious cats to the life of a noble dog? Slipping my saddle off, I turned Black Bolly loose.

Then I imagined I saw a beautiful black long-eared hound enter the glade. I rubbed my eyes. Indeed there was a dog coming. Don. I shouted my joy and awe. Running like a boy, I knelt by him, saying I knew not what. Don wagged his tail. He licked my hand. These actions seemed as marvelous as his return. He looked sick and weak, but he was all right. The handkerchief was gone from his neck but the scarf remained, and it was stuck tight where his throat had been lacerated.

Later Emmet examined Don and said we had made a mistake about the jugular vein being severed. Don's injury had been serious, however, and without the prompt aid I had so fortunately given, he would soon have bled to death. Jones shook his gray old locks and said:

"Reckon Don's time hadn't come. Hope that will teach him sense." In a couple of days Don had recovered, and on the next he was back leading the pack.

A subtle change had come over Don in his relation to me. I did not grasp it so clearly then. Thought and memory afterward brought the realization to me. But there was a light in his eyes for me which had never been there before.

One day Jones and I treed three lions. The largest leaped and ran down into the canyon. The hounds followed. Jones strode after them, leaving me alone with nothing but a camera to keep those two lions up that tree. I had left horse and gun far up the slope. I protested; I yelled after him, "What'll I do if they start down?"

He turned to gaze up at me. His grim face flashed in the sunlight.

"Grab a club an' chase them back," he replied.

Then I was left alone with two ferocious-looking lions in a piñon tree scarcely thirty feet high. While they heard the baying of the hounds they paid no attention to me, but after that ceased, they got ugly. Then I hid behind a bush and barked like a dog. It worked beautifully. The lions grew quiet. I barked and yelped and bayed until I lost my voice. Then they got ugly again. They started down. With stones and clubs I kept them up there, while all the time I was wearing to collapse. When at last I was about to give up in terror and despair I heard Don's bay, faint and far away. The lions had heard it before I had. How they strained. I could see the beating of their hearts through their lean sides. My own heart leaped. Don's bay floated up, wild and mournful. He was coming. Jones had put him on the back trail of the lion that had leaped from the tree.

Deeper and clearer came the bays. How strange that Don should vary from his habit of seldom baying. There was something uncanny in this change. Soon I saw him far down the rocky slope. He was climbing fast. It seemed I had long to wait, yet my fear left me. On and up he came, ringing out that wild bay. It must have curdled the blood of those palpitating lions. It seemed the herald of that bawling pack of hounds.

Don espied me before he reached the piñon in which were the lions. He bounded right past it and up to me with the wildest demeanor. He leaped up and placed his forepaws on my breast. And as I leaned down, excited and amazed, he licked my face. Then he whirled back to the tree, where he stood up and fiercely bayed the lions. While I sank down to rest, overcome, the familiar baying chorus of the hounds floated up from below. As usual they were far behind the fleet Don, but they were coming.

Another day I found myself alone on the edge of a huge cove that opened down into the main canyon. We were always getting lost from one another. And so were the hounds. There were so many lion trails that the pack would split, some going one way, some another, until it appeared each dog finally had a lion to himself.

It was a glorious day. From far below, faint and soft,

came the strange roar of the Rio Colorado. I could see it winding, somber and red, through the sinister chasm. Adventure ceased to exist for me. I was gripped by the grandeur and loveliness, the desolation and loneliness, of the supreme spectacle of nature.

Then, as I sat there, absorbed and chained, the spell of enchantment was broken by Don. He had come to me. His mouth was covered with froth. I knew what that meant. Rising, I got my canteen from the saddle and poured water into the crown of my sombrero. Don lapped it. As he drank so thirstily, I espied a bloody scratch on his nose.

"Aha, a lion has batted you one, this very morning," I cried. "Don—I fear for you."

He rested while I once more was lost in contemplation of the glory of the canyon. What significant hours these on the lonely heights. But then I only saw and felt.

Presently I mounted my horse and headed for camp, with Don trotting behind. When we reached the notch of the cove, the hound let out his deep bay and bounded down a break in the low wall. I dismounted and called. Only another deep bay answered me. Don had scented a lion or crossed one's trail. Suddenly several sharp yelps came from below, a crashing of brush, a rattling of stones. Don had jumped another lion. Quickly I threw off sombrero and coat and chaps. I retained my left glove. Then, with camera over my shoulder and revolver in my belt, I plunged down the break in the crag. My boots were heavy-soled and studded with hobnails. The weeks on these rocky slopes had trained me to fleetness and surefootedness. I plunged down the sliding slant of weathered stone, crashed through the brush, dodged under the cedars, leaped from boulder to ledge and down from ledge to bench. Reaching a dry stream bed, I espied in the sand the tracks of a big lion, and beside them smaller tracks that were Don's. And as I ran I yelled at the top of my lungs, hoping to help Don tree the lion. What I was afraid of was that the beast might wait for Don and kill him.

Such strenuous exertion required a moment's rest now and then, during which I listened for Don. Twice I heard his bay, and the last one sounded as if he had treed the lion.

Again I took to my plunging, jumping, sliding descent; and I was not long in reaching the bottom of that gorge. Ear and eye had guided me unerringly, for I came to an open place near the main jump-off into the canyon, and here I saw a tawny shape in a cedar tree. It belonged to a big Tom lion. He swayed the branch and leaped to a ledge, and from that down to another, and then vanished round a corner of wall.

Don could not follow down those high steps. Neither could I. We worked along the ledge, under cedars, and over huge slabs of rock toward the corner where our quarry had disappeared. We were close to the great abyss. I could almost feel it. Then the glaring light of a void struck my eyes like some tangible thing.

At last I worked out from the shade of rocks and trees and, turning the abrupt jut of wall, I found a few feet of stone ledge between me and the appalling chasm. How blue, how fathomless. Despite my pursuit of a lion, I was suddenly shocked into awe and fear.

Then Don returned to me. The hair on his neck was bristling. He had come from the right, from round the corner of wall where the ledge ran, and where surely the lion had gone. My blood was up and I meant to track that beast to his lair, photograph him if possible, and kill him. So I strode on to the ledge and round the point of wall. Soon I espied huge cat tracks in the dust, close to the base. A well-defined lion trail showed there. And ahead I saw the ledge—widening somewhat and far from level—stretch before me to another corner.

Don acted queerly. He followed me, close at my heels. He whined. He growled. I did not stop to think then what he wanted to do. But it must have been that he wanted to go back. The heat of youth and the wildness of adventure had gripped me, and fear and caution were not in me.

Nevertheless, my sensibilites were remarkably acute. When Don got in front of me there was something that compelled me to go slowly. Soon, in any event, I should have been forced to that. The ledge narrowed. Then it widened again to a large bench with cavernous walls overhanging it. I passed this safe zone to turn onto a narrowing edge of rock that disappeared round another corner. When I came to this point I must have been possessed, for I flattened myself against the wall and worked round it.

Again the way appeared easier. But what made Don go so cautiously? I heard his growls; still, no longer did I look at him. I felt this pursuit was nearing an end. At the next turn I halted short, suddenly quivering. The ledge ended— and there lay the lion, licking a bloody paw.

Tumultuous indeed were my emotions, yet on that instant I did not seem conscious of fear. Jones had told me never, in close quarters, to take my eyes off a lion. I forgot. In the wild excitement of a chance for an incomparable picture, I forgot. A few precious seconds were wasted over the attempt to focus my camera.

Then I heard quick thuds. Don growled. With a start I jerked up to see the lion had leaped or run half the distance. He was coming. His eyes blazed purple fire. They seemed to paralyze me, yet I began to back along the ledge. Whipping out my revolver, I tried to aim. But my nerves had undergone such a shock that I could not aim. The gun wobbled. I dared not risk shooting. If I wounded the lion, it was certain he would knock me off that narrow ledge.

So I kept on backing, step by step. Don did likewise. He stayed between me and the lion. Therein lay the greatness of that hound. How easily he could have dodged by me to escape the ledge. But he did not do it.

A precious opportunity presented when I reached the widest part of the bench. Here I had a chance and I recognized it. Then, when the overhanging wall bumped my shoulder, I realized too late. I had come to the narrowing part of the ledge. Not reason but fright kept me from turning to run. Perhaps that might have been the best way out of the predicament. I backed along the strip of stone that was only a foot wide. A few more blind steps meant death. My nerve was gone. Collapse seemed inevitable. I had a camera in one hand and a revolver in the other.

That purple-eyed beast did not halt. My distorted imagination gave him a thousand shapes and actions. Bitter, despairing thoughts flashed through my mind. Jones had said mountain lions were cowards, but not when cornered—never when there was no avenue of escape.

Then Don's haunches backed into my knees. I dared not look down, but I felt the hound against me. He was shaking, yet he snarled fiercely. The feel of Don there, the sense of his courage, caused my cold thick blood to burst into hot gushes. In another second he would grapple with this hissing lion. That meant destruction for both, for they would roll off the ledge.

I had to save Don. That mounting thought was my salvation. Physically, he could not have saved me or himself, but this grand spirit somehow pierced to my manhood.

Leaning against the wall, I lifted the revolver and steadied my arm with my left hand, which still held the camera. I aimed between the purple eyes. That second was an eternity. The gun crashed. The blaze of one of those terrible eyes went out.

Up leaped the lion, beating the wall with heavy thudding paws. Then he seemed to propel himself outward, off the ledge into space—a tawny spread figure that careened majestically over and over, down . . . down . . . down to vanish in the blue depths.

Don whined. I stared at the abyss, slowly becoming unlocked from the grip of terror. I staggered a few steps forward to a wider part of the ledge, and there I sank down, unable to stand longer. Don crept to me, put his head in my lap.

I listened. I strained my ears. How endlessly long seemed that lion in falling. But all was magnified. At last puffed up a sliding roar, swelling and dying until again the terrific silence of the canyon enfolded me.

Presently Don sat up and gazed into the depths. How strange to see him peer down. Then he turned his sleek dark head to look at me. What did I see through the somber sadness of his eyes? He whined and licked my hand. It seemed to me Don and I were more than man and dog. He moved away then round the narrow ledge, and I had to summon energy to follow. Shudderingly I turned my back on that awful chasm and held my breath while I slipped round the perilous place. Don waited there for me, then trotted on. Not until I had gotten safely off that ledge did I draw a full breath. Then I toiled up the steep rough slope to the rim. Don was waiting beside my horse. Between us we drank the rest of the water in my canteen, and when we reached camp, night had fallen. A bright fire and a good supper broke the gloom of my mind. My story held those rugged Westerners spellbound. Don stayed close to me, followed me of his own accord, and slept beside me in my tent.

There came a frosty morning when the sun rose red over the ramparts of colored rock. We had a lion running before the misty shadows dispersed from the canyon depths.

The hounds chased him through the sage and cedar into the wild brakes of the north wing of the Plateau. This lion must have been a mean old Tom, for he did not soon go down the slopes.

The particular section he at last took refuge in was impassable for man. The hounds gave him a grueling chase, then one by one they crawled up, sore and thirsty. All but Don. He did not come. Jones rolled out his mighty voice, which pealed back in mocking hollow echoes. Don did not come. At noonday Jones and the men left for camp with the hounds.

I remained. I had a vigil there on the lofty rim, alone, where I could peer down the yellow-green slope and beyond to the sinister depths. It was a still day. The silence was overpowering. When Don's haunting bay floated up, it shocked me. At long intervals I heard it, fainter and fainter. Then no more.

Still I waited and watched and listened. Afternoon waned. My horse neighed piercingly from the cedars. The sinking sun began to fire the Pink Cliffs of Utah, and then the hundred miles of immense chasm over which my charmed gaze held dominion. How lonely, how terrifying that stupendous rent in the earth. Lion and hound had no fear. But the thinking, feeling man was afraid. What did they mean—this exquisitely hued and monstrous canyon, the setting sun, the wilderness of a lion, the grand spirit of a dog . . . and the wondering sadness of a man?

I rode home without Don. Half the night I lay awake waiting, hoping. But he did not return by dawn, nor through the day. He never came back.

Fantoms of Peace

1

Dwire judged him to be another of those strange desert prospectors in whom there was some relentless driving power besides the lust for gold. He saw a stalwart man from whóse lined face deep luminous eyes looked out with yearning gaze, as if drawn by something far beyond the ranges.

The man had approached Dwire back in the Nevada mining camp, and had followed him down the trail leading into the Mohave. He spoke few words, but his actions indicated that he answered to some subtle influence in seeking to accompany the other.

When Dwire hinted that he did not go down into the desert for gold alone, the only reply he got was a singular flashing of the luminous eyes. Then he explained, more from a sense of duty than from hope of turning the man back, that in the years of his wandering he had met no one who could stand equally with him the blasting heat, the blinding storms, the wilderness of sand and rock and lava and cactus, the terrible silence and desolation of the desert.

"Back there they told me you were Dwire," replied the man. "I'd heard of you, and if you don't mind, I'd like to go with you."

"Stranger, you're welcome," replied Dwire. "I'm going inside"—he waved a hand toward the wide, shimmering, shadowy descent of plain and range—"and I don't know where. I may cross the Mohave into the Colorado Desert. I may go down into Death Valley."

The prospector swept his far-reaching gaze over the colored gulf of rock and sand. For moments he seemed to forget himself. Then, with gentle slaps, he drove his burro into the trail behind Dwire's, and said:

"My name's Hartwell."

They began a slow, silent march down into the desert. At sundown they camped near Red Seeps. Dwire observed that his companion had acquired the habit of silence so characteristic of the lone wanderer in the wilds—a habit not easily broken when two of these men are thrown together.

Next sunset they made camp at Coyote Tanks; the next at Indian Well; the following night at a nameless water hole. For five more days they plodded down with exchange of few words. When they got deep into the desert, with endless stretches of drifting sand and rugged rock between them and the outside world, there came a breaking of reserve, noticeable in Dwire, almost imperceptibly gradual in his companion. At night, round their meager mesquite campfire, Dwire would remove his black pipe to talk a little. The other man would listen, and would sometimes unlock his lips to speak a word.

And so, as Dwire responded to the influence of his surroundings, he began to notice his companion, and found him different from any man he had encountered in the desert. Hartwell did not grumble at the heat, the glare, the driving sand, the sour water, the scant fare. During the daylight hours he was seldom idle; at night he sat dreaming before the fire, or paced to and fro in the gloom. If he ever slept, it must have been long after Dwire had rolled in his blanket and dropped to rest. He was tireless and patient.

Dwire's awakened interest in Hartwell brought home to him the realization that for years he had shunned companionship. In those years only three men had wandered into the desert with him, and they had found what he believed they had sought there—graves in the shifting sands. He had not cared to know their secrets; but the more he watched this latest comrade, the more he began to suspect that he might have missed something in these other men.

In his own driving passion to take his secret into the limitless abode of silence and desolation, where he could be alone with it, he had forgotten that life dealt shocks to other men. Somehow this silent comrade reminded him.

Two weeks of steady marching saw the prospectors merging into the Mohave. It was naked, rock-ribbed, sand-sheeted desert. They lost all trails but those of the coyote and wildcat, and these they followed to the water holes.

At length they got into desert that appeared new to Dwire. He could not recognize landmarks near at hand. Behind them, on the horizon line, stood out a blue peak that marked the plateau from which they had descended. Before them loomed a jagged range of mountains, which were in line with Death Valley.

The prospectors traveled on, halting now and then to dig at the base of a mesa or pick into a ledge. As they progressed over ridges and across plains and through canyons, the general trend was toward the jagged range, and every sunset found them at a lower level. The heat waxed stronger every day, and the water holes were harder to find.

One afternoon, late, after they had toiled up a white, winding wash of sand and gravel, they came upon a dry water hole. Dwire dug deep into the sand, but without avail. He was turning to retrace the weary steps to the last water when his comrade asked him to wait.

Dwire watched Hartwell search in his pack and bring forth what appeared to be a small forked branch of a peach tree. He firmly grasped the prongs of the fork, and held them before him, with the end standing straight out. Then he began to walk along the dry stream bed.

At first amused, then amazed, then pityingly, and at last

curiously, Dwire kept pace with Hartwell. He saw a strong tension of his comrade's wrists, as if he was holding hard against a considerable force. The end of the peach branch began to quiver and turn downward. Dwire reached out a hand to touch it, and was astounded at feeling a powerful vibrant force pulling the branch down. He felt it as a quivering magnetic shock. The branch kept turning, and at length pointed to the ground.

"Dig here," said Hartwell.

"What?" ejaculated Dwire.

He stood by while Hartwell dug in the sand. Three feet he dug—four—five. The sand grew dark, then moist. At six feet water began to seep through.

"Get the little basket in my pack," said Hartwell.

Dwire complied, though he scarcely comprehended what was happening. He saw Hartwell drop the basket into the deep hole and carefully pat it down, so that it kept the sides from caving in and allowed the water to seep through. While Dwire watched, the basket filled.

Of all the strange incidents of his desert career, this was the strangest. Curiously, he picked up the peach branch, and held it as he had seen Hartwell hold it. However, the thing was dead in his hands.

"I see you haven't got it," remarked Hartwell. "Few men have."

"Got what?" demanded Dwire.

"A power to find water that way. I can't explain it. Back in Illinois an old German showed me I had it."

"What a gift for a man in the desert!"

Dwire accepted things there that elsewhere he would have regarded as unbelievable.

Hartwell smiled—the first time in all those days that his face had changed. The light of it struck Dwire.

2

They entered a region where mineral abounded, and their march became slower. Generally they took the course of a wash, one on each side, and let the burros travel leisurely along, nipping at the bleached blades of scant grass, or at sage or cactus, while the prospectors searched in the canyons and under the ledges for signs of gold.

Descending among the splintered rocks, clambering over boulders, climbing up weathered slopes, always picking, always digging—theirs was toilsome labor that wore more and more on them each day. When they found any rock that hinted of gold, they picked off a piece and gave it a chemical test. The search was fascinating.

They interspersed the work with long restful moments when they looked afar, down the vast reaches and smoky shingles, to the line of dim mountains. Some impelling desire, not all the lure of gold, took them to the top of mesas and escarpments; and here, when they dug and picked, they rested and gazed out at the wide prospect.

Then, as the sun lost its heat and sank, lowering, to dent its red disk behind far distant spurs, they halted in a shady canyon, or some likely spot in a dry wash, and tried for water. When they found it, they unpacked, gave drink to the tired burros, and turned them loose. Dead greasewood served for the campfire. They made bread and coffee and cooked bacon, and when each simple meal ended they were still hungry. They were chary of their supplies. They even limited themselves to one pipe of tobacco.

While the strange twilight deepened into weird night, they sat propped against stones, with eyes on the embers of the fire, and soon they lay on the sand with the light of great white stars on their dark faces.

Each succeeding day and night Dwire felt himself more and more drawn to Hartwell. He found that after hours of burning toil he had insensibly grown nearer to his comrade. The fact bothered him. It was curious, perplexing. And finally, in wonder, he divined that he cared for Hartwell.

He reflected that after a few weeks in the desert he had always become a different man. In civilization, in the rough mining camps, he had been a prey to unrest and gloom; but once down on the great heave and bulge and sweep of this lonely world, he could look into his unquiet soul without bitterness. Always he began to see and to think and to feel. Did not the desert magnify men?

Dwire believed that wild men in wild places, fighting cold, heat, starvation, thirst, barrenness, facing the elements in all their primal ferocity, usually retrograded, descended to the savage, lost all heart and soul, and became mere brutes. Likewise he believed that men wandering or lost in the wilderness often reversed that brutal order of life, and became noble, wonderful, superhuman.

He had the proof in the serene wisdom of his soul when for a time the desert had been his teacher. And so now he did not marvel at a slow stir, stealing warmer and warmer along his veins, and at the premonition that he and Hartwell, alone on the desert, driven there by life's mysterious and remorseless motive, were to see each other through God's eyes.

Hartwell was a man who thought of himself last. It humiliated Dwire that in spite of growing keenness he could not hinder his companion from doing more than his share of the day's work. It spoke eloquently of what Hartwell might be capable of on the burdened return journey. The man was mild, gentle, quiet, mostly silent, yet under all his softness he seemed to be made of the fiber of steel. Dwire could not thwart him.

Moreover, he appeared to want to find gold for Dwire, not for himself. If he struck his pick into a ledge that gave forth a promising glint, instantly he called to his companion. Dwire's hands always trembled at the turning of rock that promised gold. He had enough of the prospector's passion for fortune to thrill at the chance of a strike; but Hartwell never showed the least trace of excitement.

And his kindness to the burros was something that Dwire had never seen equaled. Hartwell always found the water and dug for it, ministered to the weary burros, and then led them off to the best patch of desert growth. Last of all he bethought himself to eat a little.

One night they were encamped at the head of a canyon. The day had been exceedingly hot, and long after sundown the radiation of heat from the rocks persisted. A desert bird whistled a wild, melancholy note from a dark cliff, and a distant coyote wailed mournfully. The stars shone white until the huge moon rose to burn out all their whiteness.

Many times, since they started their wanderings, Dwire had seen Hartwell draw something from his pocket and peer long at it. On this night Dwire watched him again, and yielded to an interest which he had not heretofore voiced.

"Hartwell, what drives you into the desert?"

"Comrade, do I seem to be a driven man?" asked Hartwell.

"No. But I feel it. Do you come to forget?"

"I come to remember."

"Ah!" softly exclaimed Dwire.

Always he seemed to have known that.

He said no more. He watched Hartwell rise and begin his nightly pace to and fro, up and down.

With slow, soft tread, forward and back, tirelessly and ceaselessly, the man paced his beat. He did not look up at the stars or follow the radiant track of the moon along the canyon ramparts. He hung his head. He was lost in another world. It was a world which the lonely desert made real. He looked a dark, sad, plodding figure, and somehow impressed Dwire with the helplessness of men.

"He is my brother," muttered Dwire.

He grew acutely conscious of the pang in his own breast, of the fire in his heart, the strife and torment of his own passion-driven soul. Dwire had come into the desert to forget a woman. She appeared to him then as she had looked when first she entered his life—a golden-haired girl, blue-eyed, white-skinned, red-lipped, tall and slender and beautiful. He saw her as she had become after he had ruined her—a wild and passionate woman, mad to be loved, false and lost, and still cursed with unforgettable allurements. He had never forgotten, and an old, sickening remorse knocked at his heart.

Rising, Dwire climbed out of the canyon to the top of a mesa, where he paced to and fro. He looked down into the weird and mystic shadows, like the darkness of his passion, and farther on down the moon-track and the glittering stretches that vanished in the cold, blue horizon.

The moon soared radiant and calm, the white stars shone serene. The vault of heaven seemed illimitable and divine. The desert surrounded him, silver-streaked and black-mantled, a chaos of rock and sand, a dead thing, silent, austere, ancient, waiting, majestic. It spoke to Dwire. It was a naked corpse, but it had a soul.

In that wild solitude, the white stars looked down upon him pitilessly and pityingly. They had shone upon a desert that had once been alive and was now dead, and that would again throb to life, only to die. It was a terrible ordeal for Dwire to stand there alone and realize that he was only a man facing eternity; but that was what gave him strength to endure. Somehow he was a part of it all, some atom in that vastness, somehow necessary to an inscrutable purpose, something indestructible in that desolate world of ruin and death and decay, something perishable and changeable and growing under all the fixity of heaven. In that endless, silent hall of desert there was a spirit; and Dwire felt hovering near him fantoms of peace.

He returned to camp and sought his comrade.

"Hartwell, I reckon we're two of a kind. It was a woman who drove me into the desert. But I come to forget. The desert's the only place I can do that."

"Was she your wife?" asked the other.

"No."

A long silence ensued. A cool wind blew up the canyon, sifting the sand through the dry sage, driving away the last of the lingering heat. The campfire wore down to a ruddy ashen heap.

"I had a daughter," said Hartwell, speaking as if impelled. "She lost her mother at birth. And I—I didn't know how to bring up a girl. She was pretty and gay. She went to the bad. I tried to forget her and failed. Then I tried to find her. She had disappeared. Since then I haven't been able to stay in one place, or to work or sleep or rest."

Hartwell's words were peculiarly significant to Dwire. They distressed him. He had been wrapped up in his remorse for wronging a woman. If ever in the past he had thought of anyone connected with her, he had long forgotten it; but the consequences of such wrong were far-reaching. They struck at the roots of a home. And here, in the desert, he was confronted by the spectacle of a splendid man—the father of a wronged girl—wasting his life because he could not forget—because there was nothing left to live for.

Suddenly Dwire felt an inward constriction, a cold, shivering clamp of pain, at the thought that perhaps he had blasted the life of a father. He shared his companion's grief. He knew why the desert drew him. Since Hartwell must remember, he could do so best in this solitude, where the truth of the earth lay naked, where the truth of life lay stripped bare. In the face of the tragedy of the universe, as revealed in the desert, what was the error of one frail girl, or the sorrow of one unfortunate man?

"Hartwell, it's bad enough to be driven by sorrow for

someone you've loved, but to suffer sleepless and eternal remorse for the *ruin* of one you've loved—that is worse. Listen! In my younger days—it seems long ago now, yet it's only ten years—I was a wild fellow. I didn't mean to do wrong. I was just a savage. I gambled and drank. I got into scrapes. I made love to girls, and one, the sweetest and loveliest girl who ever breathed, I—I ruined. I disgraced her. Not knowing, I left her to bear the brunt of that disgrace alone. Then I fell into terrible moods. I changed. I discovered that I really and earnestly loved that girl. I went back to her, to make amends—but it was too late!"

Hartwell leaned forward a little in the waning campfire glow, and looked strangely into Dwire's face, as if searching it for the repentance and remorse that alone would absolve him from scorn and contempt; but he said nothing.

3

The prospectors remained in that camp for another day, held by some rust-stained ledges that contained mineral.

Late in the afternoon Dwire returned to camp, to find Hartwell absent. His pick, however, was leaning against a stone, and his coat lying over one of the packs. Hartwell was probably out driving the burros up to water.

Gathering a bundle of greasewood, Dwire kindled a fire. Then into his goldpan he measured out flour and water. Presently it was necessary for him to get into one of the packs, and in so doing he knocked down Hartwell's coat. From a pocket fell a small plush case, badly soiled and worn.

Dwire knew that this case held the picture at which Hartwell looked so often, and as he bent to pick it up he saw the face shining in the light. He experienced a shuddering ripple through all his being. The face resembled the one that was burned forever into his memory. How strange and fatal it was that every crag, every cloud, everything which attracted his eye, took on the likeness of the girl he loved!

He gazed down upon the thing in his hand. It was not curiosity; only a desire to dispel his illusion.

Suddenly, when he actually recognized the face of Nell Warren, he seemed to feel that he was paralyzed. He stared and gasped. The blood thrummed in his ears.

This picture was Nell when she was a mere girl. It was youthful, soft, pure, infinitely sweet. A tide of emotion rushed irresistibly over him.

The hard hoofs of the burros, cracking the stones, broke the spell that held Dwire, and he saw Hartwell approaching.

"Nell was *his* daughter!" whispered Dwire.

Trembling and dazed, he returned the picture to the pocket from which it had fallen, and with bent head and clumsy hands he busied himself about the campfire. Strange and bewildering thoughts raced through his mind. He ate little; it seemed that he could scarcely wait to be off; and when the meal was ended, and work done, he hurried away.

As thought and feeling multiplied, he was overwhelmed. It was beyond belief that out of the millions of men in the world two who had never seen each other could have been driven into the desert by memory of the same woman. It brought the past so close. It showed Dwire how inevitably all his spiritual life was governed by what had happened long ago.

That which made life significant to him was a wandering in silent places where no eye could see him with his secret. He was mad, blinded, lost.

Some fateful chance had thrown him with the father of the girl he had wrecked. It was incomprehensible; it was terrible. It was the one thing of all possible happenings in the world of chance that both father and lover would have declared unendurable. It would be the scoring of unhealed wounds. In the thoughtful brow, the sad, piercing eye, the plodding, unquiet mood of the other, each man would see his own ruin.

Dwire's pain reached to despair when he felt this insupportable relation between Hartwell and himself.

Something within him cried out and commanded him to reveal his identity. Hartwell would kill him, probably, but it was not fear of death that put Dwire on the rack. He had faced death too often to be afraid. It was the thought of adding torture to this long-suffering man whom he had come to love.

All at once Dwire swore that he would not augment Hartwell's trouble, or let him stain his hands with blood, however just that act might be. He would reveal himself, but he would so twist the truth of Nell's sad story that the father would lose his agony and hate, his driving passion to wander over this desolate desert.

This made Dwire think of Nell as a living, breathing woman. She was somewhere beyond the dim horizon line. She would be thirty years old—that time of a woman's life when she was most beautiful and wonderful. She would be in the glare and glitter, sought and loved by men, in some great and splendid city. At that very moment she would be standing somewhere, white-gowned, white-faced, with her crown of golden hair, with the same old haunting light in her eyes—lost, and bitterly indifferent to her doom.

Dwire gazed out over the blood-red, darkening desert, and suddenly, strangely, unconsciously, the strife in his soul ceased. The moment that followed was one of incalculable realization of change, in which his eyes seemed to pierce the vastness of cloud and range and the mystery of gloom and shadow—to see with strong vision the illimitable space of sand and rock. He felt the grandeur of the desert, its simplicity, its truth, and he learned at last the lesson it taught.

No longer strange or unaccountable was his meeting with Hartwell. Each had marched in the steps of destiny, and as the lines of their fates had been inextricably tangled in the years that were gone, so now their steps had crossed and turned them toward one common goal.

For years they had been two men marching alone, answering to an inward and driving search, and the desert had brought them together. For years they had wandered alone, in silence and solitude, where the sun burned white all day and the stars burned white all night, blindly following the whisper of a spirit. But now Dwire knew that he was no longer blind. Truth had been revealed—wisdom had spoken—unselfish love had come—and in this flash of revelation Dwire felt that it had been given him to relieve Hartwell of his burden.

4

Dwire returned to camp. As always, at that long hour when the afterglow of sunset lingered in the west, Hartwell was plodding to and fro in the gloom.

"I'm wondering if Hartwell is your right name," said Dwire.

"It's not," replied the other.

"Well, out here men seem to lose old names, old identities. Dwire's not my real name."

Hartwell slowly turned. It seemed that there might have been a suspension, a blank, between his usual quiet, courteous interest and some vivifying, electrifying mood to come.

"Was your real name Warren?" asked Dwire.

Hartwell moved with a sudden start.

"Yes," he replied.

"I've got something to tell you," Dwire went on. "A while back I knocked your coat down, and a picture fell out of your pocket. I looked at it. I recognized it. I knew your daughter Nell."

"You!"

The man grasped Dwire and leaned close, his eyes shining out of the gloom.

"Don't drag at me like that! Listen. I was Nell's lover. I ruined her. I am Gail Hamlin!"

Hartwell became as a man struck by lightning, still standing before he fell.

"Yes, I'm Hamlin," repeated Dwire.

With a convulsive spring Hartwell appeared to rise and tower over Dwire. Then he plunged down upon him, and clutched at his throat with terrible, stifling hands. Dwire fought desperately, not to save his life, but for breath to speak a few words that would pierce Hartwell's maddened mind.

"Warren, kill me, if you want," gasped Dwire; "but wait! It's for your own sake. Give me a little time! If you don't, you'll never know. *Nell didn't go to the bad!*"

Dwire felt the shock that vibrated through Hartwell at those last words. He repeated them again and again.

As if wrenched by some resistless force, Hartwell released Dwire, staggered back, and stood with uplifted, shaking hands. The horrible darkness of his face showed his lust to kill. The awful gleam of hope in his luminous eyes revealed what had checked his fury.

"Comrade," panted Dwire, "it's no stranger that you should kill me than that we should meet out here. But give me a little time. Listen! I want to tell you. I'm Hamlin—I'm the man who broke Nell's heart. Only she never went to the bad. You thought wrong—you heard wrong. When she left Peoria, and I learned my true feelings, I hunted her. I traced her to St. Louis. She worked there, and on Sundays sang in a church. She was more beautiful than ever. The men lost their heads about her. I pleaded and pleaded with her to forgive me—to marry me—to let me make it all up to her. She forgave, but she would not marry me. I would not give up, and so I stayed on there. I was wild and persistent; but Nell had ceased to care for me. Nor did she care for any of the men who courted her. Her trouble had made her a good and noble woman. She was like a nun.

She came to be loved by women and children—by everyone who knew her.

"Then some woman who had known Nell in Peoria came to St. Louis. She had a poison tongue. She talked. No one believed her; but when the gossip got to Nell's ears, she faded—she gave up. It drove her from St. Louis, I traced her—found her again. Again I was too late. The disgrace and shock, coming so near a critical time for her, broke her down, and—she died. You see, you were mistaken. As for me—well, I drifted West, and now for a long time I've been taking to the desert. It's the only place where I can live with my remorse. It's the only place where I can forget she is dead!"

"Dead! Dead all these years!" murmured Hartwell brokenly. "All these years that I've thought of her as—"

"You've thought wrong," interrupted Dwire. "Nell was good, as good as she was lovable and beautiful. I was the one who was evil, who failed, who turned my back on the noblest chance life offers to a man. I was young, selfish, savage. What did I know? But when I got away from the world and grew old in thought and pain, I learned much. Nell was a good woman."

"Oh, thank God! Thank God!" cried Hartwell, and he fell on his knees.

Dwire stole away into the darkness, with that broken cry quivering in his heart.

How long he absented himself from camp, or what he did, he had no idea. When he returned, Hartwell was sitting before the fire, and once more he appeared composed. He spoke, and his voice had a deeper note, but otherwise he seemed as usual. The younger man understood, then, how Hartwell's wrath had softened.

Dwire experienced a singular exaltation in the effect of his falsehood. He had lightened his comrade's burden. Wonderfully it came to him that he had also lightened his own. From that moment he never again suffered a pang in his thought of Nell. Subtly and unconsciously his falsehood became truth to him, and he remembered her as he had described her to her father.

He saw that he had uplifted Hartwell, and the knowledge gave him happiness. He had rolled away a comrade's heavy, somber grief; and, walking with him in the serene, luminous light of the stars, again he began to feel the haunting presence of his fantoms of peace. In the moan of the cool wind, in the silken seep of sifting sand, in the distant rumble of a slipping ledge, in the faint rush of a shooting star, he heard these fantoms of peace coming, with whispers of the long pain of men at the last made endurable. Even in the white noonday, under the burning sun, these fantoms came to be real to him. And in the dead silence, the insupportable silence of the midnight hours, he heard them breathing nearer on the desert wind—whispers of God's peace in the solitude.

5

Dwire and Hartwell meandered on down into the desert. There came a morning when the sun shone angry and red through a dull, smoky haze.

"We're in for sandstorms," said Dwire. "We'd better turn back. I don't know where we are, but I think we're in Death Valley. We'd better get back to the last water."

But they had scarcely covered a mile on their back trail when a desert-wide, moaning, yellow wall of flying sand swooped down upon them. Seeking shelter in the lee of a rock, they waited, hoping that the storm was only a squall, such as frequently whipped across the open places.

The moan increased to a roar, the dull red slowly dimmed, to disappear in the yellow pall, and the air grew thick and dark. Dwire slipped the packs from the burros. He feared the sandstorms had arrived some weeks ahead of their usual season.

The men covered their heads and patiently waited. The long hours dragged, and the storm increased in fury. Dwire and Hartwell wet scarfs with water from the canteens, bound them round their faces, and then covered their heads.

The steady, hollow bellow of flying sand went on. It flew so thickly that enough sifted down under the shelving rock to weight the blankets and almost bury the men. They were frequently compelled to shake off the sand to keep from being borne to the ground. And it was necessary to keep digging out the packs, for the floor of their shelter rose higher and higher.

They tried to eat, and seemed to be grinding only sand between their teeth. They lost the count of time. They dared not sleep, for that would have meant being buried alive. They could only crouch close to the leaning rock, shake off the sand, blindly dig out their packs, and every moment gasp and cough and choke to fight suffocation.

The storm finally blew itself out. It left the prospectors heavy and stupid for want of sleep. Their burros had wandered away, or had been buried in the sand.

Far as eye could reach, the desert had marvelously changed; it was now a rippling sea of sand dunes. Away to the north rose the peak that was their only guiding mark. They headed toward it, carrying a shovel and part of their packs.

At noon the peak vanished in the shimmering glare of the desert. Dwire and Hartwell pushed on, guided by the sun. In every wash they tried for water. With the forked branch in his magnetic hands, Hartwell always succeeded in locating water, and always they dug and dug; but the water lay too deep.

Toward sunset, in a pocket under a canyon wall, they dug in the sand and found water; but as fast as they shoveled the sand out, the sides of the hole caved in, and darkness compelled them to give up. Spent and sore, they fell, and slept where they lay through that night and part of the next day. Then they succeeded in getting water, quenched their thirst, filled the canteens, and cooked a meal.

Here, abandoning all their outfit except the shovel, the basket with a scant store of food, and the canteens, they set out, both silent and grim in the understanding of what lay before them. They traveled by the sun, and, after dark, by the north star. At dawn they crawled into a shady wash and slept till afternoon. Hours were wasted in vain search for water. Hartwell located it, but it lay too deep.

That night, deceived by a hazy sky, they toiled on, to find at dawn that they had turned back into Death Valley. Again the lonely desert peak beckoned to them, and again they wearily faced toward it, only to lose it in the glare of the noonday heat.

The burning day found them in an interminably wide plain, where there was no shelter from the fierce sun. They were exceedingly careful with their water, though there was absolute necessity of drinking a little every hour.

Late in the afternoon they came to a canyon which they believed to be the lower end of the one in which they had last found water. For hours they traveled toward its head. After night had set in, they found what they sought. Yielding to exhaustion, they slept, and next day were loath to leave the water hole. Cool night spurred them on with canteens full and renewed strength.

The day opened for them in a red inferno of ragged, wind-worn stone. Like a flame the sun glanced up from the rock, to scorch and peel their faces. Hartwell went blind from the glare, and Dwire had to lead him.

Once they rested in the shade of a ledge. Dwire, from long habit, picked up a piece of rock and dreamily examined it. Its weight lent him sudden interest. It had a peculiar black color. He scraped through the black rust to find that he held a piece of gold.

Around him lay scattered heaps of black pebbles, bits of black, weathered rock, and pieces of broken ledge. All contained gold.

"Hartwell! See it! Feel it! Gold! Gold everwhere!"

But Hartwell had never cared, and now he was too blind to see.

Dwire was true to such instinct for hunting gold as he possessed. He built up stone monuments to mark his strike. Then he filled his pockets with the black pebbles.

As he was about to turn away, he came suddenly upon

a rusty pick. Some prospector had been there before him. Dwire took hold of the pick handle, to feel it crumble in his hand. He searched for further evidence of a prior discoverer of the ledge in gold, but was unsuccessful.

Then Dwire and Hartwell dragged themselves on, resting often, wearing out, and at night they dropped. In the morning, as they pressed on, Dwire caught sight of the bleached bones of a man, half hidden in hard-packed sand. He did not speak of his gruesome find to Hartwell; but after a little he went back and erected a monument of stones near the skeleton. It was not the first pile of white bones that he had found in Death Valley. Then he went forward to catch up with his comrade.

That day Hartwell's sight cleared but he began to fail, to show his age. Dwire saw it, and gave both aid and encouragement.

The blue peak once more appeared to haunt them. It loomed high and apparently close. The ascent toward it was heartbreaking, not in steepness, but in its league after league of long, monotonous rise.

Dwire knew now that there was but one hope—to make the water hold out, and never stop to rest; but Hartwell was growing weaker, and had to rest often.

The burning white day passed, and likewise the white night, with its stars shining so pitilessly cold and bright. Dwire measured the water in his canteen by the feel of its weight. Evaporation by heat consumed as much as he drank.

He found opportunity in one of the rests, when he had wetted his parched mouth and throat, to pour a little water from his canteen into Hartwell's.

6

When dawn came, the bare peak glistened in the rosy sunlight. Its bare ribs stood out, and its dark lines of canyons.
It seemed so close; but in that wonderfully clear atmosphere,
before the dust and sand began to blow, Dwire could not
be deceived as to distance—and the peak was a hundred
miles away!

Muttering low, Dwire shook his head, and again found
opportunity to pour a little water from his canteen into
Hartwell's.

The zone of bare, sand-polished rock appeared never to
have an end. The rising heat waved up like black steam. It
burned through the men's boots, driving them to seek relief
in every bit of shade, and here a drowsiness made Hartwell
sleep standing. Dwire ever kept watch over his comrade.

Their marches from place to place became shorter. A
belt of cactus blocked their passage. Its hooks and spikes,
like poisoned iron fangs, tore grimly at them.

At infrequent intervals, when chance afforded, Dwire continued to pour a little water from his canteen into Hartwell's.

At first Dwire had curbed his restless activity to accommodate the pace of his elder comrade; but now he felt that he was losing something of his instinctive and passionate zeal to get out of the desert. The thought of water came to occupy his mind. Mirages appeared on all sides. He saw beautiful clear springs and heard the murmur and tinkle of running water.

He looked for water in every hole and crack and canyon; but all were glaring red and white, hot and dry—as dry as if there had been no moisture on that desert since the origin of the world. The white sun, like the surface of a pot of boiling iron, poured down its terrific heat. The men tottered into corners of shade, and rose to move blindly on.

It had become habitual with Dwire to judge his quantity of water by its weight, and by the faint splash it made as the canteen rocked on his shoulder. He began to imagine that his last little store of liquid did not appreciably diminish. He knew he was not quite right in his mind regarding water; nevertheless he felt this to be more of fact than fancy, and he began to ponder.

When next they rested, he pretended to be in a kind of stupor, but he covertly watched Hartwell. The man appeared far gone, yet he was cunning. He cautiously took up Dwire's canteen, and poured water into it from his own.

Dwire reflected that he had been unwise not to expect this very thing from Hartwell. Then, as his comrade dropped into weary rest, the younger man lifted both canteens. If there were any water in Hartwell's, it was only very little. Both men had been enduring the terrible desert thirst, concealing it, each giving his water to the other, and the sacrifice had been all for naught. Instead of ministering to either man's parched throat, the water had evaporated.

When Dwire made sure of this, he took one more drink, the last. Then, pouring the little water left into Hartwell's canteen, he threw his own away.

Hartwell discovered the loss.

"Where's your canteen?" he asked.

"The heat was getting my water, so I drank what was left and threw the can away."

"My son!" said Hartwell gently.

Then he silently compelled Dwire to drink half his water, and drank the other half himself.

They did not speak again. In another hour speaking was impossible. Their lips dried out; their tongues swelled to coarse ropes. Hartwell sagged lower and lower, despite Dwire's support.

All that night Dwire labored on under a double burden. In the white glare of the succeeding day Hartwell staggered into a strip of shade, where he fell, wearily lengthened out, and seemed to compose himself to rest.

It was still in Dwire to fight sleep—that last sleep. He had the strength and the will in him to go on a little farther; but now that the moment had come, he found that he could not leave his comrade.

While sitting there, Dwire's racking pain appeared to pass out in restful ease. He watched the white sun burn to gold, and then to red, and sink behind bold mountains in the west.

Twilight came suddenly. It lingered, slowly turning to gloom. The vast vault of blue-black lightened to the blinking of stars; and then fell the serene, silent, luminous desert night.

Dwire kept his vigil. As the long hours wore on, he felt stealing over him the comforting sense that he need not forever fight sleep.

A wan glow flared behind the dark, uneven horizon, and a melancholy, misshapen moon rose to make the white night one of shadows. Absolute silence claimed the desert. It was mute. But something breathed to Dwire, telling him when he was alone. He covered the dark, still face of his comrade from the light of the stars.

That action was the serving of his hold on realities. They fell away from him in final separation. Vaguely, sweetly, dreamily, he seemed to behold his soul.

Then up out of the vast void of the desert, from the silence and illimitableness, trooped his fantoms of peace. Majestically they formed about him, marshaling and mustering in ceremonious state, and moved to lay upon him their passionless serenity.

MAX BRAND

THE MASTER OF TWO-FISTED WESTERN ADVENTURE